Terrible Love

A
NOVEL

IN LIFE, AS IN FILM,
FIGHT FOR THE ROLE YOU WANT

JAYE VINER

Editor: Sarah McGuire
Cover Designer: Damonza Designs
Interior Book Formatting by: Authortree | https://www.authortree.co/

ISBN: 979-8-9878525-2-1

Other books by Jaye Viner

Jane of Battery Park

Elaborate Lives

To Hannah, the brightest light
1987-2022

Terrible Love

"Humans cast into a prolonged state of emergency will tend towards more subtle physiological changes. Blood volume will increase, potassium will be shed in the body's excretions, the immune system will stand down its battalions, and the brain will unwind. The mind doesn't distort reality necessarily, but its memory will suffer. Because the more a stressful memory is recalled, the less accurate, and the more prone one's brain may be to puncture holes in the narrative that we have convinced ourselves might freeze the melting snowcaps of our memories."

The Inland Sea
Madeleine Watts

Teaser

He opened his arms and gently closed them around her. After a moment of holding onto her resistance, she folded her arms up against his chest and leaned into his embrace. He tightened his arms around her. They stood like that, the first time he'd ever truly held her. The first time she'd ever shrunk herself down to fit within his grasp, a small surrender writ large.

The faint ticking of an analog clock sounded from an adjacent room marking the time. Their breathing unconsciously synchronizing to it, to each other. He closed his eyes and tried to feel every part of her that touched him, to tell his mind this was the woman he wanted. This was her shape, this was her heat, her breath, her soft shivers as she came down from the climax of her rage and softened into him.

The smell of her shampoo, which had startled him before because it was not a smell he associated with the Queen, shocked him less now. The weight of her head against his did not feel so much a stranger's. Just as he was about to say he liked the smell, she pulled away from him, her face open with surprise. He thought at first she'd felt his growing erection, but then her hand went to her mouth.

"Oh no."

She made a sloppy dash to the bathroom and dove through

the door. A moment later, he heard her retching into the cold hollow of the toilet bowl.

Playlist

- Larisa's Playlist
- Titanium (featuring Sia) by David Guetta
- Come Together by Aerosmith
- California Gurls by Katy Perry
- S&M by Rihanna
- I Won't Run by The National
- Autumn in New York by Billie Holiday
- New York, I Love you But You're Bringing me Down by LCD Soundsystem
- You'll Never Walk Alone – Gerry and the Pacemakers
- Girl on Fire by Alicia Keys

Prologue

Therapy

"So, you're dating Quinn for real this time." Dr. Bade's tone came to Larisa a bit warmer than usual, but then she might be imagining it, wanting her therapist to subconsciously bestow her blessing on Larisa's choice.

"When Quinn and I were pretending to date, I was focused on finding someone who would just get me through this stage, to make my mother happy, to keep people from writing me off. I didn't believe love was possible."

"What's changed?"

Not enough, thought Larisa. A fission of panic slithered up her spine making her hot and cold at the same time. She'd been putting off this session because she didn't want to have to think about the things that hadn't changed. The very good reasons she'd been chronically single since graduate school.

One good reason. His name was Lucas.

"I'm ready to dream again," said Larisa. "I feel safe dreaming with Quinn. He's capable of caring for me."

"Have you figured out what you want that to look like?"

"What to look like?"

"How he'll care for you?"

Larisa shifted in her seat. Dr. Bade had moved out of the hospital and into a private practice office. The chairs were leather, visually stimulating but not broken in yet. "He'll care for me however he wants."

"That's very accommodating."

"What's wrong with accommodating?" asked Larisa even though she knew what was coming.

Dr. Bade smiled. "It's a thing you do."

"Yeah, well. Wanting something closes doors."

"It also allows you to go deeper with someone."

Instead of thinking of Quinn, Larisa pictured Lucas. The last time she'd allowed herself to dive deeper, to make demands of desire, it had betrayed her.

"Do you feel he's worthy of your trust?" asked Dr. Bade.

For a moment, Larisa struggled to remember which name went with Dr. Bade's use of the pronoun. Not Lucas, Quinn. Because she loved Quinn. She would do anything for him.

"Trust." Larisa turned the word over her tongue.

"Your relationship with Quinn started with deceit—"

"Necessary deceit."

"Is that how Quinn feels about it?"

"You've agreed with me total honesty is not always the best."

"I'm not asking you to bare your soul. I'm asking you what you'll trust him with. How you'll ask him to love you."

"I'll have to think about it. But it's fine. We're going slow."

"The next time you see me," said Dr. Bade.

Larisa nodded in agreement. It was easy enough to make appointments for therapy, then cancel them.

The Kandinsky print in his therapist's office never failed to reveal new aspects of itself. Quinn sat in the corner of the overstuffed couch, which was the opposite corner from where he usually sat. From here, the print appeared more orange than red, the chaos of shapes and shadows trapped within it, somehow smaller, less organized than he'd thought.

I need a cheaper therapist, thought Quinn. This was almost always the thing on his mind after sitting in the well-appointed waiting room, then being shown into the session room by an attendant in a small tight skirt. And now, sitting, waiting for the therapist as though he was waiting for a regular doctor, and it was part of their job to make him wait. He didn't think therapy was supposed to have those top-down power dynamics.

The door opened to the doctor's private room and Dr. Edagwa entered in his four-piece suit and matching tiepin and cuff links. "Quinn. Here you are again." The way he said it made the feeling of misplacement even stronger. His therapist hadn't expected him to return, so why had he?

"What's new?"

"I'm dating again," said Quinn. "For real this time."

"How long has it been? Five months?"

"Six."

"Very fast given what you went through."

Quinn wondered if Dr. Edagwa remembered what he'd been through. "Well, we both know I don't like wasting time."

"Being single is a waste of time?" Dr. Edagwa's eyebrows furrowed. Quinn thought there was something not quite right about them. They'd been filled in or partially painted.

"We're good together," said Quinn. "It's a partnership that'll get us where we want to go."

"Ambitious."

"You would be too if you didn't have any job security or savings."

"Is that all of it?"

"What?"

"The material aspect? When you first came in, we talked about your parents. Your father left when you were young. And in high school, your mother followed him."

I just want to talk about Larisa, and how I can stop being confused she's not the Queen, thought Quinn. But he didn't want Dr. Edagwa to read into his evasion, so he said, "I suppose I feel I need to justify my existence. Make up for what I cost her."

"Quinn, let's get serious for a moment." Dr. Edagwa leaned forward. After a beat of trying to decide if this could be avoided,

Quinn also leaned forward, rested his elbows on his knees. "Do you love yourself?"

"I'm not sure what you mean by that."

"Do you look in the mirror and like what you see? Do you believe people when they say nice things about you? Do you take care of yourself?"

"I've always been good at caring for other people," said Quinn.

"And you let them run over you."

"Not always—"

"The ones who can, do. That's why I worry about dating now. Do you trust this new person to not take advantage of you like the last one? Is she going to give you as much as you give her?"

Quinn wanted to lean back into the safe distance of the couch, but this would have revealed something about him, so he stayed in place, tried to maintain eye contact as he pulled words down out of the haze at the top of his brain.

Finally, he said, "Honestly, I don't know. But I'm going to try it. And if she ruins me, I guess I'll be seeing you more than once a month."

Chapter 1

Conspiring Trees

The trees were conspiring against her.

Overnight, the long heat of October had finally broken, the wind had come in, and with it, the whispers. Larisa raked her gel manicure through the long white fur of her Persian beauty, Sabrina, with the performed tranquility of a zen garden as she glared up at the trees. Behind her, through the half-open door of the solarium, she could hear the less subtle whispers of her publicity team as they waited for her mother.

"Don't you think ruined is a strong word?" said Rockie, her publicist.

"What would you call it then?" asked her agent, Julie.

"Is it even possible to be ruined these days?" asked the new junior asset manager who worked with Rockie, name forgotten. "I mean, we could just wait a year, then get her on *Dancing with the Stars*. She'd kill that."

Larisa tapped the screen of her phone. No new messages. Quinn was in his last interview of the day, but she couldn't help checking. The vibration of her phone gave her a small thrill every time it went off. It had become the most simple, most beautiful promise of delight. That delight had become the center of her world. So much so that she barely remembered early summer when her phone had vibrated with portents of dread. Or after, when it had gone eerily silent, as the scandal of Larisa de France-Kahn, the sadomasochist psychiatrist faded. The conversation had moved on, but the stain remained.

11

Above her, the late afternoon sun flickered through the swaying branches of the trees. Sabrina had turned her face up into the sun and Larisa tried to do the same, to soak in that benevolent warmth. But her peace quickly became plagued with thoughts of skin cancer. And she heard the leaves of those trees cackling, giving her a look as though they knew this appearance of peace was just that, an appearance. How sad that she felt the need to put on an appearance just for the trees and the publicity team. They weren't even paying attention to her.

"Performance is halfway to truth," she said.

Sabrina yawned.

The phone vibrated. Larisa resisted the urge to take it greedily in her hands and devour whatever message had come in. It wouldn't be Quinn. It would be something else, something banal, one of those routine things that was a necessary but uninteresting part of life. She paused to scratch Sabrina's chin, then tapped the screen.

Three messages.

> Jaden: Ready to par-tay? Costumes optional.

> Jaden: Adults only.

The third message came from Larisa's cousin, Hannah, in Minnesota, a picture of the fall foliage as seen from the deck of her parents' farmhouse. In the years since Larisa had finished med school and moved to LA, this annual missive from Hannah signaled the beginning of the holiday season.

Larisa studied the autumnal glory of Minnesota and tried to remember the smell of leaf decay, the chemical release of soil under early morning frost, the feel of heavy sweaters and hats that ruined salon blowouts. Sometimes, she couldn't believe she'd survived four years in that unforgiving climate. Sometimes, she thought it would have been better to stay in the Midwest than come home.

> Larisa: Beautiful.

> Hannah: Miss you.

> Larisa: You only miss me in the fall.

She did not add, *And only when you're single.*

> Hannah: How are things?

> Larisa: Good.

> Hannah: All recovered from that mishap this spring?

> Larisa: More than recovered.

"This won't fade the way it does for men," said Julie from the solarium. "Women aren't forgiven. Did you see the *Times* yesterday? She's become an allegorical punchline against which they're now comparing other scandals."

"Annie Sunderland's hardly a comparable scandal," said the junior asset manager. "Can we talk about my book idea now?"

"The book won't work."

"Did you read my notes?"

Larisa's phone vibrated with another message. This one from Rosa, who was very pregnant and often irritable. She'd started a group text that apparently did not include Jaden.

> Rosa: What does she mean, no children? It's Halloween. She expects me to leave them at home on Halloween?

> Krissy: The childless don't know what it's like.

Larisa checked the time. Ten minutes until Quinn might be done with his interview. She thought of sending him a barrage of emojis. Instead, she took a short video of the trees in the wind.

Larisa: The trees know a secret, do you?

She smiled to herself as she sent it. Eight days earlier, at her mother's autumn masquerade, Quinn had stood almost exactly where the publicity team now sat and spoke the most beautiful words to her. It hardly mattered that none of them included a declaration of love. She'd felt seen in ways that had never felt possible. It felt as though he had invited her into a secret alliance; the two of them against the world even as they outwardly worked to be as much a part of it as they could.

Love would come. A man could not throw himself so fully into a woman's life and not want to love her. But at night, alone in her childhood bed, thinking of him while she stroked herself off, Larisa hoped Quinn wouldn't take too long to decide he loved her. Every hour in his presence, it took every ounce of her being not to fall on him like the starving rabid thing she'd become.

He loves the Queen. Larisa pushed the thought away. Thinking too much ruined the pastel-flavored bubble of new-relationship infatuation they'd constructed. The giddy rush to share every thought no matter how ordinary or strange, the craving to constantly be in each other's presence. It all faded if she thought too much. Even now, as she smiled to herself picturing Quinn finishing the interview and seeing her message about the trees, she worried he didn't feel the same way she did.

"The book is about a naïve college student who's taken in by an experienced billionaire," said Rockie. "Completely different situation."

"It speaks to audience," said the junior asset manager. "The people reading this book might be sympathetic to Larisa."

"The book was self-published," said Julie with enough disdain in her voice that she killed the conversation.

Larisa stroked the soft triangle of Sabrina's head like a Bond villainwithout an evil plan to take over the world. "You have no idea how good you have it," she whispered.

"But I think you're right that maybe there's a cultural shift," said Rockie. "There's a window of opportunity here. We should at least get her a high-profile interview. Maybe not Oprah, but *Good Morning America*? Something bright and cheerful. Not to talk about the book. Just visibility."

"A place they never talk about sex," said Julie.

"Yes! That's exactly it. Larisa recontextualized."

"Maybe she could apologize," said the junior asset manager.

"I like how you're thinking. But how would that work?"

"I don't like the implication of 'apology,'" said Julie. "Let's avoid *Vanguard Trial* shame here."

"That show's popular for a reason," said the junior asset manager, relentless. "People like seeing a shamed celebrity."

Larisa's phone vibrated. The sans-Jaden chat was blowing up.

> Kahleah: @Rosa if you're worried about staff, my nanny has already committed to the whole night. Your kids can come over for a sleepover.

> Rosa: But it's Halloween! Aerial is so sensitive. She shouldn't be alone. Besides, we already have plans to trick or treat at the church.

> Krissy: We should all be there to support Jaden. You know she's nervous. @Larisa, you're coming, right?

The chat fell silent as though each of Larisa's sorority sisters had paused their lives at various places around Los Angeles to wait for her response. Quinn had been so busy with his movie she hadn't had the chance to ask him about Jaden's party. They communicated all day, every day but they hadn't really talked. Not about what they were doing together, or about the future, or what exactly this relationship would be. Larisa knew Quinn didn't particularly like her friends. But he also wasn't going to say no to a party where he'd have the chance to network with the future mayor of LA and a scientist with a network of hundreds of people with money that might one day finance his films.

The problem: Larisa did not want to be seen.

In the solarium at her back, another kind of silence fell. The distant clipping of heels began to sound as her mother, retired model, Suzette de France, now fashion consultant and manager of her own beauty line, marched down the stairs from the family wing where she'd been in conference with her stylist in preparation for an interview she was taping for Milan Fashion Week. The footsteps grew louder, then stopped. She'd arrived. Larisa resumed raking Sabrina's back, her eye tracking the slow descent of purple and silver nails through the air, their disappearance into the white fluff, the neat rows they left in their wake as she moved her hand from neck to rump. Sabrina didn't like having her butt touched and reflexively arched it into the air every time Larisa went too far down.

"So, we're making progress?" asked Suzette. A pause. "Larisa, what are you doing out there?"

"Sunning," Larisa called back, a nonsense answer sure to irritate her mother. It was that kind of day. Actually, every day that week had been that kind of day. The giant house and grounds had never felt so small.

"You've had enough. Come here."

Larisa pulled Sabrina to her chest, put her phone in the pocket of her joggers, and entered the house. Only the junior asset manager turned to welcome her back.

"We were considering an interview," said Rockie.

"I think Larisa should make herself available on the topic of BDSM," said the junior asset manager. "There's this new novel—"

"I've been able to generate some interest in a *Drama Queen* revival," said Julie. "But they want to focus on the secret Larisa, which I think will work against us in the long run."

Larisa snorted. "I could be the next *Girls Gone Wild*. Except I'm almost thirty and there's only me. Maybe I could pull Kahleah in? Then you'd have me and a politician's wife being kinky on late-night reality TV. And Krissy—"

"Don't even think about it," snapped Suzette. "We need to pursue the fashion week angle. It's tame, glamourous, and exactly what she needs. I was just on the phone with Marnie at Fast69. They're doing some of their own rehabilitation since Peter was fired. They will sponsor Larisa for a week to do behind-the-scenes featurettes. And she's sitting in with me for part of the guest of honor interview today."

"I'm what?"

She expected Quinn would come over as soon as he finished work. She didn't have time for an interview; she still hadn't decided what she was wearing for him. *Does she think I'm still twelve?* Larisa glared at her mother until Suzette glanced her direction.

"You wish to add something, Larisa?"

"I'm just wondering what you expect me to talk about. What a great mother you were? Stressed out trying to stay runway skinny? Disappearing for months at a time? Chain smoking?"

"You'll talk about fashion and history, and what it means to your generation."

"Fuck that."

"Larisa!"

Her name hissed out of her mother's mouth. She felt it deep in her chest like a long-festering splinter, sometimes forgotten, but alarmingly painful even when slightly touched.

"What's wrong with you today?"

"I haven't whipped anyone since March?" The words escaped before Larisa could stop them. Rockie frowned. Julie cut her gaze toward Suzette as though to commiserate over their shared problem.

The junior asset manager laughed. "Hell, if that's what it takes, I'll volunteer."

Sabrina squirmed in Larisa's arms. Larisa realized her mostly angelic cat was panicking because she was being crushed. She released her grip, allowing Sabrina to fall/leap, as cats did, to the floor, and run out of the room. She tried to breathe, to be *reason-*

able, as her mother wanted. Because the state of crisis remained. Because the embarrassment of Parish's live stream at Club D in April couldn't be limited to Larisa's embarrassment. It was her mother's and her father's. And she was being selfish.

I don't even know if I want to do bondage anymore, thought Larisa.

Maybe this thought underlined all the rest. Not that she'd been humiliated, but that something precious had been lost. Since college, bondage had been her refuge, the mind space where she felt most alive, most certain, most in love with herself when other forms of love failed. Now, the great love affair with herself and the power she wielded had crash-landed, unlikely to rise again.

I'm grieving.

How long before Quinn wants something from me that I can't give him?

"Fine," said Larisa. "I'll do the interview. But I'm not going to Milan." She picked up her phone to respond to the still silent group chat.

> Larisa: I'll be there on Monday, costume and dancing shoes!
>
> Larisa: It's Jaden's hostess debut! Whoooo! #MarriedLife

Chapter 2

Toy Story Dating

After a full day of what felt like a giant, jumbled mass of words bubbling in a cloud around his head, Quinn knew he didn't have anything left for the final interview. He'd come into it tense, irritable, braced for more of the same banality that made him and his work feel like regurgitated plastics.

But the *Film Comment* reporter had asked all the right questions. They'd given Quinn the chance to talk about cinematography and the difficulty of realizing an artistic vision. He liked that this reporter had assumed his film was artistic even though on the surface it looked like just another blockbuster spy thriller. He liked that this reporter had seen his two previous films and drawn connections between them and *The Key*. Quinn lost track of the time. He felt his answers stretching into that dangerous length of 'boring for everyone else.'

"I think I could sit here and talk about this all day," said Quinn with a laugh.

The reporter made an echo of appreciative laughter in agreement. "It's really fantastic to see anyone make the leap into big budget and bring back the soul of the blockbuster."

"Are you sure you watched *The Key*?"

Another appreciative laugh. The reporter looked down at their notes. "I know we're out of time, but if you'll allow it, no conversation about you is complete without touching on what happened this spring with your former girlfriend and Larisa de France-Kahn.

Quinn nodded. He'd already weathered two other interviews with questions about the events of that past spring. He knew what to say. But those other reporters had been hacks for the industry marketing machine. They'd asked popcorn questions and seemed to have already written their articles with his assumed answers penciled in. In contrast, this reporter seemed to have met with Quinn under the mistaken impression that their writing meant something to the world.

"So, how would you characterize your sexuality?" asked the reporter.

Not the question I expected. Quinn allowed his gaze to soften into a middle distance to the left of the reporter's head. He'd done this for other questions when he'd been reveling in possible answers. Now he did it to hide the spike of panic driving into his gut.

"Well, that's certainly a question."

"I think it's an important one." The reporter appeared so serious, so sincere. "Doesn't an artist bring all parts of themselves to their work?"

Somewhere beyond the walls of this room, Eddie, Quinn's executive producer, was going about his life, sitting in meetings, eating disgusting takeout, sleazing his way through phone calls with no idea that this, the most unimportant interview of the day, was about to blow sideways.

"As you said, the modern blockbuster tends to be a little soulless," said Quinn, stalling as he tried to find the right words. *So many words spent today.* His tongue felt as mushy as his brain. "The nature of mass market film is to appeal to as many people as possible at the same time. I think a smart artist only pulls out the parts of themselves that serve that purpose."

"But you've made an extremely risky decision turning the femme fatale archetype into a man who seduces another man, a *homme fatale*. How did you ever get approval for that?"

"It was the right decision for the story we wanted to tell. If people think its revolutionary, then that probably says more about how they see the world than how I see it."

"How do you see it?" asked the reporter.

"I see infinite possibility everywhere I look."

"So, you're a pansexual?"

Unbidden, and so very inconvenient, an image flashed across Quinn's mind. The polished slate gray floor of Club D, the twin, splotchy orbs of his bare knees, hands cinched tight at the small of his back, the heels of the Queen's boots impaling his screaming heart.

Quinn blinked. *God, what's happening here?* He took a breath he hoped just looked like a normal breath and not the panicked gulp that it was. "The idea for Dansby's character to seduce the general actually came from Larisa. When she started to help me navigate my work, it was one of her first significant suggestions. And it was a market one."

"What do you mean by that?"

"She suggested that women who wouldn't normally see a thriller would be interested in watching a beautiful, young male spy go through this age-old struggle of the femme fatale, tiptoeing between love and manipulation, between duty to a cause and self-preservation."

"Interesting." The reporter seemed disappointed. "You still have a great deal of respect for Larisa."

"Why wouldn't I?"

The reporter smiled down at their notes like they knew this was a trap question. But then they decided to answer it anyway. "She isn't very good for business, is she? No one really wants to be associated with closet sexual violence mixed up with mental health professionals. She practically ran her own cult."

Heat rushed up Quinn's face. Mind dangerously blank for untold seconds before he reeled it back to a thinking place. He needed to make his exit before he said something to make this worse. Reporters had no respect. Here he was in good faith, representing his film, representing the studio. A perfect conversation had devolved into sex and gossip.

"That's an interesting story," said Quinn, standing. "Maybe you should write a novel." He started toward the door, then stopped. He was so tired of people acting like all the trash generated in Larisa's name had any connection to reality. "We're dating," said Quinn. "Maybe you should lead with that, it'll get you more hits."

He pulled his phone out of his pocket before the door swung shut behind him, messaging Sid, who'd been elevated from manager to manager/chauffeur since the studio had leased Quinn a BMW SUV.

Quinn: Time to leave.

In his haste to leave, to cloister himself and simmer in his rage, Quinn almost missed the tree video Larisa had sent him. And then, he couldn't process it, the frivolity of conspiring trees while he was in high defense mode, skin bristling, an overwhelming feeling of wrongness. Quinn's first instinct was to reply to the text with the news that he'd just told a reporter they were dating. But that would only spread his overabundant emotions to Larisa, so he wrote:

Quinn: On my way.

Immediately, he felt better. Three words, but they felt like a promise. They felt like the future. He'd never been so happy to have a phone as he had these past ten days. It felt like passing notes in high school, with the jittery anticipation of an answer being almost as exciting as the actual response.

Now, new love had the power of nearly instant communication. What did he choose to say to Larisa? Since six o'clock that morning, the earth-shattering truths of linguistic locution included:

Quinn: Are you up yet?

Larisa: Yes.

Quinn: Sleep good?

Larisa: Sabrina was up at three. She thought I should be up at three too.

Quinn: I enjoyed talking last night.

Larisa: Me too.

Then, after he'd arrived at the studio:

Quinn: Eddie thinks I should do my hair even though I won't be on camera.

Larisa: Eddie thinks many things.

Quinn: The movie is out in six weeks. 😱

Larisa: It's going to be great.

Quinn: What if it's too great?

Larisa: Worry about that later.

Quinn: My lunch is with a producer at DuckNCover.

Larisa: Don't let him feel you up before he pays for the food.

Quinn: 👀🙈😂

Before lunch:

> Larisa: 🙄😅

After lunch:

> Larisa: How was it?
>
> Quinn: I don't know why Hollywood does job interviews in restaurants. I think I hate it.
>
> Larisa: So…?
>
> Quinn: It went okay.
>
> Quinn: Sid really likes the new car. He thinks I should sit in the back.
>
> Larisa: You should.
>
> Quinn: What are you doing right now?
>
> Larisa: A jigsaw puzzle.
>
> Quinn: What about Sabrina?
>
> Larisa: She's eating the jigsaw puzzle.

They had as much sexual tension as a G-rating. Maybe that was okay. He knew she wanted to, but she wasn't going to push until he knew he wanted her. Not the Queen, Larisa.

Not the Queen, Larisa. Two people who were actually one person, but he couldn't get his mind to believe it.

The BMW pulled up, a black tank of gleaming metal and tinted windows that spoke of important passengers. As Quinn climbed into the passenger seat, Sid gave him a salute.

"They work you hard?"

"I never thought talking about myself could be so boring." Quinn massaged his jaw. "I feel like that Barbie in *Toy Story*. But from talking not smiling."

"*Toy Story*?"

"We watched it the other night."

Sid arched an eyebrow. Quinn felt his judgement but couldn't see the shape of it. Neither of them had ever been in a relationship when, in the heady early days of infatuation, *Toy Story* had been the movie of choice.

"I assume we're going to Larisa's?"

"I'm going. You have to entertain yourself."

"For how long?"

"When you pick me up tomorrow morning. We have an eleven o'clock at the Beverly Hilton."

Sid clucked his tongue with disapproval. The Beverly Hilton was the place Quinn had met his ex, Parish, for lunch on the last day his life had been normal. She'd drugged him, taken him to the Club D bondage lounge, and staged her dramatic sabotage of Larisa's life to an audience of video game broadcasters who recorded, then shared and reshared the recording until it felt the entire world had seen it.

"What was I supposed to do? Ask them to change it? The producer called me himself."

"You should let me manage your social schedule," said Sid.

"I don't have a *social* schedule. I have meetings. And our future depends on them. I should've had a next project lined up six months ago."

"I can do it," said Sid.

"You do enough."

"Well, you shouldn't be letting people dictate the terms to everything."

"You don't know how it works."

"So, I pick you up at her place?" asked Sid.

"At my house. If something changes, I'll text you."

Again, Sid's knowing silence.

"We're going slow."

"Nothing wrong with that," said Sid.

"It's weird sometimes, being with someone who feels so familiar but at the same time isn't. I mean, I think she feels familiar because she's been with me since the beginning, but I haven't been with her. Does that even make sense?"

"You're dating a shrink. Everything and nothing will always make sense."

I'm dating her. It still didn't feel real. Was that why he'd told the reporter? He wanted the world to know. He didn't care what people thought they were doing in the bedroom.

They'd be bored, he thought. There hadn't been a bedroom. Since that night at the masquerade, when she'd taken him in her arms and kissed him for the first time, there hadn't been much of anything. He knew she wanted him. She was holding back, trying to be considerate of just how strange it was.

Sometimes.

It was strange sometimes.

And other times, it felt like he was in Willy Wonka land, sailing down a river of chocolate.

"She's perfect," he said.

"That isn't always a good thing," said Sid.

"I don't want to mess this up."

"Hard to imagine what more you could do at this point that would drive her away."

Quinn smiled. Sid had a point. There was a certain kind of comfort that came from making this choice, to be together, to try and make it work for real this time, after they'd been through so much.

But then, as he stood uncertainly on the front steps of the columned edifice of the Kahn estate, Quinn wondered about the inherent delusions of thinking there could be a future for him in this world. He'd texted Larisa thinking she'd be there to greet him, but she hadn't replied. And now, even though he'd stood on these steps almost every day that week, he felt the impulse to turn and run after the BMW's taillights before they reached the front gate.

Sarah, the house manager, opened the door with one of those studiously blank expressions that always made Quinn self-conscious. He saw the thinking brain behind that wall, judging him, his appearance, his posture, his expression, which displayed the full range of his doubts as he hesitated three beats too long before stepping over the threshold.

"Larisa was pulled into the taping at the last minute. You'll find them in the second-floor drawing room. Can I get you a drink?"

"I'm fine, thanks Sarah." He made a point of saying her name because he wanted her to know he knew her as a person and not just an anonymous person who ran the house. But as soon as he said it, his mind returned to the same thought he'd had yesterday when he'd thanked her for clearing away the dishes he and Larisa could've cleared themselves: Sarah knew exactly what kind of fraud he was and no amount of remembering her name was going to make her think better of him.

The second-floor drawing room where he and Larisa had chastely watched all three *Toy Story* movies had been transformed into a film set with lighting illuminating a corner by the floor-to-ceiling windows. The love seat had been turned to face a matching, straight-backed chair. A dozen people stood outside of the pools of light watching a man wearing some complicated garment that looked like a jumper interview Suzette.

Suzette wore a plunging shirtwaist dress with a burgundy blazer over it. Quinn noticed how she sat up straight without appearing severe. How, even when she was thinking, her gaze didn't drift the way he had during his interviews that day. She kept her hands soft against her thighs as she spoke. Only her voice reflected movement. And even it seemed modulated, controlled in a way Quinn imagined would also help the viewers feel comfortable.

"Cut!" called the director's assistant, as Suzette finished her thought. "That's great. Let's pause, stretch, then finish with Larisa."

"Will there be time for that?" The man in the sparkly shirt leaned over the arm of the chair and checked his phone. "Suzette, I really think we can—"

"We agreed on this, Peter. It's just a little extra. And it's important to me."

"They'll just edit it out. This is your moment."

"My daughter is part of it." Suzette still spoke in her interview voice, with a light airiness that softened the warning in her eyes. A look Quinn recognized from Larisa. He smiled.

Behind him, somewhere from the cavernous bowels of the house, the echoing reverberations of heavy footsteps. A shiver ran up Quinn's spine. For a moment, he closed his eyes and transported into Club D, standing with his arms pinned above his head, spread out, exposed, waiting for his Queen and simpler days. *When she was lying to me,* he thought.

Quinn withdrew into the wall of the sitting room, almost into the drapery, so he would not be seen as Larisa entered. When he opened his eyes, she stood ahead of him, a silhouette at the edge of the stage lighting. Her shoulders were the same but everything else about her felt like a stranger.

Why did she feel it was so important to deceive me?

Larisa wore a knee-length black dress that hung from those shoulders in a straight line, concealing the shape of her body beneath. She wore tights and little ankle-length boots. So little skin showing. In that at least, she resembled the Queen. They were clothes he approved of, not that Larisa would ever ask for his opinion.

But he felt none of the Queen's commanding presence, nothing of that invitation to surrender into her magnificent will. He watched Larisa check in with the director, a bright smile pressed onto her face as she said how happy she was to be part of the celebration, and did he have any suggestions for her? Everything self-deprecating, that smile going ahead of her as though she needed an ambassador, the softness of her posture telling everyone she could be told what to do. As she joined her mother on the love seat, she seemed to shrink even more, her shoulders turning in on themselves, her neck drawing down as Suzette inspected her.

"Good enough," she said.

Larisa smiled at Peter. "Thanks so much for doing this. Your spring collection was so lovely. The choice to do the bias cut with the sleeves...."

"Well, it was the obvious choice, wasn't it?" said Peter. "You look at those lines and your mind immediately says—"

"Peter?" Suzette gave him a look as smoothly polite as butter yet unassailable in its silent command.

"Yes, we're here to talk about you." He straightened back into interview mode.

Peter only asked a few questions. Larisa kept her answers short but full of that same warmth she'd used with the director. She spoke of the power of fashion to change lives and define generations. When Peter asked specifically about Suzette's legacy, Larisa hesitated only a moment before saying exactly the right thing. Suzette had redefined how women could see themselves. She made fashion something everyone could own.

The interview ended. Mother and daughter stood in tandem, not acknowledging each other as they went out to glad-hand the crew. They moved like two mirror images, the way they leaned in to whoever they spoke with, the way they tilted their heads just so as they listened. But while Suzette acted like a queen meeting her subjects, Larisa's every breath felt like obeisance.

The crew began to pack up. Larisa broke away and approached Quinn. He wondered when she'd seen him standing there, in the shadow of the drapes. He would have liked to see her face change when she saw him. But perhaps it was better he hadn't. Whatever expression he saw there, he would have ruminated on for days.

Larisa stepped into the drapes and wrapped herself up until

only her face peeked out from the folds. "You look tired. Do you want to go home?"

"I just got here."

"I don't want to keep you."

He stepped into the opposite side of the drapes and wrapped himself up so the two of them stood facing each other, overstuffed drapes with human heads. "I want to be here."

"Okay." She glanced at him, almost shy, like his words meant everything to her. "My parents want to have dinner on the patio. Then we might work on the puzzle? Do you like puzzles?"

"Sure."

"Come with me while I change?"

She led him across the balcony of the atrium, then down a hallway that split into two. They turned right and walked down another hallway, this one with a series of doors on one side and windows out to the backyard on the other. A whole house of windows.

After another turn, Larisa finally opened a door and led him into a miniature sitting room with a desk and a round sofa set up beside a picture window where Sabrina lay curled up in a fluffy white ball. A row of award certificates framed one wall, along with pictures of a much younger Larisa posing with friends he didn't recognize, and landscape photos of an idyllic European-looking countryside. An Italian villa on a hill. On the floor, an overburdened bookshelf held a range of titles from pop psychologists and self-help gurus to college textbooks, spiral-bound photo albums, romance novels, and thrillers, all of which looked stale in a long-undisturbed way, though he didn't see any dust. More recent additions of true crime paperbacks and a few hardcovers stood in precarious piles on the floor beside the bookshelf and along the edge of the window.

Larisa continued into the adjacent room where a four-poster bed, complete with frilly white curtains, sat between end tables marked with frosted globe lamps. He wondered if she expected him to follow her. He hadn't been in this part of the house before.

There was a certain irony that, just an hour earlier, he'd been thinking of how there'd been no bedroom action in their relationship and now here he stood, hesitating on the threshold of that sacred room as she continued on into a closet almost the same size as the sitting room.

"How was your day?" she called.

"Good, I think. It's all blurry. You know, for my last film I did three interviews in a month. Today, I did three interviews in six hours. And I had a lunch."

"That's right. With DuckNCover. Was it hot?"

"If it was, I missed it."

"I've always heard Duck only brings on a certain kind of person. All his producers work with their hands." She poked her head around the doorway to give him a knowing smirk.

"We just talked and ate. The project they have isn't really—I told him I'd think about it."

"You know my client was married to him. They've been fighting for years. Sometimes they get back together, and they still fight."

Quinn caught a flash of skin as Larisa pulled her dress up over her head. A puff of heat, like a struck match, burned deep in his stomach. She hadn't been wearing anything underneath except her tights. For a moment, she disappeared, then she was back, even more fully in his line of sight than before. Her back to him, she tucked her fingers under the waistband of the tights and slid them slowly down her thighs.

He felt the buzz of blood rushing to his groin, the flickering match bloomed into a true flame. It would've been easy to cross the bedroom and go to her, touch her. She was offering herself, and yet he stood still with his right foot pressed up against the side of the doorway as though to hold himself in place. The flame died out as quickly as it had come.

"Larisa?"

"Hm?"

"I told one of the reporters we were dating."

She leaned out of view, came back with a pair of bikini briefs. He averted his eyes as she slowly slid them on. Even knowing she wanted him to watch her, it didn't feel right, not when he was still looking for the Queen in Larisa's body.

"Did you? Well, then I guess we'll be newsprint official soon."

He couldn't tell what she was thinking. A flash of something crossed her face. He might have been able to interpret it if not for his worry. Something was off, the table tilting as he watched flatware slowly slide off. He didn't know how to ask the question he needed to ask so he said, "I don't remember when the article is supposed to come out. Could be tomorrow. Or it could be after the press junket. Oh, did you—"

"Your capsule wardrobe is coming, plus two outfits for just NYC. One coat. One hat." She pulled on a T-shirt and yoga pants, then turned to give him a knowing smile. "One hat means just wear it one day, okay?"

She picked up her phone and began to type a message. As she typed, her tongue came out and was trapped between her teeth. She looked like a child imitating an adult in deep concentration.

"Something wrong?"

"Just telling my team we're official. They don't like to be surprised. What outlet was the interview with?"

"*Film Comment.*"

She nodded as she continued to type. "I hope they're nice to you."

"Why wouldn't they be?"

She shook her head at her phone, then tucked it into her pocket. "They will be. Any other news I should know about?" She sat down on the bed and looked at him expectantly. Another invitation. He could join her on the bed. Her childhood bed, where she now slept because his ex-girlfriend had ruined her life.

"Tomorrow I'm meeting with an executive at FilmStreams. Kyle?"

"Oh good. I was beginning to think he was going to pass."

She continued to sit on the bed, waiting. Quinn continued to stand planted in the doorway. "Pass on what?"

"You. He lost his director for the new *Poseidon* project. I told Dad to recommend you months ago. Maybe Kyle's one of those men who likes to make it seem like all good ideas are his own ideas."

Something hard and tight clenched in Quinn's chest. This woman. Every time he thought he knew what to expect from her she did something else.

"You don't look happy," she said.

"You think I could do a superhero movie?"

"It's not. I mean, yes, it's kind of like that. But it's not like I volunteered you to churn out a thing for Marvel. You don't want to do it?"

Quinn opened his mouth and realized he didn't know how to answer that. He'd never even considered the possibility of something that big. To cover his shock, he said, "Any news I should know?"

"Today was uneventful. I might have a second client. My mother's more herself than usual, so dinner won't be pleasant. We've been invited to a Halloween party at Jaden's on Monday. Just the sisters and husbands, no kids. Maybe a couple of her other friends."

"Costumes?"

"Optional."

"Fun."

"I'm not sure we're going." She abruptly stood up from the bed and crossed the room to him. "Estelle says dinner's ready." Right beside him, she stopped, as though she'd found a hidden barrier. He couldn't tell if it was something he'd built, and she was respecting, or something she'd built. Neither made much sense. He thought again that she was waiting on him, holding herself back. He could feel the hot center of her restraint vibrating off her skin, the heat of her breath puffing into the air between them. He wanted to reach out and close that distance. To take her in his arms, to release her from that restraint. But it didn't feel right. The scene felt overwrought, the characters uncertain of who they were supposed to be, and even more uncertain of what was expected of them.

At Club D, their roles had been assigned. She'd led, he'd followed. Not just followed, he'd curved the entirety of his existence around the kernel of her direction. There had been nothing outside it. No choices he needed to make, no doubt. Fulfilling the tasks she'd set for him had been Quinn's only challenge. Endurance had never been one of his problems. And even when she'd pushed his limits, the only lasting fear he'd felt was failing her.

What did that mean for them now? He still wanted to follow her. But Larisa was not the Queen. She didn't always want to command him. Still, the idea that he might initiate, that she might want to be the one folding herself around him, seemed impossible.

There was nothing more surreal about his new life than walking into the palatial kitchen and seeing that Suzette had a glass of chilled seltzer waiting for him, along with one of those smiles that made it difficult to remember his name. Even after three such dinners, his disbelief remained. There would need to be a hundred or more of these dinners, informal at the kitchen table or out on the patio with torches lit to compliment the string of overhead lights, candles on the table, the darkness beyond the patio pressing in to make the scene even more intimate, before he would believe this was really his life. He wanted an invading paparazzo to sneak a picture of him, Quinn VanderVeer, sitting with Gunter Kahn, director of the PGA, giant behind many of the films Quinn watched as a kid, Suzette de France-Kahn, the woman who'd turned runway fashion on its head forty years earlier, and their daughter.

"I recognize that look," said Gunter. "You should have something stronger."

They knew Quinn avoided alcohol. But as drinking people they didn't quite understand it.

"I could try," he said, "but that might make things worse. I'm not sure I can do full sentences at this point."

"Very few people read the director coverage," said Gunter. "They just want the stars."

"That's good because Dansby's doing better than I am."

"They were talking about him at the salon today," said Suzette. "He needs a manager, hon. Things are moving fast. He'll miss things."

"What about you?" Gunter asked Quinn. "You're having meetings, right?"

"Just a few," said Quinn, careful to sound casual, as though the corners of his brain didn't keep him up at night worrying that he didn't have enough options.

"Tomorrow he's meeting with Kyle at FilmStreams," said Larisa, pointedly not taking the seat next to her mother.

"Ah yes. Good. What are they offering?"

"We're just having lunch."

"You should always know what they might be offering before going in. You don't want to be surprised in person. And you don't want to have unreasonable expectations either. Let me make a call, and I'll find out for you." Gunter strolled off the patio and disappeared into the darkness of the lawn.

"So much happening." Suzette peered at him over the rim of her wine glass. "The interview taped today. I saw you came for the end. They decided to have Larisa sit on for a segment to give a different perspective."

"You decided," muttered Larisa.

"They want her to come to Milan with me in February for the

anniversary. Do a little behind-the-scenes work. Don't you think that'd be fun?"

Quinn couldn't decide if he was supposed to speculate if Larisa would have fun or if the thing itself sounded fun. He settled for, "I've never been to Italy."

"Oh, it's beautiful. Everything, the food, the people, the music. Did you know Larisa went through an Italian opera phase? She spent the summer there when she was in college, and all she talked about was the music. You should come with us."

"I don't really do opera."

"How could you not do it if you've never tried it?" asked Larisa. "Ignorance isn't the same as not liking something."

Suzette continued as if she hadn't spoken. "I'm the same. But fashion week is like Italy within Italy. Parties, dinners, and old friends. You'd love it."

Quinn couldn't help but laugh. Had she really just invited him to fashion week in Italy?

"He's not going," said Larisa.

"He can go if he wants," said Suzette. "In fact, I think we should make a big event of it. I'm going to invite the girls. I think—"

"For fuck's sake, Mom. I said no. I've been saying no for six months."

"But it's my fortieth anniversary. I want to celebrate."

"You want to show off."

"Maybe I do. And you should be grateful I'm still interested in showing off my daughter."

"What's that supposed to mean?"

"Exactly what I said."

"No. It means, aren't I lucky you haven't disowned me like everyone else. Aren't I lucky I have such understanding parents who stand by their embarrassing daughter?"

Suzette's wine glass returned to the table with a hard landing. "Do I wish that video hadn't happened? Of course. Am I embarrassed my daughter is a sexual being? No."

"But you wish I was different."

Suzette opened her mouth for a quick reply, then thought better of it. She sipped her wine.

"Imagine if you had grandchildren to take to Milan."

"I knew years ago that was never going to happen." Suzette took a breath and turned to acknowledge Quinn. "Do you want children?"

"No."

"I suppose that's why she's keeping you."

Quinn glanced at Larisa, wondering what kind of past conflict he'd stepped into. "I'm happy to be kept," he said. Instead of looking happy, Larisa's face turned melancholy. She broke eye contact to watch her father as he returned to the table. "What happened?"

"Just your daughter being herself," said Suzette. "What did you learn?"

"It's promising." Gunter clapped Quinn on the shoulder as he took his seat. "After we eat, we'll talk, jah? It's time to decide what kind of career you want to have."

"Great." Quinn felt like this was an inadequate response, but he couldn't think of anything else to say. He'd sit through a lifetime of arguments between Larisa and her mother if it meant Gunter Kahn wanted to pull him into strategy meetings after dinner, especially if they began with that tantalizing question: *What kind of career do you want to have?* As though there were multiple options, as though he had the power to choose instead of just grasping desperately at whatever offers came along.

Hidden Larisa

Larisa: I've got an invite to dinner with the hottest new hostess in the city.

S'Wonderful: When?

Larisa: Monday. Costumes Optional.

S'Wonderful: What are you wearing?

Larisa: You'll have to come and find out.

S'Wonderful: Send me the deets.

Larisa to Jaden:

Larisa: Is it okay if I've invited an extra guest Monday? I promise you'll like him.

Jaden: I always like your friends.

Quinn and her father stayed together late into the night. At first Larisa sat in with them, half-listening, half-reading the detective novel inspired by the 1920s Black Dahlia murders. Not that she could concentrate enough to read. Just being in the same room with Quinn made him the only thing she could think about. More importantly, watching him talk to her father made her horny. Her father probably had nothing to do with it. She was just wound up and unable to spend the energy where she wanted it, filling her hands with Quinn's pert little ass as she plundered those perpetually swollen lips of his.

She'd told herself this desire came out of wanting him to be successful. When her father asked him questions he didn't know how to answer, she wanted to rush in and offer suggestions, to ease away his discomfort. She had all the answers for him; she knew how this game worked. Her father could open doors. The fact that he'd taken an interest should have made her relax, instead she kept wanting to insert herself in the conversation with tidbits that made Quinn look more impressive.

In the end, she'd started sending texts to help cover the itchy-finger feeling of inactivity. Her father would give advice but acting on it—like the suggestion Quinn make time for two strategic social events a week—wasn't something Quinn would do unless she forced him. And based on her father's estimation of Film-Streams's need for a director, the best she could do was introduce *Poseidon's* star, Steve Helston, to Quinn and make sure he made a good impression.

They'd still been talking when she'd excused herself and gone to bed. She'd stared at the twinkle lights trapped in the white cloud of her canopy and thought about Quinn's shy smile, which came more easily now than it had before. The way he cut his food into small bites, then only finished half of them, not a healthy habit, but endearing, nonetheless.

When she closed her eyes she could feel him, the willow stick of his body crushed into hers in the rush of emotion that had followed his speech at the masquerade. The hard press of his lips rushing to hers. But no, that hadn't been what happened. She'd kissed him. She'd *devoured* him. And now, even though all she wanted to do was devour him again, she was waiting for that kiss to be returned. She would not, could not give any more of herself to him until he could come that far.

Soon Lucas will know I've decided to keep him. And then what?

"Earth to Dr. Larisa." Parish's voice broke through Larisa's thoughts. The world came slowly into focus. She'd come to visit the private clinic where Parish remained a patient in court-mandated care. They were sitting together in what had been the pool room when the clinic had been a hotel. Now it was a gym. Parish sat on a yoga mat maneuvering her swollen body through her prenatal exercises.

"Where did you go?"

"Reliving a fight with my mother," said Larisa. She knew better than to outright lie to Parish. Eight months pregnant, the girl still looked like a manic pixie pop star, but she picked out bullshit faster than anyone Larisa knew, and she didn't care about being polite.

"About what?" asked Parish.

"Everything and nothing."

"You know I'm having a girl?"

"Do you want her to be like you?" asked Larisa.

"What else would she be?"

Larisa shrugged. She didn't feel like getting into a parenting discussion with the last woman on the planet who she expected to be a good parent.

"My doctor says I'm doing better. I might be able to have her in a regular hospital."

"That's great," said Larisa, painfully aware of how detached she sounded. She'd tried and tried again to focus on Parish, to be in this moment. Instead, her mind kept skirting around to other thoughts, unformed worries lurking in the shadows.

"My parents are excited. Mom's set up a nursery right next to my room."

"You'll have custody?"

"Why wouldn't I?"

Larisa shrugged again. Another thing it seemed better not to get into. In the abstract, usually late at night when she couldn't sleep, Larisa hated Parish with all four corners of her being. But here, in the cold institutional lighting and the hard stink of disinfectant that couldn't be disguised by the expensive air refresh system, Parish was someone Larisa could pity, someone she felt the need to protect.

"They said they called Quinn but he hasn't responded. My friend Pattie says I should write him a letter." Parish wrinkled her nose. "But Pattie is like ancient, so I guess that's all she knows how to do."

"Letters are slow."

Parish rolled onto her back and pulled her knees up with a groan. "I can't wait to be skinny again."

What will he do when he finds out? wondered Larisa. She checked her phone, which she'd managed to only do once since she'd arrived; her habit of checking for a message every other minute would've drawn Parish's interest. Her heart did a small leap when she saw a new message from Quinn. His last meeting of the day had been canceled.

> Quinn: Do you want to go out to dinner?

Larisa's mind flashed through all the possible ways a dinner out could go wrong, the number of people who would notice and feel the need to comment. She typed:

> Larisa: Come over instead.

"You're smiling," said Parish.

"So are you," said Larisa.

"Do you have a new secret?" Parish's voice slanted with dangerous interest, her eyes lighting with a preternatural glow that belonged in horror movies.

"Do you ever think about this spring?" asked Larisa.

"What about it?"

"What you did."

"Fucking Quinn at the Beverly Hilton or liberating you of your sins?"

"Sins?" First her PR team, now Parish. She was tired of people throwing around religious language without any true meaning. "If sins were what I had, only a deity could liberate me from them."

"That's what they say on those trial shows. Have you ever watched one? My friend and I—not Pattie, Kas—watched the last one live because there's absolutely nothing else to do here. And we've been following the Vanguard boys ever since. I think Bones is the hot one. But Kas likes Enoch because he's tall. I didn't know about them before. If I had, I would have nominated you for a trial. They help a lot of people."

Larisa didn't remember the Vanguard terrorists putting on another of their show trials that year. Last she'd heard, people had been speculating that the group had disbanded because the FBI had closed in. Then, without notice, her mind jumped back to what Parish had said.

"You had sex with Quinn that day?"

Parish gave her a smug look. "He did everything just as I said. It was the best sex ever. We did it in the bed, in the shower, and—"

"But you drugged him. It wasn't consensual."

Parish let out a cackle. "Details, Dr. Larisa. If you didn't get stuck on the details, you'd have so much more fun."

"So, you're only six months pregnant?"

"Yep. Why?"

Larisa stood to leave. She needed time to compose herself before Quinn arrived and, as it stood, if he was leaving the studio now, she'd barely beat him there.

"You shouldn't be stretching your back that far. My friend Rosa's six months pregnant, and her doctor said you can't reliably feel your lower back anymore even though your brain says you can. If you hyperextend your back, it can cause all kinds of problems."

"Like what?"

"I don't know. Ask your OB."

"Are you upset?"

"Yes."

"Because I said you were sinful?"

"Because you hurt people, and you don't feel bad about it."

Parish's voice followed her across the echoing tile of the walls. "Shouldn't you be glad I don't feel bad?"

Quinn had already been planted in her parents' kitchen when Larisa arrived. Sarah had let him in and sent him to the kitchen to watch Estelle finish batch-cooking freezer meals for the next week. She was going on vacation and had decided not to trust Gunter at his word when he'd said he could manage the kitchen in her absence.

"You're here." Larisa stopped herself from rushing up to smother him with a hug. He looked happy to see her, but tired. She turned and went to the fridge for a water instead. *Why do I keep thinking he doesn't want to be here?*

"I can make you chicken before I leave for the night," said Estelle.

"We'll just eat leftovers," said Larisa.

"You went out?" Quinn's voice sounded scratchy, like he was just coming down with a sore throat. Or he was just strained from talking so much the day before.

"Just an errand." She motioned for him to follow her. They walked together to the solarium, their hands at their sides almost close enough to touch. How she wanted him to touch her.

"I didn't hear much from you this morning."

"I wanted to focus for the lunch. And then things went long."

"In a good way?"

"Maybe. I mean the project is interesting. Your dad really helped. If I'd gone in unprepared . . . it was just weird being there again. Distracting."

"Where?"

"The lunch was at the same place I met Parish the day after Jaden's wedding."

"Why would you schedule a lunch there?" Larisa laughed off the sharpness she heard in her voice, which had more to do with what Parish had told her than feeling Quinn was a naïve idiot for not managing his schedule better.

Larisa turned on the solarium lights, illuminating the garden beds and the fountain her father had brought her mother from Greece, the lounge chairs, and the table covered with puzzle pieces. Quinn walked past her into the room. At night, this room felt like their special place, enchanted with soft shadows and guardian plants. She watched the shape of his back shift as his arms swung at his sides, then as his hands shoved into the pockets of his old Walmart hoodie.

She wished he'd turn around and look at her.

"I thought she took me straight to Club D after lunch," he said. "But when I was there, it felt . . . " He paused. She took a step toward him. "I don't think the Queen . . . I don't think you're the last person I had sex with." His voice dropped, something broken inside the sound. Discarding her resolve to respect his unspoken boundaries, Larisa closed the distance between them and wrapped him in her arms. He pressed into her, leaned his head back to rest on her shoulder.

"I'm sorry," he whispered.

"You have nothing to be sorry about."

He turned his head into her neck and inhaled her scent. And then, right at the moment she thought he might kiss her, he pulled out of her grasp. "You don't even smell like her."

Larisa took a moment to realize he meant the Queen, not Parish. Everything from that day was jumbled together. Of course, thoughts of Parish would mingle with his memories of the Queen, of his mind still trying to understand the lengths Larisa had gone to deceive him.

Someday maybe I'll be able to tell you.

"When do you think I should have told you?" she asked.

"What?"

"When would you have been ready for the truth?"

"At the beginning. When we sat at the bar with your friend Charity, and she did all the talking."

"And then what? Some night you're sleepy or drunk with friends, and you let slip about this amazing time you had at a bondage club with Larisa de France-Kahn."

"I wouldn't have."

"How would I know? How could you have promised that?"

"You led me on. That whole time, you planned to walk away instead of trust me, like what we had there was nothing."

Yes, she thought, *I always planned to walk away. You won't want me when you know what I am.*

"Telling you would've changed everything."

"That's my point."

He'd drifted toward the puzzle table, his back to her again.

"I've never been in that environment with someone who knew who I was."

"Okay."

"Haven't you ever wanted to be anonymous?"

He turned and stared at her.

Stupid Larisa. Stupid, stupid. She went over to the stereo and turned on the CD player. NSYNC poured out of the speakers at top volume. Across the room, Quinn swore, "Jesus!"

"Sorry. What are you in the mood for? Beatles' greatest hits? Édith Piaf? The National? How about The National? This is their newest. And if you don't like it, there's always opera." She wiggled her eyebrows at him and was rewarded with one of his ghost smiles.

"You want to talk about your mom and Italy?"

"Not really."

"Can I know enough so I don't make an ass of myself the next time it comes up?"

"We're not going to Italy. If fashion week is really on your bucket list, we can go to Paris or New York."

"Are we avoiding more than your mother's anniversary?"

"It's not avoidance. It's being smart."

They came together at opposite sides of the puzzle table. His eyes held hers, waiting for more, but she couldn't help but think of him as a foal in the woods, one cracked branch away from fleeing. And she wanted to keep him. She so desperately wanted to keep him.

She stirred the puzzle pieces with her hand.

"When you said you'd started a puzzle, I thought you'd have put some pieces together," he said.

"It's organized. You just can't tell. These are the blue pieces. These are also blue but they're the sky. And the rest is the rest."

"Where's the lid with the picture?"

Larisa glanced around. "Upstairs maybe. This is the third time I've done this puzzle this year. I do it a little every day until its done, then I break it up and start over."

As though this made perfect sense, Quinn nodded. He pulled up a chair, turned it around so the back pressed against the table, then straddled it as he surveyed the chaos of pieces. "Well, I guess I'll work on the blue ones."

She laughed. "Your sense of humor is underrated, you know that?"

"This music is forcing it out of me." He grimaced. "It must be art if it's depressing and obtuse, right? What are they even singing?"

She flicked a puzzle piece at him. "It's atmospheric."

"Well, it's not *The Sound of Music* that's for sure."

"Do you like *The Sound of Music*?" she asked in surprise.

He shrugged. "I remember there was a nice bit with Julie Andrews singing on top of a mountain."

"I love *The Sound of Music*. This one time, there was a storm so we reenacted the gazebo scene. Costumes, dancing, singing, thunder and lightning outside—the whole thing."

Quinn's head remained bowed over the puzzle, but he'd gone still in a way she knew he was no longer focused on the puzzle. Then she realized.

We.

Because she'd been thinking about Italy as much as she'd been trying *not* to think about it. Because once she let one memory in, they all came bubbling back up and resumed their places in her history, like a wrong turn she'd retraced trying to erase its existence.

"'We' being you and your college boyfriend?" asked Quinn finally. "The one who betrayed you by selling your story to the papers?"

Kind of.

"'Betrayed' is a strong word." Larisa squirmed. Why did she feel the need to defend Lucas?

"He introduced you to bondage."

She hadn't told him this, which meant he'd gone looking for it. Probably read the exposé in question, seen the descriptions of 'little submissive Larisa,' like she'd been a nubile Lolita to Lucas's Humbert.

"Among other things. A lot actually."

"But you just said you'd never done it with anyone who knew who you were."

"I wasn't a dominant with Lucas," she said, hoping this level of truth wasn't a mistake. "The way I was with him . . . there wasn't much of a line between role playing and real life. I did what he wanted."

Silence rushed in to fill the room. Larisa felt its judgement, tried not to watch the top of Quinn's head too closely as he made connections she didn't want him to make. Finally, he said, "What happened when that wasn't what you wanted?"

Something inside her that had been solid began to melt. Of all the questions he could ask. And more than that, the way he'd asked, as though he sensed how hard it was for her to talk about, how much she didn't want to go there with him. He was so very gentle, she wanted to pull him against her and hold him until he understood how completely perfect he was for her.

"Then I changed what I wanted." She watched Quinn's long, boney fingers rise up from his lap to triumphantly match two blue pieces together. They'd been still in his lap until now, not fidgeting, because Quinn didn't waste energy on extra movement. She wished she could change the subject, to just pour out how much she loved him and have that be enough.

It wasn't enough. Maybe, if they'd met before, this conversation wouldn't be necessary. But if they'd met before, she wouldn't know how to love him. She wouldn't notice his hands, his stillness, his careful questions. His silences would've scared her off before the third date.

Say something, she thought. *Help him understand.*
Trust him.

Larisa retreated to the stereo. "You know, you're right. This album's really a mood killer." Instead of turning it off, she skipped forward to track eight and stood still, listening until the circular guitar seeped into her legs, and she began to sway, then hum along with the naked voice of Matthew Donald Berninger singing about his refusal to run from the end of the world. And when he told her to throw her arms into the air, she did so, moving back and forth in the promise of the lyrics, or at least, what she thought the lyrics said. "I won't run." As she sang, tears slipped from her eyes.

If Quinn had joined her then, she would have said, "Isn't this the most heartbreaking song you've ever heard that isn't about heartbreak?"

But Quinn stayed at the table. Maybe he watched her, or

maybe he didn't. She didn't need to know. One of the many things she'd learned after Lucas was the value of owning a moment for herself. She wasn't great at it with people. But in music, at least, she had good luck claiming a space of her own where she lived for her own eyes, and her own feelings, and her own dreams.

Chapter 4

This Isn't the Right Party

The *Sound of Music* comment lodged in Quinn's mind and refused to budge. She'd sounded so happy remembering that time with her ex. *Lucas.* It felt so present in her mind, that joy, a thing huddled just below the surface of her current self. The more he thought about it, the more significant it became. Not just a happy memory, but a symbol of what she wanted in a relationship. Someone spontaneous and carefree, someone who liked musicals and dancing.

The next day, they worked on the puzzle. It was quiet in the beginning, and Quinn thought maybe they were making progress, being able to just sit together in silence. He thought maybe the past was the past and if Larisa wanted him instead of her ex, he didn't have anything to worry about. But then Larisa started humming. She drew back from the puzzle and stared out the window.

What is she humming?

Does it remind her of him?

Unreasonable thoughts. Larisa's life was a bundle of chaos she somehow kept trapped in her mind. While they'd been working, she'd received over a dozen text messages from her PR team and the sisters. All of them had made her draw her eyebrows together as though in pain, as though her life pained her. The silence between them became something less comfortable, as though she was purposefully holding herself in a place he couldn't reach.

Finally, he said, "You have a lot going on in your head today."

"Just the usual."

"What's usual?"

"I'm not sure about this party. It sounds like there'll be more people there than I thought. Jaden's foundation friends." Larisa hitched her shoulders up around her ears like she was cold, then shook them out. "But it's fine. We should support her."

Who supports you? he wondered.

"You know you can talk to me, right?" It sounded like he thought she needed counseling instead of just an invitation to share her inner life with him. The look she gave him, like he couldn't begin to imagine what went on in her head, made it impossible to say anything after that.

When Sid picked him up that night, Quinn felt like he'd stepped out of an alien atmosphere and returned to the safety of Earth where he could finally breathe comfortably.

"I think she was thinking about someone else the whole day."

"Maybe you didn't give her a better option," said Sid.

"What's that supposed to mean?"

"If you're really into her, she might wonder why you haven't gotten your shit together, yeah? It's been like two weeks."

Sid said it like going from being in love with one woman to falling for someone entirely different was something that could happen in a set amount of time. Quinn didn't tell Sid that getting to know Larisa better made it feel even less likely that they would last. In Quinn's bruised mind, Larisa and the Queen were two separate people. Before *The Sound of Music* comment, he'd thought of them as islands formed out of generalized life experiences like everyone else, separated out of an entirely understandable self-preservation instinct.

But by the time he arrived at the studio on Monday, Quinn had become convinced that the only thing linking the two was Lucas. It felt like he'd been with them the entire weekend in the things Larisa chose not to say, in the habits that couldn't be traced to her parents or her friends. Quinn felt it in the way she looked out at the backyard with her mind lost in another time and place.

He felt it in the way she hummed to herself, then abruptly broke off as though expecting him to finish the tune, and in the meticulous way she'd organized a playlist for their drive down the PCH that weekend. He might learn to enjoy some bands and maybe movie soundtracks, but he was never going to catch up to her enough that it'd be something they'd share.

She doesn't expect that, thought Quinn, as Discovery's chief of marketing clicked through a PowerPoint on the distribution of advertising dollars for *The Key.*

But she might want it. Down the road she'll be dissatisfied.

Don't think about the future. All you know is now.

I want her in my future.

This felt like a breakthrough. When the thought had come to him, he'd pictured Larisa not the Queen. He enjoyed being with her. That morning, she'd been sending him costume ideas for the party. They'd exchanged several heated texts arguing over the all-time best Halloween candy. It was fun. Larisa was fun, which seemed a revelation. He'd never have imagined the woman who'd sat in that grungy public health consultation room in her over-sized designer clothes and cold eyes would ever start an argument about Halloween candy.

As the meeting ended and Quinn checked his phone for her latest message, someone came up to him and gave him a thumbs up. "Saw you're official. Good luck."

Quinn supposed this meant the *Film Comment* article had been published. His first thought was guilt, as though he should have asked someone's permission first. Later, when he and Sid were driving over to pick up Larisa for Jaden's party, he realized it was the ex-boyfriend he felt he should have asked. He became so caught up in this thought he didn't even realize they'd arrived until Sid let out a low whistle.

"That woman's wasted on you, bud."

Sid had inexplicably decided to wear only the pants portion of a white stormtrooper uniform and one of those Venice Beach T-shirts printed with Arnold Schwarzenegger's chest. This look made the comment seem more sleezy than insulting, even though Quinn knew Sid was warning him yet again that he felt the relationship had been stamped with a giant, red FAILURE sign.

Quinn got out of the front passenger seat and saw Larisa walking toward them. She was wearing a jumper costume that was black in the pants part and blue on the top with a little silver badge fastened to the side of her chest. She'd painted brown markings all along her temples and forehead.

"I thought you were joking when you said *Star Trek* costume," he said.

"I was joking about *you* wearing a *Star Trek* costume," said Larisa, as she blinked her eyelash extensions at him.

He held the back door open for her to get in, then climbed in after her.

"So, are you a human or alien or what?" Quinn waved at the patterned spots she'd painted along the side of her face and forehead.

"She's Jadzia Dax from *DS9*, obviously," said Sid.

"I don't know what that is. Am I going to be the only person at this party not wearing a costume?"

Larisa grinned at him. "I guess we'll find out." And then, as though thinking he was really freaked, she scooted across the bench seat and gave him the kind of hug an adult gave a child who was afraid of the dark. "You'll be okay."

I am okay, he told himself. Together, they would survive the party. He could count on her to guide him through it. The rest of what was making him crawl out of his skin wasn't real.

Jaden and Adrian lived in a mansion on top of a mountain. Half a mile out, both sides of the road up the mountain were lined with parked cars. For each minute that rolled by with cars encroaching out the windows, Quinn's low-grade anxiety about being the only one without a costume ballooned into a true pulse acceleration. This was not like the birthday party he'd been to that summer. This was a *Hollywood* party.

He heard it before he saw it, the rumble of the bass like thunder. Sid pulled up to the valet stand and the din of what seemed liked thousands of voices rolled down the front walk toward the car.

"Should've brought a swimsuit," said Sid, as he hopped out and ran around to pass the keys off to the valet.

"What's wrong?" asked Larisa.

"This isn't what I expected," said Quinn.

"Yeah. It looks like she went a little overboard." Larisa's mouth turned upside down with sour irritation. "Want to go home?"

He looked at her in surprise. It was too dark to see if she was offering for his sake or because she also didn't want to do this. All he saw were those spots, which weren't just spots, they were squiggles and curves, a design that had taken her hours, that he didn't understand well enough to appreciate.

"Let's give it thirty minutes," he said. "We're already here."

"And Sid's excited." Larisa nodded out the window to Sid bounding up the front steps.

"Sid thinks large groups of intoxicated people are fun."

"He's never had a crowd turn on him." Larisa sucked in a breath. "Alright. Thirty minutes. If he's not ready to leave by then, we can hide in one of the bathrooms. There are nine."

"Nine?" Quinn tried to think of how many bathrooms were in the Kahn estate.

"Only seven," said Larisa before he could ask.

"How did you ever manage?"

Her face lit up with delight. She leaned in as though she would kiss him, then reached across him to open the door. Nudging him with her hips, she said, "Out. We're holding up the line."

As he got out of the BMW, Quinn saw there were several cars lined up waiting for the attention of the valet. When had Larisa noticed? He'd felt as though all her attention had been on him and yet, somehow, she'd noticed the cars, and she'd noticed Sid. It reminded him of how much of Larisa's mental acuity was going to waste as she passed her days sitting in her parents' house instead of helping people solve their problems.

Her hand slipped into his as they climbed the stairs up to the front of the house, which was landscaped with a bridge over a reflective pool, a magnolia hedge, and a rock garden with ceramic frogs. Inside, there was textured plaster walls painted in neutral-toned ombre waves and brightly colored sporty pseudo-art. After the entryway, the walls became invisible boundaries confining and funneling people in a tangled intestine of chaos.

His grip on Larisa's hand tightened as she led him through the press of bodies. How was attending this kind of party going to improve his career as Gunter had suggested? What even was the point of standing in a room with a hundred other people so close together you couldn't see anything? And if someone spoke, they had to shout in someone's ear to be understood. Even that would've been almost impossible because it seemed most people were dancing. Why would someone choose to dance in a place where there wasn't enough space to breathe?

They burst out of the press onto the palatial pool deck. The glowing azure square was marked out from the party by a thick frame of gyrating bodies. Steam rose from it into the cool night air that only existed above the water. Quinn wished the pool was one of those painted illusion floors so he might go out and sit down right in the middle of it. Alone.

A smaller, elevated deck overlooked the pool deck. Here, in a corner by the railing, they stopped. Quinn liked how Larisa planted him against the railing, then stood between him and the crowd, though the few people already on the deck were focused on a man wearing a ball cap and several diamond chains around his neck. One of Adrian's baseball teammates.

"You okay?" asked Larisa, as she scanned the deck, then moved her gaze to the mass of people down below.

"Sure."

She turned to look at him as though she didn't take him at his word. Her hand came up, fluffed out his hair, then pushed the long top part to the side so it hung over the right of his forehead. "I don't see anyone you'd want to talk to. I thought Steve would come. I told him . . . he always says what you want him to say even if he never means it. Fuck. If you could impress Steve that would—there's Rosa. Why's she alone?" Larisa let go of his hand. "I'm not leaving you. I promise. I'm just going to go down and get her. If you see a very tall Greek god, introduce yourself."

He felt a puff of refreshing coolness as the mountain air rushed in to fill Larisa's place at his side. Quinn waved his sweaty hands through it, trying to calm down. He was just wondering if the Steve Larisa had mentioned was Steve Helston, when Rosa crested the stairs, her large stomach leading the way, with Larisa right behind her.

"But why isn't Tate here with you?" asked Larisa. "I'm going to text him."

"There was a thing at work. It's fine. I'm *fine*." Rosa laughed. "Hi, Quinn. Nice to see you again. Congrats on being official."

"Official?" asked Larisa.

"The internet knows you're dating Quinn. Don't look it up."

Something that looked like genuine panic crossed Larisa's face. It passed so quickly, Quinn almost thought he'd imagined it.

"Is it that bad?" she asked Rosa.

"Some of it made me blush." And then, as though recalling whatever she'd read, the flush on Rosa's cheeks deepened.

Larisa darted away to steal a chair from a pair of teenagers who'd decided the baseball player was boring and were ready to move on. "It can't be that bad," she said, as she returned. "I'm just an unscrupulous mental health professional who likes to beat men." As though realizing she'd just said that aloud, she glanced around. Her gaze narrowed. "There's Steve. Neither of you move!"

Once again, Larisa plowed down the deck stairs and began to wade through people to reach an epicenter of gravity forming by the door.

She's avoiding me, thought Quinn. An irrational, overblown thought, but still potent.

Rosa eased herself down into the chair. "I didn't think it would be like this."

"Me neither."

"I wouldn't have come." Rosa laughed. Quinn thought he heard a tinge of bitterness in it. "So, how's it going? And you don't have to lie. I know Larisa can be challenging."

Quinn glared at the drainpipe of the roof just a few feet above the baseball player's head. *She just rescued you from all those people,* he thought. *And she brought you a chair. Don't apologize for her.*

"It's good." He wondered if Larisa had ever felt the need to apologize to her friends about him. He certainly wasn't easy. Rosa was looking up at him with that veiled caution one gave a person they didn't know how to talk to. But what else was there to say besides 'it's good'? They were at a party. Any minute Larisa was going to walk up the stairs with a movie star in tow and Quinn would have to be charming, or at least moodily artistic. Because he did want the job directing the new *Poseidon.* If he made that, he could do anything he wanted afterward. There would be no more uncertainty. The questions about his future that Gunter Kahn had asked him on Thursday night would have answers.

A new song began to pound out of the stereo system. Quinn thought he recognized it from their drive that weekend, which reminded him of how it'd felt to be with her feeling like half the time she was thinking about someone else.

"What was Lucas like?" he asked.

"Charming, sophisticated, extremely wealthy. How much do you want to know?"

How was he with her?

How did he treat her?

Was there any warning when it ended?

The biggest question: *Do you think she's gotten over him?*

"I only met him once," said Rosa. "He came to graduation. Obviously, there were problems. But it was her first big relationship. She loved that he wasn't connected to her parents or impressed by them or anything like that."

When he'd met with Gunter, essentially canceling their evening doing the puzzle, had she been upset? Did she resent his desire to know her parents?

"Anyway, it was messy when it ended. We all went out to Minnesota. She was in med school living with her cousin, not eating, not sleeping. She was put on academic probation. I swear I didn't think she'd ever come out of it."

"And then?"

"And then, one day she just clicked back into place. Told us she was fine. Sent us home. Became a doctor. We all feel it's best to pretend he doesn't exist. That's why it's so surprising she agreed to this Italy trip. He lives there, you know. In Tuscany."

Quinn's gut churned. He moved to the other side of the railing for a better view of down below. Larisa had reached the unmistakable tall blond, god-like figure of Steve Helston. But instead of moving toward the stairs, they started dancing together. Not just dancing, leading everyone around them in the pulse of the song. He thought he recognized Krissy and Jaden in the crowd.

"She didn't agree to Italy," he said.

"Then what . . . Oh." Quinn thought Rosa was going to say something terrible, though entirely deserved, about Suzette. Instead, she said, "Well, that's too bad. I would've loved to get away. Suzette said she'd hire a nanny for the baby to travel with us."

"It's a little weird, isn't it? Avoiding an entire country because one person lives there?"

"Yeah, I guess. I never thought about it. But you know Larisa, she doesn't do anything halfway."

Down below, Larisa, Jaden, and Krissy threw their arms in the air like they were at a club. For a moment, they danced, unified in their movement, then Krissy leaned over and shouted something in Larisa's ear. Larisa went still, her head snapping around to look at Krissy as Krissy and Jaden continued to dance unaware of the shift in their friend. But Quinn recognized it. That shift was the full stop of the bottom dropping out, of dread washing through a body so it was no longer aware of anything but the one thought that had triggered it. Larisa now knew her mother had invited Larisa's friends on an all-expense-paid trip to Milan for fashion week.

He texted Sid:

> We need to leave. Where are you?

In the moments it took him to type and send the message, Larisa recovered. When he looked up, she was dancing again. She moved back to Steve, then to the people around him. She took a drink right out of someone's hand and downed it.

"I bet we could convince Larisa to change her mind," said Rosa. "I've never been to Italy. If Suzette has made all these plans, it would—"

"Would you like a ride home?" Quinn asked.

"Uh, well I should at least say hi to Jaden." Rosa pushed herself up to her feet. "Do you see her? Oh! Is that Steve Helston?" Rosa moved to the stairs. "Why didn't you tell me?"

Quinn caught up with her in time to offer his hand as extra support going down the stairs. Back on the ground, the little breathing room they'd found on the deck disappeared. People jostled and pushed into his space like he was invisible. Rosa, though she was a foot shorter than him, led the way, steering with her elbows pointed out.

In no time at all, they'd reached the circle gathered around Steve. On the side opposite Quinn, Larisa's body was a rage of motion as she sang at the top of her lungs. She waved at people to encourage them to sing along. When she saw Quinn, she lurched toward him.

"Quinn! I was just coming to get you. This is Steve. Steve?" She grabbed the movie star's giant bicep and pulled him around. "Steve, this is Quinn. He should do your next *Poseidon*."

Quinn barely registered Steve's huge grin as he stuck out his hand to shake. He stared at Larisa, shocked by how loose she seemed after one drink.

"You're a director, huh?" asked Steve.

"I guess so."

Larisa gave him a look like, *Seriously, Quinn? Do better.*

"Cool. I'd love for you to do the new movie. Just know I have my way of doing things. Right? Like the character, and all that, is established."

"Yeah." Quinn moved toward Larisa, but somehow the distance between them remained the same. He called out for her to stop moving. Oblivious, she pressed onward and disappeared into the mass of bodies. He found himself between Jaden and Krissy.

"It's Quinn!"

"Quinn! You're official for real this time. Congrats!"

In his pocket, his phone vibrated. He ignored it and kept moving until he fell into the current of people and followed it inside. There, several people ahead and to his left, Larisa's hair caught the light and drew his attention. She turned and disappeared down a hallway. Someone grabbed his arm and said, "Hey man, you know where Steve Helston is?"

"Patio."

Quinn kept moving. The more he walked the less likely it felt he would find her. He began to do what that guy had done to him, hands on sleeves, pressing into other people's space, and asking, "Have you seen Larisa de France-Kahn?"

"That kinky whore?"

"Hey, aren't you that guy?"

"Seen Larisa?"

"Who?"

"Tall brunette?"

"There was a model who went that way." A woman pointed toward the ceiling. Entirely unhelpful.

By now Quinn didn't remember his last satisfying breath, and he'd sweated through all three layers of his clothes. He opened the first door he found. A bathroom. He stepped inside and closed the door, stood there until he caught his breath. His phone vibrated.

He'd missed two messages and a call from Sid:

> Sid: I'm at the bar.

Then, ten minutes later:

> Sid: Got Larisa. We'll meet you at valet.
>
> Quinn: Coming.

He splashed water on his face, took a breath, and opened the door.

The bubble of the BMW felt like the silence of a gothic mansion after the turmoil of the party. Besides the occasional clicking of Sid turning the blinker on and off, the only sound was Larisa's rings knocking against the neck of the bottle of vodka she'd stolen from the bar. They made it all the way to West Hollywood before she said, "Did you know?"

"Rosa just told me."

"Fucking bitch cunt."

"Is that really necessary?" asked Sid from up front.

"Fuck you, Sid." Larisa took a long pull off the bottle. "Actually Sid, I really love you. I think you're wonderful. Can we go somewhere else?"

"Not the parental manor?"

"How about my apartment? It's just-just take a right here, here, here" —she jabbed her finger toward the windshield— "and pop into Santa Monica."

Larisa's apartment was one of six units in a squat, square building off a courtyard full of birds-of-paradise. She hopped out of the car without saying goodnight.

Quinn climbed out of the car and stood by the driver's side door. Somewhere in the shadows, he heard Larisa swearing as she dropped her keys while trying to punch in the gate code.

"I'll text you later," he said to Sid. "I don't have any early meetings tomorrow. I'll just get a car to the studio."

"Good luck." Sid held out his fist to bump, then rolled up the window and pulled away. Quinn hurried to catch the front gate before it locked him out.

Larisa had managed to unlock her door. She stood still on the threshold, a silhouette in pink light cast by an unseen lamp. "It smells in here. I thought Sarah was sending someone to clean every week." She stumbled forward. Quinn followed her.

This was the place she'd lived until April when reporters had besieged the front gate, demanding answers to questions no one needed to know but felt entitled to, nonetheless. It was a small place with a combined kitchen, dining nook, and living room. The pink light came from a fuzzy pink scarf draped over a lamp. No doubt a fire hazard, but it added character to what was otherwise a spare space. The hi-fi stereo took up an entire wall.

"Welcome to my den of iniquity." Larisa gave him a crooked smile that held only a moment before it crumbled. "I always hated this place. I was working fifty hours a week at the hospital, and I still needed my parents' help to afford a dump like this. Fucking LA."

"It's nicer than anything I had until last year."

"Do you think Sid is mad at me?"

"No."

"Are you mad at me?"

"Why would I be mad at you?"

Larisa shrugged. "It feels like there are lots of reasons." She held up the vodka bottle and squinted at the level of liquid inside. "This went fast."

"Time to switch to water?" Quinn moved past her toward the kitchen. As he did, she leaned into him and trapped him against the island counter.

"I can do better."

"Larisa—"

"I know this weekend wasn't great. I'll talk more. Be more open. What do you want to know? Ask me anything."

For all the things he'd wondered and felt unable to ask over the past two weeks, at that moment, Quinn couldn't think of a single one. She was so warm. Her energy radiated into him like a muted police siren. In and out, in and out with her rushed breath. The current of it seeped into him, recalling old fantasies he'd nourished. What he would do to the Queen when he'd finally made himself worthy enough for her to remove her mask. Before he could stop himself, his hand went to Larisa's hip, traced upward to the high the waistband of her pants and—

No.

He couldn't come onto Larisa like he was one of her lotharios full of swagger and ego. After what he'd brought into her life that spring, he'd never make himself worthy doing the regular things. The horror of it covered him like a second skin and now, that skin was touching the furnace of her velvet-smooth belly. It pulsed against him, as much an invitation as a mockery. He withdrew his hand.

"I'm sorry about your mom," he said.

The breath slowed. She twisted away from him. But he caught her around the hips and pulled her back. These hips, in their, bicolor *Star Trek* costume, so solid in his hands. Finally, familiar.

"Everyone's going to hate me if I call it off."

"I won't hate you."

She stiffened against him. "I'm so tired of being disappointing."

He opened his arms and gently closed them around her. After a moment of holding onto her resistance, she folded her arms up against his chest and leaned into his embrace. He tightened his arms around her. They stood like that, the first time he'd ever truly held her. The first time she'd ever shrunk herself down to fit within his grasp, a small surrender writ large.

The faint ticking of an analog clock sounded from an adjacent room marking the time. Their breathing unconsciously synchronizing to it, to each other. He closed his eyes and tried to feel every part of her that touched him, to tell his mind this was the woman he wanted. This was her shape, this was her heat, her breath, her soft shivers as she came down from the climax of her rage and softened into him.

The smell of her shampoo, which had startled him before because it was not a smell he associated with the Queen, shocked him less now. The weight of her head against his did not feel so much a stranger's. Just as he was about to say he liked the smell, she pulled away from him, her face open with surprise. He thought at first she'd felt his growing erection, but then her hand went to her mouth.

"Oh no."

She made a sloppy dash to the bathroom and dove through the door. A moment later, he heard her retching into the cold hollow of the toilet bowl.

At first, Quinn thought he'd give her privacy, but then he saw the force of the expulsion had captured all her focus. Her hair was falling forward into the toilet. He stepped over her feet on his way to carefully perch on the side of the bathtub.

"Go away!" she gasped between the violent convulsions of her stomach.

He leaned over her and began to gather her hair in his right hand.

"Leave it." Her left hand shot out as though to wave him off. Just as quickly, it came back in and clutched her stomach. "Oh God."

"You have very big hair," said Quinn. "Thick. It's thick, huh?"

"Would you just—"

"If I move, I'll have to drop it."

"Fuck you."

He smiled down at the back of her head. "I was sick a lot in high school. Junior year was just a solid eight months of 'my gut hates me.' A stress reaction, but it didn't feel like that then. I felt calm. My mom had said she was leaving. The guidance counselors kept having us take all these life-goal tests to see what kinds of careers we should have. They kept talking about how important college was. Everyone was freaked, but I felt calm. I don't remember eating much besides instant cup ramen, saltines, and Pepsi."

Larisa lifted her head from the toilet and slowly drew herself back. He moved with her, still holding her hair. His thumb moved absently over the silky softness of the twist he'd made in his palm.

"I like your hair."

"Thanks."

He released it, stood, stepped over her to the sink where he found a hair tie in one drawer and a washcloth in another. He soaked it with warm water and held it out to her.

"This is so embarrassing." Larisa wiped her mouth, folded the cloth, then wiped down her entire face.

"Ready to stand?"

"Hmm, maybe not yet." Larisa pulled out her phone and scrolled through her notifications. "Jaden wants to know where I am. Poor thing. Everyone probably hates her." Larisa typed a message. "My agent says that *Film Comment* piece got mentioned by the *Hollywood Reporter*. Shall we see what it says?"

"You're going to read it on your phone?" Quinn sank down on the floor with his back against the cabinet, facing her.

She composed her face with exaggerated focus on her phone screen. "'I recently had the honor of sitting down with Quinn VanderVeer, director of Enterprise Studios' *The Key*, a holiday season release starring Vince Rocks and newcomer Dansby Vaast.'

Da . . . ta da, la, la, and summary of the film. Boring, boring. 'VanderVeer is most animated when discussing film, gesticulating with the energy of a child on Christmas morning as he describes the revelation of watching *2001: A Space Odyssey* as a boy. Besides Kubrick, his favorites are Kurosawa and Todd Field'—seriously?"

"What?"

"Those people all make boring movies."

"They make beautiful, technical masterpieces your father should have taught you to appreciate."

Larisa rolled her eyes. "He tried, believe me. But that's not my point. You're not like them."

"You haven't seen *The Key* yet. It's better than Kubrick."

"If you'd bring me a screener, I'll watch it and tell you all the ways it's better for not being like Kubrick." She paused as though suddenly worried she'd been too forceful, or maybe she was exasperated with his insecurity the way Sid was sometimes. "You have more sugar," she said. "They're basically all red meat."

He arched an eyebrow at her. "Are you still drunk?"

"I'm serious. It's like . . . "

He held back laughter as he watched her face contort itself, nose scrunched, alien spots smudged, searching for better words. He'd never seen her like this. Beautiful on her own terms, wholly herself without worrying what anyone else thought of her.

"Like the difference between literary and upmarket commercial fiction."

"I don't know what those are."

"Literary is like artful writing books. Like what they require you to read in school. And upmarket commercial is like Stephen King. Or maybe just the new book he did about Kennedy is upmarket. Most of his work is just plain commercial."

"This isn't getting any clearer."

"Upmarket is the middle ground between pop entertainment and high art. It's like a balanced meal."

"But you said I'm sugar."

"A balanced meal people want to eat has sugar. They don't eat it because it's good for them."

"I'm going to tell your father you said that."

"He'd probably agree with me. Sugar sells well. Anyway, this conversation won't make sense in the morning."

Make it be night forever. Quinn's back already hurt but he didn't want to be anywhere else except sitting on this bathroom floor across from her, the stink of vomit and vodka fuming the room. Finally, finally, he felt they were in the same place together.

"What does it say about us?" he asked.

Larisa hit the button on her phone to illuminate the screen. "'VanderVeer has many reasons to be giddy about his life these days. Besides *The Key*, there's rumors he's been tapped to take on the latest *Poseidon* installment for FilmStreams. And he's dating Larisa de France-Kahn, daughter of the legendary producer Gunter Kahn. When asked if he felt any added pressure now that he's moving up in the world, VanderVeer said, "the biggest pressure has always come from myself. That will never change. I don't want to waste a single day being ordinary."'"

"Kind of disappointing he felt the need to attach you to your dad," said Quinn.

"That's typical, especially now when people don't know what to call me. I'm not a trendsetter, or an actress, or a model, or even a doctor. So, I'm the 'daughter of _____,'" she drew her hand in a line through the air like Meg Ryan in *You've Got Mail*, "until you keep me around long enough people start thinking of me as the 'girlfriend of _____.'"

"You'll have your practice set up before that happens."

Larisa shrugged.

"We should think of a name for you."

"Like a pseudonym? I think I've had enough role playing."

"No, like a stage act or a tag line that teaches people your value."

"I don't have value, Quinn. My one client is an aging actress who's fallen in with some feminist cult of other actresses and wants to know why men hate her."

"Why don't you work with Dansby? He's got money now. Probably needs help managing all the attention." Quinn pictured Dansby as he'd looked when they'd briefly crossed paths at the studio the week before. His actor had been coiffed and strutting like a peacock that had just discovered exactly what beauty could do for him. He'd seemed fine. Much more fine than Quinn would've been under that kind of limelight. But then Dansby wasn't troubled by thinking too deeply about anything.

"I think I'm ready to stand."

Quinn got to his feet and stood, ready to catch her if she fell.

"I appreciate you being willing to go on record," she said.

He cupped her elbows in his palms as she swayed, then found her balance. "I don't think you're as difficult as you think."

She gazed at him for a long moment as though searching for the hint of a lie in his expression. Then she nodded and motioned for him to move toward the door. "We'll see how you feel tomorrow."

What Is Love

L arisa didn't return to her parents' house until her PR meeting Thursday afternoon.

"There you are. I was beginning to wonder," said Suzette.

They'd all been in discussion before Larisa walked in and disturbed the air.

"Wonder if I was mad enough not to show up?"

Rockie and Julie exchanged glances. But the junior asset manager, name still unknown, perked up as though something was finally happening. Perhaps in response to this enthusiasm, Larisa said, "My dearest mother invited all my friends to Milan without telling me."

"I'll go in her place, Suzette," said the junior asset manager, who then received a chastising glare from Rockie.

"Anyway—" Larisa flopped into a chair— "what are we discussing this week? Ya'll are so serious you'd think I'd been caught murdering puppies."

"The relationship revelation hasn't hit well," said Julie. "We can't wait for Milan to start real damage control."

"I'm not allowed to be in love?" asked Larisa.

Rockie and Julie exchanged another look, then Julie looked to Suzette.

It feels like someone has died and they've been in here planning the funeral, thought Larisa.

"You know how people like to talk," said Suzette, easing into whatever bombshell was coming. Larisa's diaphragm tightened the way it did at the top of a roller coaster. That pause before the plunge was the worst part. She always wanted roller coasters to take off and never slow down until the end. All thrill, no dreaded anticipation.

"And you give them so many excuses."

"I didn't sign up to be famous," said Larisa. "That's something you gave me, *Mother*."

"There were pictures leaked of you with Steve Helston at a party."

"Everyone dances with Steve. That's how he is."

"And someone said you're sleeping with him to get Quinn the *Poseidon* job."

"Don't forget the radio guy," said the junior asset manager. She looked like she enjoyed this. Maybe not Larisa's humiliation, but the abstract idea of it, cause and effect, being so close to a woman who could shake the national conversation just by dancing at a party.

"And a radio host held a call-in for listeners to answer the question of why you hate men so much you'd want to beat them. It's been picked up and reported by several major outlets."

Larisa opened her mouth and closed it. Responding felt less than useless.

"For the record, I think it was picked up because everyone's talking about this book." The junior asset manager waved a paperback in the air.

"The Discovery rep called me this morning and asked why we didn't warn them," said Julie.

"Quinn doesn't know how these things work," said Larisa. "He just . . . it came out during one of his interviews."

"They're concerned how this will look for the film. His sexuality has been questioned."

Larisa let out a small incredulous laugh. "What do we do?" she asked.

"You need to break your silence," said Rockie. "It's time to join the conversation."

"I'm not going to go on a radio show and talk about why I beat men. Anyway, before Quinn, I beat plenty of women. My skills were in high demand, believe it or not."

"Do you still go?" asked the junior asset manager.

"I'm talking to Oprah," said Julie. "In the meantime, we'd like you to be wholesomely visible."

"What the fuck does that mean?"

"Volunteering? Dog walking. Green smoothies. Wearing modest clothing."

"I don't have a dog."

"Are you planning to go to events with Quinn for the film?" asked Rockie.

"Not if I'm going to get egged."

"Is Jordan still your stylist?" Rockie pulled out her phone and began making a note. "I'll want to approve all your looks. We don't want anything too edgy."

"Oh my God, are you serious?"

"This isn't just about you anymore, dear," said Suzette. "You don't want Quinn to see you as a problem, do you?"

An unanswerable question, the kind that made Larisa seal her lips and cross her arms to pout like a child. Behaving like a child could be extremely satisfying. Though this time, it did nothing to ease the reality of the hurt. It had been years since her mother had trapped her so cruelly.

Larisa hadn't said anything else for the rest of the meeting. She'd wanted to be angry, to rage against her handlers for cruelty that wasn't their fault. But the bottom line was the conversation needed to be productive. They drafted a press release officially announcing the relationship. They were going to set up an appointment at an animal shelter and invite cameras. They were going to ask the studio about Larisa sitting in on one or two interviews for *The Key* press junket, so people could see her as a nice, supportive girlfriend.

As the group had made their exit, the junior asset manager gave Larisa the BDSM novel to read. Larisa, wrung out and spoiling for a fight, followed her mother to the kitchen.

"We need to talk about Milan," said Larisa.

Suzette began to set the table. "We need to talk about the holidays. Alison called today."

Alison was Gunter's brother's wife, Hannah's mother, and holdfast of the Kahn family festivities since their mother had passed on. Everyone except Gunter and one of his second cousins still lived in Minnesota, so all celebrations took place there except when Gunter decided to host everyone in LA, which didn't happen very often because most of them didn't like paying for it.

"I want to talk about how you went behind my back to my friends."

"It works best for us to be there for Christmas," continued Suzette. "But if you want to do separate holidays, I suppose you can go there for Thanksgiving, and your father and I will go for Christmas."

"I don't want to go anywhere with you."

"Your father will be disappointed."

Larisa glared at the kitchen table. And in this case, her mother wasn't even being manipulative. Gunter loved Christmas in all its technicolor glory and consumerist splendor. He'd already mentioned how happy he was she'd be free to come this year.

"I haven't thought that far ahead," said Larisa, as she deflated.

"Will Quinn come?"

"I haven't thought that far ahead."

"It'd be good for you to be out in the world with him so it seems like a real relationship. You're so formal with each other. I wonder if we could—"

"Mom, stop. I'll commit to Minnesota Christmas. I'll ask Quinn about it. But neither of us is going to Milan. Do you understand that?"

The security system pinged an arrival at the front door.

"Anything else?"

Suzette sighed. "I don't want you going back to that apartment while this is going on."

"This is my life, Mom. It's been 'going on' for thirty years." She stood to go answer the door. "We'll eat when you leave."

"Don't be so petty," her mother called after her, loud enough Quinn heard her in the atrium.

"You okay?" he asked.

"Let's go outside." She led the way to the backyard. They left the path that led from the patio to the gazebo and walked onto the lawn. She watched Quinn's eyes stray to the gazebo then look away, and thought he was remembering what she'd said about recreating that scene from *The Sound of Music* with Lucas. She reached over and took his hand. "Can we be frivolous and nostalgic tonight?"

"I'll follow your lead."

She flopped down into the grass. He more carefully laid down beside her. Overhead, the trees cackled in the wind, laughing at her louder than ever. Their leering made the rotten feeling in her stomach worse.

"Did you ever have girls over to your house?"

"Once maybe. We were studying for the SAT."

"Studying or pretending to study?"

She loved the way his face turned pink as though they weren't years away from being embarrassed by adolescent hormones.

"I made the mistake of trying to impress her with my vocabulary. She was an English, bookish person, so she wasn't impressed. But we did make out on the kitchen table."

"The same table you have in your house now?"

"The very same."

"And after that?"

"She graduated."

She slapped his arm. "Come on."

"Well, if you're asking about past significant relationships, it's not very interesting. I went to a Fourth of July block party freshman year and lost my virginity to my neighbor Kayla, who went around telling everyone I was terrible at it. After that, I got smart and only had sex with people at work."

"No."

"Yep. But it was easier than it sounds. Everyone was kind of sleeping with everyone. And it broke up the long hours."

"What about love?"

"Well, I love Sid." He laughed. "And there was Patrice junior year, who sat two rows in front of me in chemistry. She wouldn't give me the time of day. Which is typical, right? But I thought if I worked hard enough, I'd see her at the reunion and be so impressive she'd just throw herself at me." He paused. "And I was pretty gone for this writer in college."

"Screenwriter?"

"No, poet. For some reason, I loved how he'd write about me as this neurotic, mad genius, always brooding and silent until I had a good idea, then I'd just blab it all over everyone."

"True love."

"It felt like it." Quinn paused. "I think love is being seen. And being appreciated. And filling in each other's gaps." He laughed as though surprised by how quickly the conversation had turned serious.

"Gaps," said Larisa. "Like what they're not good at?"

"Not very flashy, is it?"

"But nice. Romantic." She thought of her earlier fear that Quinn had not said, 'I love you,' at the autumn masquerade. Maybe he'd felt it unnecessary given everything else he'd said.

In so many ways they fit together. And yet.

"What about attraction?" she asked.

"What about it?"

I'm not anything like Parish physically, she thought.

Behind them, the patio door swished open just enough for Gunter to stick his hand out and wave. "Kitchen's vacant." He hesitated there as though he'd planned to say more, but then retracted and closed the door.

"He's not going to defend me against my mother," said Larisa.

"Did you talk about what she did?"

"She's acting like she didn't do anything wrong, and he's acting like nothing happened. They're thinking about the holidays."

"Big party to plan?"

"You wish." She toyed with his fingers. It felt good to be connected to him. "She's done this before. It's like an army attacking right before a storm, then the storm comes in and erases all evidence of what they've done. In this case, the storm's the holiday season. We'll all be busy, forced into good family cheer until the first week of January. And by then, the jet will have been chartered, the rooms purchased. And I'll just have to say yes to Italy."

"Which you don't want to do."

"Obviously not."

The silence of Quinn thinking, then the inevitable question. "Why is it obvious?"

"I think you should pick the movie tonight," she said.

"We're doing a movie? Let me text Sid. He was going to hang around a bit."

"You weren't planning to stay?"

"I wasn't sure you'd want me to." He ducked his head over his phone to send the text.

She watched his hair fall forward across his forehead, watched his concentration, which was much more intense than necessary for a text. *He's always so focused. Everything he does, precise, as close to perfect as possible.* Even lounging on the grass, he'd arranged himself the way an actor would look in a Henry James film if he was at a seaside picnic, propped up on one elbow with his shoulders back, his legs with a soft cross at the ankles.

Why did he think I wouldn't want him with me tonight?

"Done," said Quinn. "Alright, since we've moved back to the real world. I'd like an answer to my question. It's easier for me to support you if I understand."

"Or you could just trust that I have my reasons."

75

Trust, whispered Dr. Bade's voice in Larisa's head.

"I do."

"Then it can wait." Larisa jumped up and led the way back into the house.

They sat at the kitchen table with the two place settings Suzette had left. Larisa watched Quinn decide not to press his question. She loved that he was willing to drop it. And hated that she couldn't give him an answer. Dr. Bade would've said they were building an unstable foundation for their relationship. Larisa would've answered that they lived in LA, home of teetering tectonic plates. Stability would always be an illusion or a choice.

She prayed it could be a choice.

"I like that they eat together," said Quinn. "Not many families make time for that."

"Don't be too impressed. It's not real," said Larisa. "When I had my reality show, the producers wanted us to be down-to-earth. So, we always ate dinner together. Or what was filmed as dinner. Sometimes it was lunch or eating dinner food for breakfast because one of them had to be away for work during actual dinner."

"But it stuck."

She shrugged. "My parents aren't in love."

"Why are you so sure about that?"

"He doesn't touch her."

"They've been together thirty years. So, don't you think love might look different after so long?"

"You're an expert?"

Quinn leaned back in his chair. "I have an imagination."

"About my parents?"

"About people not being so straightforward as we think."

"I'm straightforward," said Larisa, only partly serious. "I'm really just a girl sitting in front of a—"

"I don't buy that."

Larisa struggled to keep the smile on her face. "Love is such a thing, isn't it? You think you have it figured out, you think you know what you're doing, that you've made good choices. But then it turns on you. Nothing looks the same. Everything you depended on has turned false. How can anyone be straightforward when that's what they sign up for as a human being?"

Quinn cut off a slice of his dinner and chewed thoughtfully. "We're good at not thinking about all that. Biology helps."

"Believe it or not, I'm trying really hard to be simple for you."

"I didn't ask for that."

"It's necessary, I promise."

"You know what I think? I think I'm not enough for you."

"Quinn—"

"I mean there's the obvious 'I don't know what the hell you're doing with me' part. But also sexually." He poked his fork in the air toward her. "You'll get bored."

"Because I'm not sure how I feel about bondage right now?"

"Because you're immense." He threw open his arms. "Who am I to think I'll always be the body you're going to want for the rest of your life?"

She stared at him. She hadn't even considered Quinn in 'the rest of her life.' She worked very hard never to think about anything that involved those words. But what he was saying made a strange kind of sense. It startled her that he could be right about something she hadn't ever thought about. All she could think to say was, "That isn't how it works."

"Well, it could, right? If we trusted each other. If there was always just us at the center and the rest of the world revolved around that center?"

"I'm not sure I'd want to share you."

He held her gaze, the light illuminated their depth as though her words meant the world to him. And yet, he didn't love her. *Why am I so stuck on that?*

Because he hasn't given himself over.

"Beware the romantic full of beautiful words," she murmured.

"Is that a quote?"

"Yes."

"By who?"

She saw the question that wasn't quite suspicion in his eyes. It might as well have been labeled Lucas. *Am I really that obvious?*

"Do you envision Parish as part of this equation?" asked Larisa.

"Obviously not."

"Why obviously?" She hid her irritation behind a smile.

"Because she betrayed us. And she'd probably do it again if she could."

"Then why isn't it obvious to you why I won't go to Italy? What if I said I wanted Parish to be part of our life?"

"Why?"

"I just do."

"I'd say that's not good enough. Are you serious?"

She shrugged. "No, I guess not."

"Is your ex going to be part of our life more than he already is?"

"What's that supposed to mean?"

"Exactly what it sounds like."

"We were together for years."

"He hurt you."

The way he said it, that flash across his face, like what Lucas had done was a crime worthy of summoning an army to the cause of vengeance, made Larisa's heart pound, and not in a good way. The last thing she needed was Quinn feeling she needed to be avenged. She didn't want him to feel that, to think he had that place in her life when he hadn't even said he loved her. She suddenly felt the need to put him in his place.

"Have you ever been in love, Quinn? I mean let's be serious now. You haven't. Not like that. Not the kind that pulls you in and drowns you, colonizes your mind so it's the only thing that keeps your heart beating. You talk of love like it's a business deal because you've never stood in the rain and wanted to rip someone's clothes off. You've never been trapped in a public place trying to keep calm while your skin is starving for another person's touch."

She finished in a breathless rush, overheated and vehement, as though they'd been arguing. Or she'd been having an argument with herself. Quinn sat calmly at his side of the table, thoughtful, studying her as though he'd just seen something new, and he was trying to decide what he thought about it.

But what had she expected? For him to lunge across the table, suddenly enflamed with the very passion she'd accused him of never having experienced? She took a breath.

"That isn't what I want from you. I was just saying." She reached for her water glass as though to hide behind it. After she'd drained it, and there was no good reason for her to keep holding it, she set it down and managed to look at him. "Aren't you going to say something?"

"I think you've just proved my point. You'll need more than me. I'm not . . . you're right. What you're describing is not something I'm likely to experience."

"I know."

He nodded as though that was the end, even though she thought perhaps he wanted to go back to the question of Lucas and Italy. Because unlike most men, Quinn didn't lose track of things when she avoided giving him answers, especially when it was something he didn't understand.

I don't know how to explain, she thought. *There aren't words for what Lucas is.* But then, she thought if she said that and couldn't follow it up, Quinn would only wonder more. So, she smiled and playfully snatched the uneaten part of his chicken from his plate to eat herself.

"Have you decided on our movie? Did you finally steal a screener so I can see *The Key*?"

"You should choose," he said. "I might find something without enough sugar." His eyes glimmered at her, that devious little smirk. If he was worried about Lucas, it didn't show. It probably wouldn't ever show.

Two weeks in and we're already burying our questions for the sake of harmony, thought Larisa. It was her fault, but she didn't know how to fix it.

"What did you love as a kid? Before you were going to be a serious, artistic filmmaker who likes Kubrick and all that?"

"Are you going to judge me for this answer?"

"Yes."

"Spielberg. From *ET* on. *Indiana Jones. Jurassic Park. Back to the Future. The Goonies. Hook.*" He paused, then tilted his chin at her as though recognizing that she'd somehow tricked him. "*Star Wars. Home Alone.* Movies used to feel so large. Maybe it was the film stock or something." He shrugged. "They felt real. Enchanted."

She gazed at him for a moment trying to absorb that light in his expression as though he was the one enchanted. Then she said, "You know, most of those movies got their magic from their film score and brilliantly placed music cues."

"I knew you were going to say that."

"Let's make it a Harrison Ford weekend. Three original *Star Wars.* Three original *Indiana Jones.* I promise I won't masturbate during *Temple of Doom.*"

"It wouldn't bother me if you did."

Quinn hadn't exactly lied to Larisa when he'd agreed with her that he'd never been taken by passion. But her acceptance of his answer surprised him, as though she had no idea what the Queen had done to him. Everything Larisa had described, except ripping clothes off in the rain, which just seemed like a passion killer, he'd felt for her. For those few months at the start of the year, she'd been his beacon of light, the source of all possibility, the beginning and the end of a journey he was suddenly not walking alone, clinging to his dreams by the skin of his teeth.

He almost said, "I fell for you. And you broke my heart." But that would have ruined the night, if not the weekend. And now that it felt they were finally coming together, he didn't want to ruin anything. He'd rather she be frustrated by his reticence than be reminded where it came from. Part of him was just putting one step in front of the other until things got better, but he didn't want her to know that. It wasn't fair to either of them. The whole thing wasn't fair.

They'd sat on opposite sides of the couch with Sabrina ensconced in a blanket on the middle cushion. After restraining themselves through the first two movies, they'd jump-quoted all the best lines from *Raiders of the Lost Ark*. And then, in the thin hours of the morning, before the Death Star blew up Alderaan, Larisa had stolen Sabrina's blanket, stretched her legs out so they invaded his side of the couch, and fallen asleep.

For the rest of the movie, he'd been distracted by those feet, the fancy painted nails, the soft skin so well-tended it glowed in the light of the TV. When it was time for the first Death Star to have its comeuppance, he'd worked up enough courage to set his hand on her ankle. *This woman loves me,* he thought, as he stroked his finger along the line of bone. He didn't understand why that was so hard to believe. He couldn't interpret the iron line of resistance that held him fast to his side of the couch. With any other person, at any other time in his life, he would have stretched himself out beside her. Instead, he settled for this hairsbreadth of connection, skin to skin, a meditation on stolen moments of peace.

Chapter 6

Debut of a Social Pariah

"I don't know how to answer that," said Anastacia Sinitsina, as she reclined on the chaise in her front room, her two giant Pyrenees sheepdogs on the floor beside her. The actress liked to hold their counseling sessions in the aviary of her replica nineteenth-century mansion.

"I mean really," continued Anastacia. "What's true about desire except that it changes? I look at Duck, and I think I'm not in the least attracted to him. I'm afraid I only let myself go there because I was attracted to the idea that he would want me."

"That isn't nothing," said Larisa, as she doodled vaguely phallic shapes on her legal pad.

"But I want it to be pure. I went out with this guy this weekend, had a good time. But afterward, my only interest in seeing him again was that I'd get more out of it now that there'd been a practice round."

"You didn't desire him?"

"In the moment, sure. But in that other way? Building a life with someone is exhausting."

"You don't like being alone," said Larisa gently.

"Well, that's the thing."

Anastacia paused long enough Larisa felt a sizzle of anticipation in the back of her neck. She wasn't a thoughtful person, and now she'd paused to think. It felt like a breakthrough. Finally, Larisa was helping her dig down past the surface level of her problems with men.

"I don't want to be alone, but I don't want what I've had."

Larisa made a note. "Why 'exhausting'? Some people might say it's an exploration, or even a creative activity."

"People who say that still trust other people."

That word again. Larisa scribbled a shaded square on the margin of her legal pad as though it would make her less of a hypocrite. Just that morning, she'd canceled her next appointment with Dr. Bade.

"Do you say that because you can't imagine being in a trusting relationship or because you don't have one in your life right now?"

"It's both, right? At my age, you feel you know people. They become predictable. And I don't like what I see."

Larisa's phone vibrated with her muted alarm. "Sorry, but we're almost out of time. Maybe this is something to think about this week?"

Anastacia rolled onto her side and studied Larisa. "Do you have one of those relationships where you trust your partner in everything?"

"Same time next week?"

Anastacia reached to stroke her dogs' heads. "Did my friend Lea call you yet? She's the manager at Kellee, a great new boutique. NYC import, I think. Anyway, she's having a rough time. I'll nudge her again. You know, it's hard to take that first step if you've never been in therapy before."

And hard to stay in it when you don't want to talk to your therapist, thought Larisa.

As she walked out to her Bentley, Larisa pictured all the unhappy women in West Hollywood sitting pensively by their phones, trying to force themselves to take that first step to make an appointment with her. If only five of them became her clients she'd feel so much better about her life.

She unlocked her phone screen and scrolled through her messages as she pulled out of Anastacia's driveway.

> Rosa: Are you okay?
>
> Larisa: Can you be more specific?
>
> Rosa: You're in the news again.

Oh yes, that. She'd been so preoccupied with Quinn she'd almost forgotten the PR fallout from the *Film Comment* interview.

> Rosa: Come for happy hour.
>
> Larisa: Or you and Krissy can come to my parents.
>
> Rosa: Are you still hiding?
>
> Larisa: Maybe you don't want to be seen with me.
>
> Rosa: We're meeting early because Kahleah is joining. 4 pm. Cloud Nine.

Four o'clock barely left Larisa enough time to change. As she drove to the Kahn estate, she considered texting back, using the last-minute timing as an excuse to cancel. Not that it couldn't be done, but the rush felt like too much. She'd become used to a certain pace since leaving her residency program. Quinn would be coming at eight. She'd planned to use the time until then to plan her outfit and do a hydrating mask on her face and chest. She didn't want Quinn to think unemployment had turned her into a slob.

She was reading on her phone, still debating if she'd commit to what would be her first true public appearance since the spring, when she walked into her parents' house.

"She really is formidable, isn't she?"

Larisa stopped short and looked up. Standing at the far side of the atrium, gazing at the imperious oil portrait of Suzette mounted on the wall, was the junior asset manager from Rockie's PR firm.

Name, name, what's her name?

"I'm Teale." The woman stepped forward and extended her hand to shake. "I don't think we've formally met. Rockie likes to pretend I'm just one of her appendages." She flashed a smile that looked a little like Julia Roberts, big teeth, giant lips, a little too perfect.

She came to LA to become an actress, thought Larisa, as she waved Teale into the house.

"I don't think there's a meeting on the calendar today."

"Not officially," said Teale.

Larisa led the way upstairs into the family wing. "So, you've come to make your move."

Teale's face contorted, perhaps with surprise or irritation. Whatever she felt, she quickly smoothed it back. "What is my move?"

"You're going to tell me what's good for me, and it'll be something I don't want to do. And something Rockie doesn't want me to do either." Larisa opened the door to her bedroom suite. "Why do you care?"

"I want to manage your case myself."

"Rockie is one of the best."

"She also works for your mother."

Larisa's phone vibrated. *Quinn?* Her heart beat a little faster at the possibility.

> Lucas: Looks like you're having fun.

For a moment, Larisa couldn't move. She read the text over and over, wishing it away, wishing she hadn't looked, wishing she could just move her finger over to the Block button.

"Something wrong?"

Larisa pressed a smile across her mouth. "Pitch me."

"There's no good reason to be ashamed about who you are."

Larisa moved through her living room into her bedroom, stripping down to her underwear as she went.

"You allowed the world to have a conversation about you, but without you. That made you look ashamed. We're a decade into a new millennium. Sexuality is something people want to talk about without being condemned for it."

"There's more voices of condemnation than not," said Larisa.

"Do you know the hottest thing in books right now?"

"Stephen King writing about Kennedy?"

"No, that self-published BDSM romance novel." Teale pointed to the couch where Larisa had left the book Teale had asked her to read.

"The book club thing again." Larisa began to peruse her closet. What were people wearing for happy hour these days? She had no idea. Her mother had been sent some of the fall trends, but she hadn't shared them with Larisa, probably because until today she hadn't needed to be out and dressed.

"Wow, you really don't do boundaries, do you?"

Larisa glanced over her shoulder. Teale was standing back by the bedroom door, eyes hungry with appreciation for Larisa's body. For a moment, she thought it might be more fun to seduce Teale than go to happy hour. But they didn't know each other well enough for that. And Teale seemed like a normal person, therefore someone who was going to wonder about monogamy and sex leading to feelings and attachments, et cetera, et cetera.

Instead of meeting Teale's desire with something of her own, Larisa said, "I don't know anything about book clubs."

"I'm not suggesting a book club. We create an avenue for you to be part of the conversation. It already has momentum."

"Have I fallen so far that self-published erotica adds credibility?"

"I've already spoken to *The Rumpus*. They'll give you a weekly column for the month of January to discuss themes in the book."

"I'm not a writer."

"I'll help you if it comes to that."

"And then what? The haters aren't going to go away."

"No. But it'll turn you from a victim into an expert. Women are asking questions in public that they've never asked before." Teale turned on her phone and began to read. "'What do I do if spanking turns me on?' 'How do I find someone I can trust to play with?' 'Is this book feminist?'"

Larisa laughed. "Not likely." On impulse she selected two hangers from her collection and held them up for Teale to see. One was a sweater dress, the other was a soft halter top with an open back and a matching miniskirt. "Which do you think?"

"For what?"

"Apparently, I'm going to happy hour with my girlfriends."

Teale crossed the bedroom and stepped into the closet. She began to look through Larisa's clothes.

"Would you at least read the book? And every time you find yourself responding to it, send me a text."

"I don't want to be known as Dr. Bondage Slut."

"This is just step one. Step two is your brand." Teale selected a hanger with a button-down, collared blouse from among Larisa's 'doctor' clothes, then stepped back out to the doorway where she'd dropped her purse. She pulled out a folder cracking at the seams. From inside, she handed Larisa a sheet of paper with a crisp cream and black design.

Dr. Larisa de France-Kahn lifestyle consultant. Personalized guidance and support with relationships, careers, and sexual satisfaction.

Teale pulled a second sheet of paper from her folder with a similar design but different text.

Dr. Larisa de France-Kahn Mental Health Consultant. Everything can go wrong on a set, avoid costly stoppages by giving your crew the support they need.

"With your permission, I'll set up meetings with three studios that all had problems on set this past year. And I can take this first idea to a graphic designer to organize it into a half page for a magazine or web ad."

"Why?"

"Why what?" asked Teale.

"Why do you want to work on this?"

"It seems like a problem with an obvious solution, but no one wants to solve it."

"Some might argue I deserve what I got."

"Well, that's fucking bullshit."

"You're the first person to say that." Larisa followed Teale out of the closet. "What am I doing with this shirt?"

"Wear it with jeans?"

"Who wears jeans?"

"Cindy Crawford."

"I think you just made my point."

"Who needs to see your legs tonight?"

"What kind of question is that?"

"You asked me what I thought."

"No, I asked you to make the right pick and if you did, I was going to hire you without arguing about it. The right pick is the top and skirt, by the way. It's two inches longer than the dress so my legs don't stick to the booths at Cloud Nine."

Teale opened her mouth, then closed it.

"Fine, I'll do it." Larisa began to get dressed. "What do I do? Email the firm and say I'm restructuring my representation?" She waited for Teale to say thank you. Instead, the younger woman just nodded.

"Where do you come from, Teale?"

"Tennessee."

"And what brought you here?"

"Love. But I've moved past that."

"I hope it comes around again," said Larisa. "Love makes everything else brighter." She glanced toward her phone laying where she'd dropped it on her bed. The screen was black.

"You're worried about tonight, huh?"

Not just tonight. Larisa wished Quinn hadn't blurted out about their relationship to that reporter. She'd thought they'd have more time before—

It'll be fine.

"Why did you say that about my legs?"

"I just think if you're going out to meet your friends, jeans are okay," said Teale. "You don't need to show off your legs."

"What's wrong with them?"

"They're noticeable. Maybe tonight you could try to be less noticeable."

"Like a disguise?"

Teale did that opening and closing thing with her mouth again. She looked concerned in a way Larisa wasn't sure she liked and certainly didn't understand.

"Don't laugh," said Larisa, as she strode into Cloud Nine wearing ankle boots and a pair of jeans she hadn't touched since Minnesota. "They were my new publicist's idea. There. Is. Nothing. Wrong."

Rosa and Krissy glanced at her, then at each other. It was Kahleah, already halfway through a margarita, who did exactly what Larisa had forbidden and laughed. "Is there a rule against jeans at happy hour?"

"You look great," said Rosa, sipping on a non-alcoholic beer.

Krissy, also going the non-alcoholic route in solidarity with Rosa, patted the bench beside her for Larisa to sit down.

"Are people staring?"

"They always stare at you," said Krissy.

"Yes, but now it's different." Larisa glanced around the bar. The crowd was sparse this early in the evening, or was it considered late afternoon? She couldn't remember the correct terminology.

"I'm debuting as a social pariah."

"We were sorry to see that editorial in the *Times* this morning," said Rosa. "All lies, I'm sure."

Krissy also looked sympathetic, but Kahleah stuck her wrist to her forehead and threw her head back dramatically. "Woe is Larisa, who worries about wearing jeans to a bar while the rest of us run around as fast as we can, getting it done as good as we can."

"Your marriage isn't broken yet," said Rosa.

Whoa. What'd I miss? Larisa tried to focus, but she felt like people were watching, and she wanted to turn and look. Had she been recognized? How long before someone came over and said something?

"What did he do now?" asked Krissy.

"I don't want to talk about it and have Larisa try and solve things from her armchair. We're here to discuss Halloween. Let's do it before Jaden gets wise and realizes we're conspiring. Actually, I don't care if she finds out. What the fuck was she thinking? There were people doing lines on her living room table. I can't be at a party like that."

"I didn't see any coke," said Rosa.

"I didn't see you," said Krissy.

Kahleah made a hissing sound by pressing her tongue against her teeth, her trademark irritation. "That's because I got five feet past the door and turned around and left! Imagine if I'd been in those photos with Larisa. Pictures like that! Cade's wife out at a wild party like she's a twenty-year-old coed. No offense Larisa. I'm already fighting 'hood' stereotypes."

The idea that anyone would look at Kahleah, who had pressed, polished, and chemically treated every inch of herself into an almost perfect imitation of Michelle Obama and think she didn't belong in the rarified atmosphere of political wives made Larisa furious, but she was also distracted by this new underlying current in her friend's voice. It sounded like she was holding back tears.

Note to self: reach out to Kahleah one-on-one.

There was movement in Larisa's peripheral vision. She turned her head away from the table just enough to see a woman get up from a table across the room and walk up to the bar.

"It's true, we're getting older," said Rosa. "Jaden should have told us ahead of time."

"She knew we wouldn't come!" said Kahleah. "It was a total go for the gusto without telling us. I say we all block her."

"I'm fine with that." Krissy reached for Kahleah's drink and took a gulp. "We shouldn't be in that kind of environment anymore."

"So, we're all agreed," said Kahleah. "Risa?"

"I think we should talk to her first. Maybe—"

"Talk about what?" asked Kahleah. "She punked us. She deserves this."

"Uh, sure, yeah, I guess that's true." Larisa had been planning to have at least two drinks, but she felt so disoriented she wasn't sure she could trust herself to drink. It was just so strange to be here, to sit like everything was normal. Then the conversation had gone so far. *Did we just excommunicate Jaden?*

"Okay, good. So, everyone block her now." Kahleah pulled out her phone, did the deed, then held up the screen to show them.

Larisa pulled her phone from her purse and braced herself for whatever she would find on the home screen. *Why do I keep thinking Lucas will say more? He only sends one text at a time.*

You aren't ready for what's coming.

"So, how's everyone?" Kahleah pressed a smile onto her face.

"Pregnant," said Rosa.

"I'm thinking about getting a job," said Krissy.

"Why?"

"I dunno. It seems fun."

"Risa had a job. Was your job fun, Risa?"

"Sometimes," said Larisa. She didn't like to think about her job or how she'd lost it. Maybe the bitter taste rising up her throat made her say, "But I've heard it's hard to get a job once you've been out of school a while."

"What were you thinking about trying?" asked Rosa.

"Like skincare, or jewelry, or something."

As though on cue, the three friends all turned and looked pointedly at Larisa.

"What?"

"Your mom could hire Krissy."

"There's a word for that."

"Networking," said Kahleah.

"Nepotism."

"Oh, come on. You of all people?"

"What? I don't have values now?"

"I like your mom," said Krissy. "I think she likes me too."

"You're not working for my mom."

"You don't think she could do a good job?" asked Kahleah.

Larisa squinted at her across the table. *Since when has Kahleah been this hostile?* She thought about how different it was to sit with her friends at a table in a quiet bar instead of being at a party, where there were other things to do than talk. And she realized, even though they were in daily contact in the chat, she hadn't had to sit down and talk to any of them face-to-face since before Jaden's wedding, and even then, it'd just been once, at this bar, in this booth.

"Is this about Italy?" asked Rosa.

"What about Italy?" Krissy looked panicked.

"Larisa doesn't want us to go to Italy with her mom for fashion week," said Rosa.

Oh my fucking Christ.

"Why can't we go to Italy?" asked Kahleah.

Larisa glanced at the bar's front entrance. Someone was coming in, but they'd stopped to hold the door and cold air was blowing right at her. *Jeans are nice,* thought Larisa. *I could become a person who wears jeans.* She wanted to think about jeans instead of how to tell her sisters Italy wasn't happening.

Trust them with the truth, whispered Dr. Bade's voice in her head. They would be disappointed, maybe they'd even try to argue, but at least they'd understand from her perspective why it couldn't happen. Was her perspective enough? They'd say she was being dramatic. They would stare at her, unable to believe Larisa de France-Kahn, solver of all their problems, fearless leader, invincible sex queen, was afraid. She was so afraid she didn't even want to be on the same continent as the master of that fear.

"You can go," said Larisa. "But I'm not going."

"That doesn't make sense," said Krissy. "Isn't your mom's—"

"So, I have news if anyone is interested," said Larisa. "Today, I officially went into business for myself."

For a moment, no one spoke. Somewhere in the back of her head, Larisa knew she was being irrational, that these were her friends, and she should trust them, that they were in that very moment forming resentments against her for changing the subject. And perhaps these resentments were being added to older resentments, years of resentments buried away under years of deflections. Because, the truth was, Larisa had even less trust in the people in her life than Anastacia Sinitsina, and the idea that she could be in a relationship with anyone and feel free to tell them what she was thinking struck her as the absolute worst way to live one's life.

Finally, Rosa said, "You started a business?"

"I'm going to be a therapist. Not the clinical kind. Just the regular kind."

"Talk therapy?" said Kahleah. "I thought you were above that."

Larisa smiled gently. "You must be having a really bad day. Would you like to talk about it?"

"Please tell me that's not what you'll be doing." Kahleah waved to get the attention of their waiter so she could order another drink.

"Well," said Rosa, "that's very exciting. Congratulations."

"Yeah," said Krissy without enthusiasm. "Congratulations."

"There's something else. This involves all of us," said Larisa. "I'm volunteering to walk puppies at the animal shelter. And I'd love for all of you to partner with me in this worthy cause."

Chapter 7

Ghosts Looming

"And then Kahleah said I wasn't good enough to help her with whatever's going on with Cade."

Quinn looked up from the puzzle table in surprise. "She said that?"

"Strongly implied." Larisa slapped a puzzle piece into its place. "I think it would have gone better if someone had come up to the table. I kept expecting it to happen. Everyone at the bar was looking at me. But then no one said anything. I think I just didn't perform well on an interpersonal level because I was braced for a confrontation."

"They're your friends."

"Is that comment in relation to Kahleah not wanting my help or everyone in the bar looking at me knowing I'm the nymphomaniac shrink but not saying anything?"

"Never mind." This felt like the first time she had chosen to just pour herself out. Quinn liked listening to her talk, but he wished he had something better to say than a better version of, *I knew this was coming.* "I think we're missing some pieces."

"No way."

"There are six holes and four pieces." He ducked his head under the table.

"I'm not sure who I am to them now. It's been so long."

"But they agreed to do the dog walking?"

"Kahleah and Krissy did. Rosa isn't doing a lot of recreational walking right now, but she would like us to send pictures."

"Dr. Larisa, the dog walker." He drew back from the table and watched as Larisa found homes for the remaining puzzle pieces.

"It's a good idea from a PR point of view."

"Sabrina will be upset." He looked around and spotted Sabrina's white mass tucked up into a ball on the ottoman of the lounge chair. He went over and squatted down, gently stroked the line of fur from her nose to her head. She yawned and gave him a little squeak of greeting. Quinn squeaked back. She cocked her head at him and made a sound like an anime character jumping off a cliff into the air—Mi-Meowwww!—and looked at him expectantly. Quinn scooped her up in his arms and cooed at her.

This was not the result Sabrina had expected; she squirmed to get down.

"What are you doing?"

"Asking our cat if she ate the missing pieces." Quinn let Sabrina fall back to the ottoman. "You don't talk to her?"

"We use full sentences and English."

Quinn looked questioningly at Sabrina to confirm this. The cat just blinked sleepily at him.

"Here's one. My sweater caught it." Larisa plucked a piece from the lose weave of her puffy sweater sleeve. "See the other one?" She turned before him. As she did, she sashayed her hips, an invitation.

"You look good in jeans," he said.

"I'm undecided. They're very 90s." She swayed over to him and waved her sleeves for closer inspection. "See it anywhere?"

"Nope."

"Maybe its stuck to you." She pressed up against him, his hands in hers, and began to twist him from side to side as though the missing piece could be jarred loose. He caught the fruity scent of her lotion and the breeze of her hair like coconuts on a tropical beach. Neither smelled anything like the Queen, but that was okay. He was getting used to it.

"What are you looking at?" she asked.

"You." He didn't add, *I'm trying to pull you into focus from the background.*

I miss the Queen.

As though she could read something of this thought in his expression, Larisa withdrew from him and returned to the table. "Shall we start over?"

"Now?"

"Why not?"

"Don't you have other puzzles?"

"Probably. But this is the one I do."

Quinn came back to the table and looked at the finished puzzle, an Italian city landscape captured from an aerial photograph, a giant cathedral in the center under a brilliant blue sky. "Why this one?"

Larisa was pulling up the edge and folding it into the middle, her head bowed over her work as though the task needed close supervision. *To push or not to push?* he wondered. Aside from Larisa's almost frenetic frustration over what had happened with her friends, they'd had a good night together. He didn't want to derail them.

Still, he didn't like her silence. If there was going to be an ex-boyfriend between them, he at least wanted to be able to talk about it.

"Have you been to that church?" he asked.

"I have." Larisa's hands danced distractedly over the pieces, flicking them apart, sundering their little bonds. "It's nothing special, unless you like giant medieval architecture."

"Is that what you think about when you do this puzzle? Medieval architecture?"

Larisa laughed. "I think about how much human life has changed since the days of building cathedrals. And I think about what's still the same." She paused. "I was in this church when I decided to leave Lucas. Not as a tourist. I went to mass with a bunch of nonnas wearing scarves and carrying their personal roseries. Because that's mostly what mass is in Italy now, the dying generation. Or at least, that's how it was in Florence. Anyway, we were just back from a trip to an island he owns, and I'd learned something about him I couldn't accept. My heart was broken."

She paused again. Quinn thought another woman would be welling up, or even crying, but not Larisa. A stillness had come over her. Her hands were still working on disrupting the puzzle, but she was still otherwise, as though she'd banked the nuclear reactor that usually burned inside her.

"And I was going back and forth between pretending it was okay or leaving him over it. I thought I'd feel at peace, but it was close to Easter, and they were going through the stations of the cross, and I just felt all this violence. Each one of the frescos, the story, the history that comes with it, the monuments to old dead men, I hated all of it. So, I came home without telling him, and we spent the next eight months fighting about it."

"It must have been really great, what you had together."

Larisa's mouth moved like she'd tasted something sour. When she began to speak, her eyes took on a starry, faraway look. "It was exciting most of the time. I didn't really know what he was doing until the end. So, it was just . . . life without limits. He was always wanting to do new things. The world felt huge and full of possibilities. We went on an archeology mission one week and flew north for glacier hiking the next. We read books and went to concerts. One day he woke me up in the middle of the night and said, 'Do you want to learn how to polka?' I asked him why. He said, 'Because it's an important dance in Austria.' Then he ran out of the room."

"Did you learn to polka?"

"We did. The very next day after breakfast. We worked on it for so long my feet swelled up. The next day I couldn't walk."

"He didn't care about hurting you."

"It never felt like that in the moment."

Quinn waited for her to say more. He could just barely see her face, the hard determination in her expression as she took him through her memory. Part of him was relieved to find no longing there, no mournful dredges of lost love. But he also wondered if bitterness wasn't a stronger force. Did she do the puzzle over and over to excise her rage, or relive her loss, or something else?

"When I was younger, I had this idea that being hurt would make me more interesting. I'd been told my entire life I was beautiful. And I wanted more than that. Depth. Texture. Stories that made people look at me for a different reason. My therapist says it makes sense. I wanted a version of life I'd never had."

"A tragedy?" asked Quinn, working hard not to think about how different his life would be if he'd had even half the safety, and security, and adoration she'd had as a child.

"The chance to figure out who I wanted to be."

"Did you?"

"As much as anyone ever does."

The idea of Larisa throwing herself at the world so it'd hurt her made Quinn nauseous. On some level, he understood, but the idea still held horror. There were so many things that could've gone wrong.

"If you're moving back to your apartment, maybe we could box it this time and set it up over there?"

"I'm not sure I'm moving back," said Larisa. "My parents are worried."

"About what that radio guy said?"

She looked up at him in surprise as though she'd assumed he didn't know. *And she chose not to tell me*, he thought.

"I'm sorry you're part of my mess now," she said.

"The studio's handling it. I mean, I've been called worse." The truth was, Quinn hadn't heard what the radio guy had said, or what was being said online. Sid had said it was better not knowing. Quinn had decided to trust that. "You might come to New York for the junket?"

"Maybe. I've never believed in the idea that adding more words to the conversation makes the conversation better. If you don't feed a fire eventually it dies out."

"The dog walking will shut everyone up." He grinned at her. "But it's going to be hard on the family."

Larisa turned and gave a bow to Sabrina. "I apologize in advance for what I'm doing on Tuesday with your sworn enemies." Then she turned back to him and studied him as she chewed on her lip. "Maybe I'll move back to the apartment while you're in New York. By then maybe you'll want to live with me."

"I haven't said I don't want to live with you."

"But you also haven't said you want to."

She continued to chew her lip, waiting for him to say the right thing. Did she realize his desire to make her happy was sometimes the only thing getting him out of bed in the mornings? Each day he hoped he would feel ready to give her what she wanted. But in her presence, he felt disoriented and uncertain. And sometimes at night, in the twilight of sleep's descent, she came to him as the Queen. Her voice roused him. All he had to do was follow her. It was an illusion, but knowing its character didn't diminish its power.

"Did you drink at the bar earlier?" he asked.

"No. I mean, I had that virgin beer Rosa was drinking. Lots of sugar." She wrinkled her nose, and it was absolutely adorable, like a cat that had gotten wet and was fussing about it. Every day with Larisa he noticed something new about her that made it feel like he was seeing her for the first time.

I'm at the beginning and you're past the halfway point.

"So, you don't want to do the couple's interview your publicist suggested?" he asked.

"Rockie is my ex-publicist, remember?" Larisa shuffled the pieces around the table.

"Can I ask you something random?"

"As long as it doesn't have to do with Lucas."

Quinn paused so he didn't accidentally say, *It feels like everything is connected to Lucas.*

"Are you upset I told that reporter we were dating?"

There it was again, that momentary flash of blank panic. It

streaked across her face like a startled deer. She was upset about it, and she hadn't wanted him to know.

"I didn't tell you not to."

"But?"

"I think I wanted you to be my secret for a little while."

"It's funny," he said. "This spring we were faking it because we felt other people needed to see us together. Now we're together, and you want to hide."

"There are millions of people in Manhattan."

"Which could make us anonymous."

"I haven't said no yet. Obviously, I'll do whatever's best for you and the film."

"Larisa."

"What?" She looked up at him and, for a moment, there was this look on her face, a washed-out devastation that couldn't possibly have been about her flying to New York with him for the press junket.

Go to her, hold her. Stop thinking so much.

But then the look was gone, and she was smiling at him in that soft way that made all his doubts feel meaningless, a smile that made him feel silly for worrying, because she always had everything under control. The feeling that something was gunning for them, unseen over the edge of an unknown horizon, was just residual from that spring.

We're fine, he thought.

"I have a new client this week. Can you go to your fitting by yourself?"

"I just have to stand there, right?"

"Hans may ask what you like best between the three options. Just tell him you're taking all of them. One will be for the junket screening, one will be the LA premiere, and one will be the London premiere."

"I can do that."

"And Kahleah's daughter, Chloe, has her birthday party on Wednesday. You don't have to be there, but—"

"I can be there."

"Do you want me to text Sid to put it on your schedule?"

"I'm managing my own schedule."

"That's not what he said."

"Well, he's wrong."

Chapter 8

Compromised

"Did you commandeer my calendar?" Quinn asked Sid. They were parked in a no-parking zone in front of the 208 Rodeo Restaurant, waiting because they'd arrived early for Quinn's lunch with Kyle from Film-Streams and he didn't want to go in and sit by himself.

"You told me you were handling it."

"Then why does Larisa think you handle it?"

Sid shrugged. "I'll park and walk around, yeah? Your fitting is just up the road."

"You say it like you think I don't know that."

"Well, I didn't know it until I looked it up, so I wasn't sure you did. Where's Larisa getting her outfit for the show?"

"I don't know."

"You're not coordinating?"

"No."

"I think people normally coordinate. Because some fabrics don't match. And, ya know, colors are complicated."

"You're my stylist now?"

"I've been doing re—"

"There he is." Even though the windshield was tinted, Quinn turned his head to the side to hide from Kyle as he walked up the sidewalk and through the 208's entrance.

"Have you had sex yet?"

"What? No."

"Well, that explains it. You wouldn't want to look too intimate on the red carpet and all that."

"What are you even talking about?"

"It's kinda like you're still faking it."

"We're not."

"Oh-kay. You going in now?"

"Five more minutes."

"So, you wanna talk about why you and Larisa aren't—"

"I changed my mind. I'm leaving now. I'll see you at Tom Ford in an hour."

"Hour and a half," said Sid, as Quinn opened his door and plunged out.

He absolutely did not want to think about Larisa and their *Toy Story* version of a relationship just as he walked into a meeting that could change his life.

Kyle was seated on the yellow bench-seat side of a two-person table. The blue wall behind him washed out his skin and the hard white lighting didn't do anything to help. Quinn realized he was taking in the room as a filming location instead of a restaurant. *Calm down. This is just any other meeting.*

"Quinn, good to see you again."

Be a normal person. Be serious and important.

"Kyle, glad to be here."

Really, Quinn?

He should have brought Larisa. Or at least had her come for the beginning to get him through the small talk and the food ordering. Last time they'd met, Kyle had mentioned a son who played sports at some university. Quinn had thought, remember this to ask about next time, but now of course he'd forgotten.

I hate this, he thought.

"I saw you made the tabloids last week. Congrats."

He thinks I'm a confused pansy who likes to be controlled by women and would be a real man if I'd had better parents. Now, he's realizing he doesn't know anything about my parents or where I come from.

"I was surprised people are still interested."

"Well, that's Larisa. Hard to let a story like that go. She's just so ripe for it. You're brave for taking her on. Don't get me wrong, she's absolutely gorgeous. I tried really hard to get her attached to Steve when he was just starting out. Funny they were together at that party."

A pause that felt like Kyle wanted it to be significant, as though he was curious what Quinn thought about Larisa dancing with Steve Helston at Jaden's party. He could have said Steve had been invited to meet Quinn. Instead, he just let it go. "Steve's too pretty to need a wife like that."

Kyle chuckled, then rubbed his meaty hands together and transitioned the conversation. "So, we're looking to start filming this spring. I know that sounds fast, but all the pieces are in place. We would just need to recalibrate for any changes in vision you bring to the table. Have you had a chance to read the script?"

"I have."

The script was basic comic-adaptation fare except for a few creative flourishes that meant the writer probably had a future, if only the industry let him be an artist and not just a cog in the great gears of big budget monotony. But Quinn was thrilled to have the chance to be part of the great gears, and he was mostly fine with being a cog himself. He understood his job was to make something predictable and entertaining in a flashy, big feeling, small substance, sort of way. He could do that, so he tried to look like a man who was confident in his work but also flexible enough to take orders.

"I think it's doable," said Quinn. "I'm just a little concerned about the shooting schedule. I think we need to add some space to allow for weather and the limitations of lighting when shooting outside."

"This is a total soundstage production."

Quinn froze as his brain became a computer. Translation: soundstage to green screen. Translation: soulless, tedious, an infinite number of hours staring at computer screens watching to see

if the effects tech got the fake shadows right on this one inconse-
quential corner of—

Just say yes. You can make it through anything.

Quinn shook his head. "*Poseidon* should be shot in Greece."

"The others have all been done this way." Kyle offered a placid
smile as though to ask, *Are we really doing this?* Or, *How quaint
that you think a fantasy movie is shot on location these days.*

"I'm sure I can make that work."

Two hours and about three-too-many forkfuls of pasta later,
Quinn stood on the platform in the Tom Ford dressing room
trying to avoid eye contact with himself in the mirror. To his
right, Sid lounged in a sweatshirt and his usual gym shorts sipping
champagne and pestering Hans the sales associate with questions.

"But if a woman wanted to wear men's style clothing you'd
work with her, right?"

"We do that often, yes."

"For Larisa?"

"Yes, but not formalwear. She's traditional."

"Of the shops here, what would you recommend for her? To
go with what Quinn's wearing right now?"

I can't make an entire movie with green screen, thought
Quinn.

"You've shrunk since this spring." Hans pinched together the
fabric of the tuxedo jacket between Quinn's shoulders. To Sid, he
said, "Larisa knows these things. I'm sure she's already met with
the staff at Toi Beauté. They've just brought in several Marchesa
gowns to hold for special clients. Everyone wants one this year.
The belle epoch of feminine."

"Marchesa," said Sid, as he typed the name into his phone.
"I'll ask her about it tomorrow. Thanks."

"What's tomorrow?" asked Quinn.

"Hans, I know this is outside your expertise, but do you have suggestions on what to buy a nine-year-old girl for her birthday?"

Hans beamed. "My daughter's almost ten. I'm an expert in how difficult they are!"

Later, as they walked up Rodeo Drive to the store Hans had recommended, Sid said, "Admit it. You forgot about the birthday party."

"I would've remembered it tomorrow when I looked at my schedule."

"But you wouldn't have thought about a gift, or what you're wearing, or if we're driving with Larisa or separate."

"What? Do you just want me to admit you have nothing better to do than think about my life?"

"That's my job, boss."

Quinn thought Sid might be joking. Didn't he have something better to do with his life? But when Quinn looked for a ribbon of resentment beneath the words, he found nothing.

"Fine. But you don't need to worry about Larisa's wardrobe. She has a meeting with her stylist after the dog walking thing today."

"Great, then we can compare notes tomorrow. Shit. I forgot to ask Hans what color blue is in your shirt. I'll meet you there."

Ten minutes later, Quinn was standing in the world's fanciest children's store, which had surprisingly few toys and far too many pristine white bedspreads, when Sid arrived looking ashen.

"What's wrong?"

Sid shook his head. "Did you find them?"

"What?"

"Those things Hans was talking about. The roller blades that become ice skates?"

Quinn was standing in the showroom for bedroom furniture. "Imagine if I had children."

Sid forced out a laugh. "I've never once imagined you with children."

They found the roller blades and began to walk back to the car.

"I should've told him I wouldn't do it," said Quinn, as though he'd already told Sid about the meeting and how easily he'd collapsed under Kyle's lame excuse of 'this is how the others were done.'

"What now?"

"I can't shoot a green screen movie."

"Is that what they're doing with *Poseidon*? No wonder it looks so shiny." Sid pulled out his phone and began checking messages.

"I'm just going to call and tell him location shooting is nonnegotiable."

"Uh, why don't we wait on that a bit? Maybe you can send an email later."

"Why?"

"There was a thing that happened. I think it's good not to remind him you exist at this particular moment."

"What happened?"

"Someone heckled Larisa at her volunteering thing today. And she . . . uh . . . it looks like she got the dog to attack him somehow. I dunno. The video's shaky."

"Show it to me."

"Maybe in the car?"

Quinn pulled out his phone. All he had to do was type 'dog and Larisa de—' and a YouTube video came up, the original source, copies on two other socials platforms, and one very on top of things news outlet. The video had been live for ten minutes. Quinn wondered how Sid had found out about it so quickly. *How does anyone find this shit?* he wondered.

The video started mid-altercation out on some palm-lined street with hedges for fences. There was Krissy at Larisa's side but shrinking back and Kahleah, looking like she was trying to hide behind the two of them, and five dogs between the three of them, yapping and barking and straining at their leashes. Larisa was shouting at a man who'd come up and blocked their path on the sidewalk.

"Get the fuck out of our way."

"They let you touch dogs?" said the man. "You fuck them when your little friend isn't in the mood to get whipped?"

"My friend would outlast you."

"He's a dog too then. So beat he can't see there's a better world out there."

"You like dogs? You can have them." Larisa released the two leashes she was holding. The dogs leapt forward. The man screeched as he turned to run, calling over his shoulder, "No one wants to fuck you, you fucking whore."

Quinn dismissed the browser and pulled up his messages. Nothing new from Larisa.

> Quinn: Are you okay?

Which was really not the thing to say, but what else? *Fuck.* "What kind of person says that to someone on the street?"

"Celebrities, they're like public commodities or something," said Sid, entirely unhelpful. The man's voice played back in his head, as toxic as though he'd been the object of their venom.

> Larisa: It's fine. I didn't want to volunteer anyway.

> Quinn: I'll come over.

> Larisa: I'm going to Krissy's. See you tomorrow.

"Fuck."

"Is she okay?" asked Sid.

"Probably not."

"You should call her."

"And say what?"

"Well, for starters—"

"Let's just go home."

What can we do? thought Quinn. Larisa had sequestered herself at her parents' all summer. And now, just barely out in public again and this happened. He hadn't understood why she'd been so nervous. Now, it felt like Larisa's precautions weren't enough. *She needs a bodyguard.*

Does someone take a bodyguard with them to walk dogs for the shelter?

Sid's phone was blowing up, a near-constant chiming as they walked down the sidewalk.

"Everyone knows, huh?"

"Not everyone. My mom, Guilia. Teddy."

"Teddy?"

"That guy who drove the car for us."

"Right. They could text me."

"Guilia said you're ignoring her."

Quinn tried to remember the last time he'd had an exchange with the woman who'd been his director of photography for his first two films. Sometime that spring. He probably hadn't responded well. Just as he wasn't likely to respond well if he was the one with messages pouring in about Larisa.

"Thank you for doing this," he said.

"When you get a raise, I get a raise," said Sid with a grin.

"We should find Larisa one of you."

Sid laughed. "She'd never surrender control like that."

"True," said Quinn, but he thought of what Larisa had said about her life with Lucas, the submissive in their relationship. Again, he wondered if she wanted that, and if so, how was he going to do that for her.

Eddie called from the studio. "I just heard from scheduling that Larisa pulled out of the junket."

Quinn wished he hadn't answered the phone.

"You should convince her to do it. I don't like how this looks for you."

"Okay."

"All those things people say about how this is the twenty-first century and progress and yadda yadda, they're not true in Hollywood. You understand? She's making decisions that could hurt you. It's already hurting you."

"What decisions?" said Sid. Quinn realized he wasn't holding his phone to his ear but merely suspending it in some space near his head.

"What decisions?" said Quinn, as he repositioned his phone. "She was walking stray dogs. Last week she went to a party and danced with a movie star while wearing a *Star Trek* costume. What's the scandal that could've been avoided? You want her to be a hermit? She did that all summer and fall."

"I'm just trying to be helpful." Eddie sounded defensive. "If it doesn't bother you, fine. Whatever. But it looks bad. Directors with questionable sexuality don't get funding in this town. Really, it'd be better if you were the one who beat her."

"Thanks for calling."

"What do you think about the junket?" asked Eddie. "Are you going to talk to her?"

What do I think? I want to go back to lunch and tell Kyle I'm not wasting my life on his piece of shit movie.

I think Larisa doesn't deserve this.

Quinn hung up.

"There's nothing wrong with either of you," said Sid. "You know that, right? People will forget eventually."

Quinn gave Sid a look to shut him up. "Just drive."

Chapter 9

A Birthday Peacemaker

They didn't talk that night. She didn't call, or text anything except good night at ten o'clock. She sent a picture of Sabrina sitting wide-eyed in her cat bed, ready to do anything but fall asleep.

The next morning Quinn went to the studio and sat through two emergency sessions with experts brought in to discuss things he should and shouldn't say about his personal life during the junket interviews. The row of executive assistants sitting along the wall taking notes kept looking at him like they knew what he looked like without his clothes on.

And then it was time to go to Kahleah and Cade's for their daughter's birthday party. Sid picked him up. The gift had been wrapped. Larisa had texted Sid to say she was driving herself. Everything just floated along, and Quinn chose to go with it. As the BMW cruised out of Studio City, through Sherman Oaks and into Encino, he thought he was glad Larisa had these friends who made demands of her. That she could have this distraction even if it was superficial.

He felt it again, this flush of gratitude, as he walked under the giant purple and blue tunnel of balloon arches, then carried the gift to the table overflowing with other gifts. And again as he drifted toward the adults and accepted a beer from Krissy's husband Dev, who clapped him on the back and said, "You can have as many as you want." And with Rosa, beached in a lawn chair, when she motioned him over to sit so he didn't have to look conspicuous as he searched for Larisa.

"How's the baking?" he asked.

She patted her stomach. "Not done enough apparently. But the oven is certainly done." She moved her hand to his arm and patted him. "She came with her new publicist. They're in the tent watching the kids learn how to do pottery."

"Quinn, you're here. Wonderful."

He looked over and saw Kahleah approaching with a tray of iced waters. Beside her was a woman at least one life stage beyond them, perhaps two, who wore low heels and a cardigan sweater set with pearls. Quinn thought this was a strange thing to wear to a birthday, then realized Kahleah wore a similar outfit. Behind them two more women, one younger, one older, were coming along the walk.

The political wives, he thought without really knowing what that meant. They made Rosa in her Fendi maternity dress look slutty.

"This is Pam Hagan. Pam, Quinn VanderVeer. He works in the industry as a director."

Quinn shook the woman's limp hand. After a long pause that felt like antiquated gender expectations, he said, "And what do you do, Pam?"

"I'm married to Senator John Hagan. He's getting his hands dirty with our daughters right now." She waved her hand toward the tent. Quinn waited for more but there didn't appear to be anything else. He glanced at Kahleah for some clue as to what was appropriate, but she'd turned and was motioning the other women forward, repeating the introduction with emphasis on his rising career in film. It occurred to Quinn that, for perhaps the first time in his life, he was being introduced as a celebrity among commoners.

"Do you know any movie stars, Quinn?" The youngest of the wives had come around and boxed him in beside Rosa's chair.

"Larisa is really the one with . . . "

Kahleah gave him a pleading look like she was hoping he would impress these people. *I'm not your show pony, and neither is Larisa.* But then he thought, *She's Larisa's friend.* And then he had an idea.

"But the guy in my most recent film is gonna be big this year. Have you heard of Dansby Vaast?" *I can't believe I'm doing this.*

"Sounds familiar," said the wife.

"Look him up. Everyone will be talking about him in a month."

She pulled out her phone.

"V-A-A-S-T," said Quinn.

"Oh wow." The wife held up her phone to show the group Dansby's October fashion shoot photos.

"Why didn't he come with you today?" asked one of the wives.

"Schedule conflict. But maybe he'll be around next time."

Kahleah bowed her head at him in silent thanks. Two of the wives were already turning to her speculating about when 'next time' might be. Quinn had enough space to step out of their circle. As he made his retreat, he backed into a body and found that Larisa had been standing just behind him. She caught him gently in her arms and gave him a hug from behind.

"You're a good man," she whispered.

"I'm not so sure about that." He faced her and saw she was giving him a look that said she knew exactly what it had cost him to offer up Dansby as his prized connection. He looked for other things, grief, sleeplessness, some open wound from the day before. But she seemed fine. If anything, she seemed excited, vibrant.

"What?" she asked.

"I dunno. You seem . . . I think maybe you're scheming."

She leaned forward and pressed a finger to his lips. "Maybe I am. Maybe I'm not."

A woman stood slightly behind her, distracted by her phone. With short, spiky hair, gauged ears, and a black leather jacket with no shirt in evidence beneath it, Larisa's new publicist looked like she'd come to the wrong party.

At the same time Quinn saw her, the wives also took notice. All but Pam, the senator's wife, were staring at Teale. One looked interested. One looked repulsed. One looked like she wanted to run to the tent and snatch away her children before they were contaminated.

"I got the schedule from *The Rumpus*," said Teale, as though she was unaware of the stares. "Six posts starting in January. And a book discussion group on Thursday nights. They don't want the posts to have any spoilers."

"Teale is going to turn me into a literary figure," explained Larisa. "Teale, this is Quinn."

"Heya. Do you want to write something on the male perspective?"

"Of what?"

"The bondage lifestyle."

A ripple trembled through the air as though it had become a solid thing Teale had set off with a flick of her finger.

She said that loudly on purpose.

Kahleah looked like she wanted to melt into the cement. Rosa snorted a giggle, then said "Ya'll, this is Larisa. She's actually really well-adjusted given where she came from."

"In DC, there are bondage clubs on the corner of every block that borders a government building," said Pam with a knowing look.

"Obviously there's nothing wrong with it," said another. "For people who are wired like that."

Silence. No one quite looking at each other. Then the youngest wife said, "I have this friend who's still in college, and she's reading this *Twilight* fanfiction book. Have you heard about it?"

Quinn watched Larisa look back at Teale, who gave her a knowing look. Larisa squeezed Quinn's hand as a goodbye and glided into the gap he'd left in the circle.

"Everyone I know is talking about it," said Larisa. "I have a copy, but I haven't read it yet. Apparently, it's very explicit."

"How explicit?" asked one of the wives.

Quinn smiled to himself and pulled back into the shade of the house. Teale followed him. "It's a serious offer on the male perspective," she said.

"I'll think about it."

"There's a whole world of submissive males out there who're angry about how you're being treated."

"That's unlikely."

"One might wonder why you're not angry about it."

You've known me for three minutes.

"What are you going to say at the junket?"

"I haven't decided."

"Sure you have."

"Why are you here?" asked Quinn.

"Larisa didn't want to be alone? We had a strategy session in the car on the way over. She's doing New York."

"Is she traveling with me or by herself?"

"You, I think."

Quinn took a breath and nodded to himself. Okay. Good. They'd have some time together. Maybe it would be like a vacation. Room service, a change of scenery, shared purpose.

Across the lawn, the flaps of the tent parted, and a score of children began to pour out. They wore aprons that said CHLOE'S NUMBER 9 B-DAY. The aprons, their hands, their necks, their faces, their hair, and the sleeves of their designer sweatshirts were all spotted with colored swipes of clay.

In the middle of them, wearing a tiara with her hair all done up in curls, a miniature version of Kahleah was yelling, "Time for cake!" The kids around her took up the call. "Cake! Cake! Cake!" They moved in a pack into the house with a posse of nannies following them. The dads who'd been with them in the tent broke off to join Dev and the others at the cooler. The mothers who'd been in the tent swelled the size of the circle Larisa had wrapped around her little finger, still talking about a book she hadn't read.

He heard her say, "It's really got to be an amazing thing to be that free, right? To give yourself totally over to desire and not have to worry about anything else because someone's in charge of you. And you know their whole being exists to make you happy." His mind went to Lucas before he could stop it. He hated the thought, that single word with a giant plot of real estate in his mind, and how easily it mingled with his own desire to give himself fully over to Larisa, to exist only for her and making her happy. He struggled to imagine Lucas had ever been that kind of boyfriend. So, Quinn could take comfort in that, as long as he believed that was what Larisa wanted.

She paused to check her phone. A smile flushed her face with a mixture of pleasure and determination. He watched her excuse herself and walk across the lawn to the balloon tunnel.

"Where's she going?" asked Kahleah. "We're going to do cake."

Quinn was about to answer that he had no idea, but then realized the answer was obvious. There was only one thing that made Larisa light up like that. He'd seen it on set that spring when she'd been working as the studio's mental health consultant.

"She's been talking about how unhappy you are," said Quinn.

Kahleah flashed a glare at him. "What does she know? She's off in celebrity land causing scandals, worrying about wearing jeans."

"Maybe, just—"

Larisa reappeared at the end of the balloon tunnel walking arm and arm with Jaden.

"Oh no, she didn't," said Kahleah with a hiss. "Rosa, look."

"Hey, it's Jaden," said Rosa. "What do you want to do?"

Kahleah shook her head, then glanced at the political wives. Larisa and Jaden closed the distance, and Jaden came forward with a gift in her hands.

"I want to apologize for the party." She looked to Kahleah

first, then to Rosa. "I didn't realize so many people would come."

"But you invited them," said Kahleah.

"I invited some just to see if it'd work. I've never done anything like that. It just . . . anyway. I knew it had blown up before you all got there, and I didn't say anything and that was wrong."

A long silence. The cluster of wives watching. Larisa rubbing comforting circles on Jaden's back as though she was afraid her friend would cut and run under the pressure.

"I'm okay with this," said Rosa. "It was kind of exciting. There was a movie star and everything."

"Larisa did that," said Jaden. "I didn't ask her."

"True," said Larisa. "It's possible he told some people. I'm partly to blame for not thinking about what would happen."

Kahleah was still glaring, but some of the tension had eased out of her shoulders. "You have to say it to Krissy. She's inside getting the cake ready."

"Of course." Jaden hesitated, then moved forward to give Kahleah a hug. Then she bent down to hug Rosa. "I love you guys."

"Me too." Rosa's eyes welled. "Oh no, pregnancy hormones."

Kahleah took a breath, then turned to the wives to introduce them to Jaden.

As everyone shifted toward the house full of yelling children, Quinn took Larisa's hand and held it as they walked. He wanted to say something, but all his ideas felt clumsy and half finished.

They don't deserve you.

How do you have the energy?

Finally, he settled on something simple, "You're beautiful." He wished he could pull her away, make some excuse and abscond with her into the night. For all the time they'd spent together, it suddenly didn't feel like enough. He looked at her and all he wanted was more, for her to look at him, to speak to him, to laugh when he tried to be funny.

We'll have time, he thought.

Chapter 10

Playing the Wind

They'd held hands on the plane and in the airport whenever Larisa hadn't been texting. Quinn's idea, not hers. Something had changed at the birthday party. He'd started to look at her like he knew her. Sometimes his looks were bashful, openly appraising, appreciative, and when she caught him looking his cheeks turned pink. Other times he was serious, almost sad, almost scholarly in his attention. And when she looked at him, he merely tilted his head and smiled as though he knew a secret.

It's going to be a good weekend, thought Larisa, as she responded to the latest of Kahleah's texts. Yes, Quinn would be stressed out with the junket, but they'd have evenings in a hotel suite with a view of the skyline. She would coax him, tempt him, do everything she could short of throwing herself at him. Finally, they would begin. Years later, they'd look back on this weekend as the true beginning of their love.

"I think Kahleah is okay with me springing Jaden on her," said Larisa. "They're all doing happy hour tomorrow."

On the other side of the taxi bench, Quinn adjusted his new hat so he could crane his neck to look up at a passing building.

"But the two of us are going to do mani-pedis sometime after the holiday. She loves that."

"I hope Teale's plan with the consulting works," said Quinn. "It's great to see you like this."

Larisa had to agree, it was great. She'd gone from feeling absolutely horrible after the dog walking incident Tuesday to very nearly invincible at the birthday. "Helping people is the best thing anyone can do."

"But not everyone is energized by it. Or good at it." He turned from the window to look at her and Larisa felt her smile falter. He was so proud of her. He didn't seem to see anything wrong with what she was doing.

"Dr. Bade thinks I hide behind giving people what they want. I don't ask for things for myself. Or if I do, I feel bad about it."

"Because you don't trust people with yourself." Quinn nodded like this was an obvious thing. Larisa hadn't realized he'd gone ahead and diagnosed her. Heat rushed to her face. "It's difficult for people to understand. When I trust people, they fail, then feel horrible and resent me. It's just better to manage everything myself."

She held her breath, waiting for Quinn to argue. In her head, Dr. Bade reminded her relationships could only go so far without the vulnerability of trust.

"Well, my therapist keeps wanting to talk about my parents," said Quinn. "He also doesn't think I should be dating right now."

"I didn't know you were still going."

"Not really. I just went once last month." He paused. "And I went yesterday because things unraveled a bit."

This was news to Larisa. They'd been together the entire evening. He'd seemed fine, hadn't said anything about an emergency therapy session.

"I finally listened to that radio show. And it was just . . . " Quinn turned back to the window to gaze at the same midcentury building cloaked in scaffolds he'd seen five minutes earlier. The taxi hadn't moved.

"I don't want you to think you're too much," said Quinn. "This isn't your fault. It's completely reasonable that you don't trust people."

"But it is a problem. I'm working on it." A delivery person on a bicycle zoomed by. "I'm glad I came. I'm happy to be here with you."

"Me too."

Larisa hesitated. Then she decided to go for it. "And, in the interest of trust, I'll tell you that one of the reasons I didn't want to come was because the last time I was here I was with Lucas. My cousin, Hannah, and I came just after Thanksgiving to see the lighting of the tree at Rockefeller Center and all that. He showed us around. He had an apartment here. Has one still, I suppose."

With the hat and the intermittent streetlights, there wasn't enough light to read Quinn's expression. She thought he was keeping himself carefully neutral so she'd feel safe telling him these things.

Nothing about Lucas is safe, she thought.

"I've never been here," said Quinn, turning back to the window. "I might go out walking before bed, unless you have something planned."

She couldn't tell if he was telling her or asking permission. The thought of Quinn wandering late-night New York streets tightened her throat. The reaction made her feel ridiculous. Quinn wasn't recognizable on the street. He wasn't some soft, rich person who'd been riding in hired cars his whole life, sheltered from the real world. He knew how to take care of himself.

So, she kept quiet. And, once they got to the hotel and up to their suite, she waved goodbye even though she wanted to rush at him and tell him to stay, or worse, lobby for an invitation. But he hadn't invited her. And, even though he'd been more attentive since the birthday, the distance between them still poked its rotten head up often enough she understood why he'd want to be alone.

Larisa occupied herself by taking a long shower. When she thought of Quinn whispering 'You're beautiful' at the birthday, she touched herself. She drew his face in her mind as her fingers parted her labia and substituted themselves for the shaft she wanted in their place. She thought, *Maybe this weekend, we'll—*

And allowed herself to go no further.

Wrapped in one of the downy hotel bathrobes, Larisa plugged her iPod into the nightstand speaker of the master bedroom and listened to Miles Davis as she unpacked. Even though she had no intention of leaving the suite until they drove back to the airport, she'd packed for the first night an evening dress with enough give she could sit in bed and eat dinner, as well as a satin boob shirt for the second night. She'd packed her conservative negligee, including the transparent robe gifted to her from the mayor of Las Vegas, which had shocked Quinn when they'd shared a room at Jaden's wedding ceremony.

Tonight, perhaps they would share a bed, but she didn't want to presume, so Larisa carried Quinn's Tom Ford tote and garment bag into the suite's second bedroom and unpacked all his clothes.

His suit jacket rattled when she pulled it from the bag. There in the pocket, apparently untouched since that fateful day, was the bottle of Viagra and the metal handcuffs Parish had stashed in the coat when she'd called Quinn out of Jaden's wedding.

"God damn it, Parish."

Larisa shoved the cuffs and pills into the bottom of the bag in the hope Quinn wouldn't notice them until he was packing to go home.

If not for Parish—

Another thought she left unfinished. Still, the familiar bitterness rose up like poisoned water, a flood of the same feelings she imagined had sent Quinn to an emergency therapy session. They didn't deserve any of what had happened. And yet it had happened, was continuing to happen, and there was nothing they could do about it.

When you feel helpless, turn it into action, Dr. Bade liked to say.

Larisa shut off her music and dialed the clinic where Parish lived. A five-minute phone call just to see how the baby was doing would remind her that Parish was a person. Flawed, possibly a criminal-level sociopath, but still a person.

"You're calling me," said Parish.

"I am. How are you?"

"Are you alone right now but don't want to be?"

This had been a mistake. "Actually, I was really just calling to see how you were doing. I try to do that when I'm tempted to hate you."

"Why do you hate me?"

"How's the baby?"

"She's good, coming any day now. I can't decide if I want a Thanksgiving baby. I mean, it's not the same as Christmas, right? She won't feel cheated out of a birthday on Thanksgiving like Christmas babies are."

"I didn't realize you were that close."

"I'm not. They want to induce labor early. I can't remember why. They're watching something. They take my blood every day. The nurses hate doing it as much as I do. Who knew giving birth was so complicated?"

"You sound happy."

"Why wouldn't I be? Aren't you happy?"

"Good night, Parish."

"Do something that makes you happy. Forget everything else."

Larisa hung up, but Parish's voice reverberated between her ears.

What would make me happy?

Easy answer: Making Quinn happy.

For a moment, she thought she could take him to a club. There were a few good ones in the city. Or at least, when she'd been here the last time, there had been good places. She and Lucas had snuck out after Hannah, who'd kept a strict curfew so the evil big city wouldn't tempt her into sin, had gone to bed.

Memory flashed across her body, an awakening in the backs of her thighs that felt like fire, the delicious trail of a flogger along her groin, blood rushing in her ears. The anticipation of a blow. She'd tensed for it, so very ready for release. But then, when it'd come too hard and in a place she'd told Lucas never to hit, there'd been a spike of panic, the dawning realization that something was happening she couldn't stop.

They hadn't used a safe word for months. He'd said they didn't need one.

Afterward, Lucas had apologized, but she'd never submitted to him again. Telling him no had made her feel like the worst person. Withholding herself from him had felt like a punishment he didn't deserve instead of something she was allowed to do for herself.

"That's all done now. Quinn's different."

But Quinn had gone out walking alone. And she didn't know how to wait for the man she loved except to pose herself in preparation for sex, which wasn't something she believed Quinn wanted.

So, I'll set a different kind of scene.

By the time Quinn returned to the suite, Larisa had transformed the living room into a gothic fantasy with candles lining the mantel of the gas fireplace, clustered on the end tables, and in little groups on the floor. She'd drawn the curtains over the windows and turned out the lights except for one lamp. She'd draped the damask blanket she'd brought across the divan and laid down on top of it wearing her sheer robe with nothing underneath. And when she heard the door opening, she posed herself with one hand demurely resting on her pubic bone and the other over her head.

He stopped short when he saw her. She watched his eyes travel over her body, then around the room. In that first moment, interest flickered across his face. She saw his expression expand in that way she loved, like he was blossoming from the inside out as his mind went to work. But the moment passed, whatever else was in his mind caught up to that interest and muted it. He began to unbutton his coat.

"I've dressed a scene for you," said Larisa, trying not to panic.

"I see that." He laughed softly. "So many candles." And then he went into the secondary bedroom.

Larisa almost got up and chased him. But what good would that do? She turned and stared into the gas fire as her mind raced. *How can I reach him? Doesn't he want me?*

Movement to her right.

Quinn had returned. He'd removed his coat and the sweater he'd been wearing beneath it, and now stood at the far corner of the fireplace rolling up his shirtsleeves. "What scene is this meant to be?"

"Dracula." Larisa stared at the slow revelation of his forearms, the pale lines of his wrists mossed in stark black hair, thick, primal. *He has no idea what he's doing to me.* The hand resting on her pubis dipped under the seam of her robe.

"Don't do that." Quinn blew out a candle, moved down to the floor by the couch and blew out two more. He moved the lamp so it was up behind the side of the couch, then knelt beside the divan. He took her wayward hand and brought it up to curl around the side of her neck.

"You don't know yet what you're waiting for, but some part of you knows this" —he stroked a finger down the line of her neck— "is vulnerable."

"I'm not afraid enough," she said.

He nodded. The light of the fire had warmed his skin and softened his features. "And there's an element of the supernatural. A breeze blows the windows open and, on that breeze, an intoxicating scent. His hand brushed over her eyes. "You fall into a dream."

No, I want to watch you, thought Larisa. But she closed her eyes.

His hand lingered at her chin, then dropped down to her collarbone where she'd fastened the fur-trimmed neck of her robe.

With a deft flick, he released it and moved the fabric aside. "You're such a young thing," said Quinn, his voice soft, like a poet in a trance. "So hungry for an experience that will define you." His hand stroked the curve of her left breast, thumb moving across the nipple, so light she arched her chest to chase it. "You can't imagine how wrong it could go."

Fingers danced across her sternum, moving to explore her right breast, a light brush on her already erect nipple. She ached for him to take it in his mouth.

Instead, Quinn said, "This is the wind bringing you to life. And now, he has come." He rose from his knees and sat on the side of the divan, leaned over her. "He has come to do what he always does." He leaned down and released his hot breath against her neck. Larisa's skin prickled, the heat traveling down through her chest, its own kind of life-giving animation. It took all she had to stay still and keep her eyes closed.

Touch me. She could have screamed at him for all her body longed for his hands on her, everywhere on her, gentle if he must, but rough if he could manage it. And a kiss, that first certain kiss that would tell her everything she needed to know.

"But then he sees her," continued Quinn. "It isn't beauty that stops the beast, but innocence. He's not so far gone that he would take what had not already been stolen by the cruelty of the world. Instead, he attempts to give her what she desires." Quinn's hand trailed down her stomach, cupped her bone and curled his fingers around it, parting her so slowly Larisa was halfway to climax before he began to stroke her.

"Does she fall in love?"

"She falls in love with the dream," said Quinn, as he probed deeper inside her. "With the wind. It comes to her one day every year for the rest of her life."

Larisa reached for him, tried to pull him toward her, but he captured her hand in his free hand and pressed it to his lips. A brushed kiss at first, then, one by one, his lips enclosed her fingers, his tongue marking their planes. She whimpered. "Let me see you."

"I am the wind. There's nothing to see."

Her hips bucked against his hand even as she tried to keep still, to draw this out until her starving soul was satisfied, even though she knew it wouldn't be enough. She wanted him inside her, taking her as thoroughly as she had once taken him.

And then his fingers dipped between her folds and pressed into the hard knob of her center. Her floodgates opened. She cried out his name. But he did not answer her. He was there but so far away he might as well have been the wind, a dream. She might have broken his orders and opened her eyes, but she was afraid of what she would see.

Chapter 11

Junket Meet Cute

She'd been so soft.

Quinn could still feel that luscious flesh between Larisa's legs, the way she'd filled his hand when he'd cupped her bone. All morning, he'd held his coffee mug in his lap so the bulge in his pants wouldn't be obvious. He'd taken care of himself after he'd gone to his room the previous night, and again that morning when he'd woken up dreaming she'd followed him to bed.

Unfinished, his brain said. *You shouldn't have retreated.*
She whimpered.

It shouldn't have bothered him. But that sound had ruined not just the scene, but the first timid steps he'd made toward being comfortable with her. His Queen was not a woman who made such fragile, pathetic, begging sounds as whimpering. And if she didn't, how could Larisa?

So, Quinn had retreated. And, if given the same scenario tonight, he would probably do it again. Because it was one thing to give pleasure to a woman, and another thing entirely to take her and claim her as his own the way so many other men had tried to do.

Not so many, he thought. Even though Larisa's history felt crowded, there'd only been one who mattered.

That's what she wants, to be taken the way he used to take her.

The tight ache in his groin redoubled its efforts to distract him.

128

"Why a spy film?" The reporter across from Quinn had snowy white hair, a beard that hadn't been trimmed in a few weeks, and glasses he kept adjusting. "It's such a departure from your other work."

I needed the money, thought Quinn. *It was the right kind of opportunity.*

"I'm interested in fantasy," said Quinn. "Not dragons and wizards, but the fantasy of something larger than life, of not having to care about what reality is as long as there's enough scaffolding to make something plausible. And the spy thriller has been done so much, I think I liked the challenge of seeing what new things could be done with it without alienating people who really love what it's always been."

"How did you balance that fantasy element with real elements?"

Quinn's mind jumped back to the previous night and Larisa's *Dracula* scene in the suite. His hands, her skin, that look in her eyes like a caged spirit, waiting for him to release her. The only thing he wanted was her happiness. So why was it so hard to give her what she wanted?

"Well, we had a script with some great set pieces, and a lot of extravagance. Then we brought in two experts. One was a CIA counterterrorism agent, and the other was independent consulting detective for the International Monetary Fund. He'd been a consultant for *The International* a few years ago. Between the two of them, they, uh, taught us the real-life spy shit."

The reporter smiled in a way that made Quinn certain he'd never felt led to say 'shit' in his life. Too easily, his mind slipped away from the discomfort of revealing too much of himself. There were Larisa's eyes laughing at him during the birthday party when one of the kids tried to climb in his lap. Both of them agreeing children were not in their future.

"What would you say was their greatest contribution?" asked the reporter.

"The CIA agent told us most criminals operate out in the

open now. There's no hiding their faces because 'they might be identified' kind of thing. They can mask all their criminal behavior through lackies, off-books accounting, and the black web. And sometimes, because the web's so crowded, they don't even need to do that. They can't be prosecuted without proof, so the biggest challenge is finding the people who can deliver the proof. That's why the undercover agent story is so compelling in the Internet age. You can't just slip in and steal a hard drive. You have to be close to someone, trusted. And then you wait for them to slip up and tell you something you can use."

Larisa, in the closet of her childhood bedroom, making a show of stepping out of her clothes while he watched.

"But I've heard the film doesn't end with the secret being found and the CIA moving in for an arrest."

"We ultimately decided that didn't make a satisfying ending. And the IMF detective agreed with that. As someone whose job is to try and track the money for global terrorism, and try to shut down bank accounts, and put people in jail, his definition of justice has two versions. One, you trap the money, and you make it impossible for one bad guy to do his work."

"Not very exciting on film."

"No. So, we went with his second version of justice, which is impassioned execution. More bad guys are killed by their own people or by assassins, than ever see the inside of a jail cell."

"Glad I didn't go into that line of work," said the reporter.

Global terrorism or enforcement? wondered Quinn, as he adjusted his mug so that it applied a gentle pressure to his penis to relieve the ache of what it really wanted.

For the last interview, before the break that proceeded their luncheon, Vince and Dansby joined him from the rooms where they'd been interviewing on their own. He was tired of sitting, but his erection hadn't gone down. Thoughts of Larisa had only grown stronger as the day had gone on.

It was beginning to feel obscene, meeting with all these serious, mostly male, reporters who used words like 'film' and 'cinema' and 'rhetorical context,' while part of his mind was thinking of a woman hiding on the thirtieth floor and what he would say when he saw her. He thought maybe he wouldn't say anything, he'd just charge into the room and interrupt whatever she was doing and kiss her. He'd kiss her because that was what he wanted to do. And he'd fill his hands with her body. And he'd stop waiting to feel like he knew what he was doing, or that he deserved her.

Vince shook his hand. "How's your first rodeo?"

"I wish I knew bigger words," said Quinn.

"Even if you did, they wouldn't be impressed. They're never impressed by people coming out of Cali."

"I don't feel that," said Dansby, as he slurped from a fresh mug of coffee. He noticed Quinn's was empty. "I can get you a refill?"

"I'm pacing myself."

"I saw Larisa's on the schedule tomorrow. Is she here yet?"

Quinn opened his mouth and closed it when he realized he didn't know what to say. If he said yes, Dansby would want to meet her. If he said no, he'd be in trouble if she was spotted later. Not that he cared what Dansby thought. The kid was like a Ken doll with an accent and hair that had its own personality.

The reporter came in, a young woman dressed to be on camera. This interview would be filmed as part of an online web series for IMDB. Quinn looked down at his lap, then over to the camera being set up. He judged from the angle his lap wouldn't be in frame.

Even though the interview featured all three of them, it quickly became clear the questions were focused on the actors, which was fine with Quinn. They gave good answers. They exchanged knowing looks, playing off each other for the camera.

When Quinn was brought into the conversation with a question about the script rewrite, he spoiled the mood by being too serious. He told the story about the rewrite of Dansby's character being Larisa's idea and how it made sense from a marketing perspective even though a male femme fatale hadn't really been done. It came as a relief when the camera pivoted back to Dansby, who bashfully recalled the first time he'd read the rewritten pages.

"Our last question comes from our fans," said the reporter. "What would make each of you a good spy?"

"Are we supposed to answer for each other or ourselves?" asked Vince. "Because I'd only make it about thirty seconds before they caught me. I'm an actor, but I can't fake it when the stakes are that high."

"I think Dansby is pretty plausible on the seduction angle," said Quinn. "You think you could do it for real?"

Dansby stroked his upper lip in thought, a motion so innately sexual that, even looking at him from the side, Quinn found himself distracted. *Is he doing that on purpose?*

"I dunno. I mean, when we were doing it, Quinn kept feeding me these ideas that I hadn't . . . that you know, hadn't occurred to me at all. Like, trust how you look and use it. Beauty blinds people. Hide behind it."

"I like that," said the reporter.

"It was great, jah. And then he was like, this is where you test out to see what'll drive the general mad. Not like in a bad way but like lust, right? And he said, you identify your limit, you hold him there, but then be ready for him to break through it. He'll feel like he's taken you, but he hasn't because you know you have something deeper he'll never touch and that's what you hang onto when you feel like you're losing yourself."

"Wow. That's some intense advice."

"It was an intense movie," said Quinn, stunned Dansby had remembered so much. At the time, Quinn had given so many notes because he'd felt like everything he told Dansby went through his ears into oblivion.

"Of the three of us Quinn would make the best spy," said Dansby. "He thought of all that stuff he told me. And, I mean, just look at him. He's sitting there and you have no idea what he's thinking."

Quinn laughed. "I was thinking it was an intense movie." He paused, then decided it was okay, he was going to go there. "And I was thinking I pushed you too hard."

For a moment, Dansby looked nervous, as though this struck too close to the truth, but then he turned and grinned at the reporter. "You seen the film yet? Oh no, wait, that's tonight, right? Well, you'll love it."

"What a ride," said Dansby when the interview finished. He raked his hands through his hair and gave Quinn a sly look. "You're so good. I thought when she asked about the rewrite you would freeze."

"Quinn's got nerves of steel," said Vince with more familiarity than he'd ever shown on set. Quinn didn't blame him. Seeing these men again, he felt he should apologize even more than he had during the interview. But he wasn't sure how to articulate what he felt in a way that would make sense to them. That he'd been demanding? That he'd been distant? Did he think he should be friends with everyone the way Dansby was?

He pushed the feeling away. "We have a break now before lunch, right? I think I'll go take a nap."

"I bet he's sneaking up to see Larisa." Dansby gave Vince a knowing look.

"Don't keep her locked up," said Vince, as Quinn retreated down the hallway. "Have her come to the reception tonight."

The elevator dinged for Quinn's floor. As he neared the door of the suite, he found himself slowing down and listening, as though there'd be some sound that would warn him of what he'd find on the other side. And what did he expect? That she'd pounce on him? That she'd dressed herself for some impromptu afternoon delight? His body was absolutely up for it, but his earlier fantasies of charging into the room and stealing a kiss from her now felt impossible.

Larisa was tucked up under her blanket in a lounge chair by the window reading the self-published book she'd touted at the birthday party. She looked relaxed, even peaceful. He wished he could squeeze himself into the chair with her and stay there.

"Have you ever read an erotic romance?" she asked with mischief in her eyes.

"Ah, no."

"It's a trip. Here, let me read some to you. There was this good bit . . ." She began to flip through the pages.

"Do you like it?"

"Nope."

"Is it good?"

"Depends on your definition of good."

"Larisa." *Fuck, she was beautiful.*

She grinned at him. "Well, it's not what I said it was about to all those political wives. It just boils down to a powerful man trying to work out his issues by manipulating an inexperienced young woman into having sex with him. And the bondage scenes are just . . ." Larisa shook her head. "Anyway, how was your morning? Did you talk, talk, talk?"

"I did."

"Were you charming?"

"Sometimes. I saw Dansby. He and Vince think you should come to the reception tonight."

"Obviously, I'd love to see Dansby." Larisa hesitated. "What's this reception for?"

"The critics who are watching the screening this afternoon. Which reminds me, I need to go do a sound check before lunch. When we were in LA the sound was flat and the air vent on the right side of the theater kept ticking."

She gave him an amused look, partly indulgent, partly proud. "What?"

"Nothing. I just . . . I don't think you realize how different you are when you're . . . this."

"A confident rising film director ready to revolutionize the industry?"

"Happy."

He took her hand and raised it to his mouth, gently kissed the ridge of her knuckles. As he did this, he held her gaze. He thought, *This is her. This is the woman I want. Why can't I feel it?* "This is what you've done to me."

Color rose on her cheeks. He could hardly believe it. Larisa was blushing. "Well, I suppose I'll have to come down and make an appearance."

"We can stage it. You need me for something, but I'm not answering my phone. If you want, we can fight about it, then you'll drag me off early. We hide up here the rest of the night."

"I like this plan."

He went into the master bedroom and looked in the closet. All the clothes Larisa had brought were things he'd never seen her wear, going-out clothes even though they'd planned to stay in. He selected a red crepe dress with a high collar and a low draped back. He carried it back to the living room where she sat, the book forgotten on her lap, waiting for him.

"This one," he said. "And put your hair up."

She stared at him, her face inscrutable. He thought he'd pushed too far. It was so strange to give her an order. But then he saw the color on her face deepen with a thought that forced her to cough and rearrange her expression as though embarrassed. She gave him a salute. "Yes, sir."

The hotel staff knew what they were doing. They'd thought of everything Quinn had and more. The screening ended up being practically perfect. The eighty or so critics in attendance were less rowdy than the audiences in LA. They were so buttoned-up they didn't laugh at his joke about big budget thrillers being low-brow compared to their usual entertainment. But then, he probably should've resisted the temptation to try and lighten the mood with humor.

Over half of them looked like they'd walked out of window-less, bookshelf-lined offices on college campuses and found them-selves in his screening on accident. There were over a dozen bow ties, a fair number of patched-elbow tweeds, and most of the attendees were over fifty, not at all the target market for a spy thriller. He decided not to worry about that.

After he gave his opening spiel, introduced his actors, and thanked everyone for coming, he retreated to the back of the room and paced the exit aisle behind the last row of seats. For the most part, he felt it kept the audience's attention. After the climax of Dansby being rescued, Quinn felt some restlessness of people shifting in their seats, but that was expected. It was a traditionally scripted movie; everyone knew all the important things had happened and now it was just a matter of getting to the end. He'd fought with Eddie about the editing of the last sequence to try and avoid this very thing, but Eddie and the studio executive board had overruled him. So, there were ten minutes of closure when five would've been sufficient.

The next project will be better, thought Quinn. *I'll do better.*

This reminded him that he hadn't heard from Kyle at Film-Streams in response to the email Quinn had sent asking if he could submit an alternative shooting schedule that included loca-tion days.

He returned to the front of the theater for the formal Q&A. Afterward, he stood with Dansby and Vince to shake hands as the audience walked into the reception. This had also been the process for the initial LA screening, and it was definitely his least favorite part. He wasn't an actor who'd chosen a career of public appeasement. He didn't see why he should have to touch the hands of strangers and breathe their air when they leaned forward to say they liked his work. People saying the same compliment over and over created a cumulative opposite effect. By the time the theater was empty, he felt everyone who'd said how much they liked the film had secretly hated it.

"I'll wake up tomorrow to thirty bad reviews," he muttered, as he watched the last of the tweedy university types walk toward the bar.

"Don't be so sure," answered a deeply-accented voice. "They speak of what they have yet to understand."

Quinn turned back into the theater to see the speaker, a man who'd just moved on from Dansby and was coming up to Quinn. He looked like an actor from a costume drama, distinguished salt-and-pepper hair, immaculate goatee, a maroon, vampiric dinner jacket complete with cravat, and a crushed velvet vest with silver buttons.

"And they probably won't ever fully understand it," he said. "But that will be their own failing, not yours."

Wow, thought Quinn. Then Quinn's mind fell away into a space beyond language. The man had trapped Quinn in his gaze with eyes the color of chestnuts, equal parts warmth and intelligence, with a hint of what? Of malice, there in the very back? Quinn was barely aware of holding out his hand to shake. The man took Quinn's offered hand in his two gloved hands and stroked it between them.

"Shall we drink?" he asked.

Then they were walking. People passed around them, but Quinn didn't feel their attention or hear if they spoke to him. At the bar, he stood still, entranced, while the man asked the bartender about her selection of red wines, then followed up with a series of questions about how long the bottles had been open and how they'd been stored.

He's an actor, thought Quinn. *He's an actor who snuck into the screening to meet me. He's going to ask for a job. I'm going to say yes even though I don't have a job to give him.*

He's a conflicted hero.

A charismatic villain.

A chess master.

A demanding lover.

They moved to a cocktail table in the corner of the reception room.

"It's a poor year, but the vineyard is respectable," said the man, as he pushed one of the wine glasses toward Quinn.

This wasn't the moment to announce Quinn didn't drink. He took the glass and held it in his hand. Something about its familiar shape brought him back to a place of words. He remembered what this man had said about his film.

"So, what is it in my film that people saw without being able to understand?" asked Quinn.

"That cinema such as yours is a meaningless void created to keep the machine running and give them just enough pleasure they'll never stop to question if they might do something more with themselves." The man smiled in a way that made the insult feel like a compliment. He sipped his wine and watched Quinn over the edge of his glass, waiting for his response.

How could there be a response to that? Quinn felt himself crashing. His anticipation, which had blossomed so quickly, imploded into gas and dissolved without a trace. "You don't have a press badge," he said.

"How astute."

"Who do you write for?"

"Whoever I like."

"What do you wish you'd spent the past two hours doing instead of watching my film?"

"Bending you over a table and fucking you while she watched."

The erection that had died while he'd been busy with the screening, suddenly came back to life, even more insistent than before, the pain in his groin a sharp, needy fire. Quinn thought he'd frozen in place, stunned by the violence of the man's words as though he'd been struck, but his expression must have given something away because the man's smile deepened.

"Lucas."

"Very good." Lucas set his glass on the table. With what seemed both the slowest and the most graceful movement Quinn had ever seen, the hand that had held the glass reached out and traced the line of Quinn's jaw. "You're rather rough, aren't you?"

Quinn didn't move away even though he wanted to. Walking would be excruciating. Maybe he didn't exactly want to leave, but he didn't like the look in Lucas's eyes when he touched him, like he knew the exact nature of every moment of Quinn's life since he'd met Larisa and saw that it was nothing compared to what they'd shared.

Somewhere far away, Dansby's irrepressible cheerfulness called out, "Larisa!" Because he was glad to see her and couldn't conceive of a situation where that joy wouldn't be shared by everyone around him. He certainly couldn't imagine that she might have wanted to be anonymous.

"She's here," said Lucas with soft knowing in his voice that spread Quinn's pain outward into his hips, the backs of his thighs, tightening muscles so deep between his hips he'd never felt them until that moment. "What do you think she'll do?" Lucas's hand had dropped down, his fingers dipping beneath the collar of Quinn's shirt, memorizing the line of his collarbone.

Still, Quinn didn't move. He was going to explode. He couldn't breathe for fear of it.

"Security!" The cold iron in his Queen's voice brought him out of the spell. Quinn flinched away as Larisa marched up to the table, inserted herself in front of him and began to push him back toward the exit. His vision filled with her neck, the curve of her hairline where she'd swept her hair up just as he'd asked.

"How dare you."

"Hello, Larisa," said Lucas.

"Get out."

"Wonderful to see you."

"Security is on its way. Leave or be arrested."

"Leaving is always your solution, not mine." Lucas's voice was like honey in sunlight, but it seemed a dim stream compared to the torrent of Larisa's rage. Quinn felt his groin going liquid, his heart quivering. Any moment now, he'd lose it. What would she think of him when she realized it? Each overheated exhale felt like a sob.

He bowed his head. "I'm sorry," he whispered into her neck.

"Not now," said Larisa.

He clenched his jaw shut, but the words pressed against him, insistent, needy just like every other part of him in that moment. He set his hand against the small of her back and rested his forehead along the hard ridge of her shoulders. "Please."

"I'm surprised," said Lucas. "He really is yours."

"Security!"

To Lucas, she said, "Don't approach him again or I will end you."

"We could have a drink. The three of us—"

"The winery," said Larisa.

Quinn barely registered the long silence that followed. It was the silence of Larisa winning, but all he could think about was the smell of her skin, the long smooth planes of her shoulder blades, that voice.

Command me, he begged.

Punish me.

He grasped the skirt of her dress in his fist and clenched so hard his nails dug into his skin. The pain only amplified what he felt. She was ignoring him.

"Larisa," he whispered.

"Quiet!"

Somehow, her command was enough. He managed to bank his fire, pull himself together, and wait with his eyes on the floor, watching the veiling and unveiling of her feet beneath the curtain of her skirt when the breeze of passing people disturbed the red crepe. The people passing were hotel security. They wanted identification but Lucas didn't have any. Quinn heard Larisa being softer, almost apologetic as she asked that they please escort Lucas out of the hotel.

Then she was pulling on Quinn's hand. He gasped at the pain, all his concentration focused on keeping his feet under him as she dragged him through the reception to the elevator atrium, the arriving bell chime, the doors sliding closed. And then the explosion.

"Oh my fucking Christ, how could you be so stupid?"

He stared at the floor, an imitation-stone tile so polished it acted as a mirror. He could see his pink face staring back at him and Larisa staring at the top of his bowed head, the column of her body heaving up and down, back and forth, as though she was coming apart with the strain of some internal pressure.

No, that was what he felt. The pressure. His need.

"I'm sorry," he whispered. "I didn't—" He stopped. Arguing felt wrong.

The elevator chimed their arrival. He didn't move.

"Out!"

Under her command, he walked down the hall. His pulse pounded through his throat, his breath came in little gasps. Closer and closer, that door, and the future lay behind it. *Please don't leave me like this,* he thought.

She unlocked the door. It slammed shut behind them. Silence.

You should comfort her, he thought. *This was a shock. The last thing she's thinking is—*

"Take off your clothes."

Tears burned Quinn's eyes as he scrambled to obey. He almost fell trying to get his pants down without showing her his erection. It was the worst possible thing to be like this at a moment when she was certainly feeling something else. He should have explained earlier that she'd been in his head all day, that Lucas alone hadn't done this to him.

"Put your hands against the wall and present yourself."

As he followed her instructions, he heard her behind him, moving his clothes around. He felt a delicious sinking relief when he heard the zing of her yanking his belt from his pants.

"I can't believe you," she said with all the derision he remembered. "You think I'm going to fuck you after that? You're just tainted meat now."

The belt whistled through the air and cut a line of fire along his right ass cheek. He jumped in surprise. He'd forgotten how the first blow was always the most shocking. He resettled his position, resolved to hold it, already he felt better.

More, please.

She gave him five strikes and then dropped the belt. For a moment, a complete stillness. He waited, not daring to breathe for fear it would upset her, and she would retract.

Just when he began to imagine she'd snuck away and left him to hold his position without an audience, she dug her nails into his hips and turned him, slammed him against the wall as she set her hand along his jaw exactly as Lucas had, her eyes black embers of fury. He'd never seen her so angry. Even though she'd beaten him, the torrent of her rage remained unquenched.

"No one touches you except me."

"Yes, ma'am."

"I did not give you permission to speak."

For a moment, Quinn thought he'd misjudged the scene. That she really had beaten him out of anger. But then he saw the rage wilt from her eyes and that familiar tenderness rise up in its place as though she couldn't even look at him without her heart melting. He still didn't understand how anyone could look at him like that, especially her.

Now was not the time for doubts. He wanted her. Larisa. His Queen. He tilted his cheek into her palm, and before she could retract her hand, he licked it.

Her eyes widened, nostrils flaring. He thought she would slap him. Maybe he wanted her to slap him. Instead, she drew aside the front panel of her skirt and took his swollen, aching length in her hand. She guided him to her clit and began to massage an agonizing circle over the lace of her panties, then she pulled the lace aside and pushed him inside her.

"I'm sorry," he whispered, as her pulsing warmth enveloped him. He wanted to thrust, but she hadn't given him permission. It took all he had to stay still as she moved herself upon him, eyes locked on his with that dark warning that told him he was in trouble. "I'm sorry," he said again, and it felt like the words took on everything that had happened between them, and all he had failed to do, and perhaps even what he would fail to do in the future.

"Shhh," she whispered.

Her throbbing tunnel took in the rest of his length, drowning him in one delicious stroke that drove away his shame. He took her hips in his hands and began to thrust, once, twice, and then release. As he came, he clung to her, the two of them finally one as they shivered through the ripples of their shared pleasure.

He wanted to hold her forever. But even before he had completely withered, she was withdrawing. "Wash yourself and meet me in the living room," she said without even looking at him. She was gone before he could ask if she wanted him to be dressed.

In the shower, weak-kneed and blissed out of his mind, Quinn went through the motions. It was impossible to think, but he was aware he wanted to be thinking, that his mind was reaching for meaning, trying to fill in gaps. He decided clothes were best. He wore the luxury cotton lounge clothes she'd bought for him, so fresh and new they still smelled like the store.

Larisa had also showered. She wore briefs and a satin shirt that emphasized her breasts. While he'd been in the shower, she'd pulled all the pillows off the couch and arranged them on the floor around the coffee table where room service had delivered charcuterie and a tea service. On the table beside the chrome tea pot were a pair of handcuffs.

"You brought those?" he asked.

"They were in your bag. Sit."

He came forward and knelt beside the cushions. His ass ached from the belt. It took some maneuvering to figure out how to lay on the side of his hip without pain.

"Are we going to use them?"

"Maybe later. You're tired."

"I'm fine." *Better than fine,* he thought. Except that her coldness made him nervous. Still no real eye contact. She'd come to sit beside him, but she kept fussing over the table, distracted. "Larisa, what just happened?"

She adjusted a cushion at his shoulder. From the wooden board on the table, she assembled a stack of rice crackers, cheese and Italian cured ham, and held it before him. When Quinn reached out to take it, she batted his hand away. The pointer finger of her right hand stroked the line of his lips. "Open." She fed him the stack. The explosion of flavor in his mouth mirrored the explosion that had rushed from between his legs. He had the feeling of floating, of the most intimate pleasure. The touch of her finger lingered on his lips. He opened his mouth for more.

She fed him cheeses that melted over his tongue, salty meat so soft it came apart in threads, and a sweet fig sauce that he licked from the end of her finger. Finally, what she offered him was her own mouth with its own sweet lips, and pungent breath, and ripe desire.

When his mouth was not enough for her, she moved to other parts of him. His body bloomed to life as she nibbled his ears with her teeth and carved a gully around the base of his neck with her tongue. Her mouth tongued his nipples, then bit them so that his back arched up off the floor as currents shot through him, explosions that felt like the beginning of creation.

By the time she stroked her soft lips down the line of black hair that led to his bush, he was hard again. She mounted him and rode him as though all she lived for was the moment of his ecstasy. She was so tight and so wet, and yet he felt every quiver of her muscles around him, felt the rush of heat pouring out of her as she cried out toward the ceiling, a hiccupping laugh of a cry, like diamonds bursting with joy. And still, she moved on his length, driving him forward, then pulling back, leaving him breathless on the edge, then pushing him over to plummet into a place he'd never been.

After, Larisa held him.

"I'll always love you," she whispered, as he drifted off to sleep. He thought it was a strange thing to say, almost like a goodbye, but he didn't think any more of it until he woke up the next morning and the suite was empty.

Chapter 12

Larisa's Last Secret

Snow fell as the sun rose over Central Park. Larisa hadn't planned to be outside on this trip, so she hadn't packed any appropriate outerwear. She bought gloves from a vendor at the Columbus Circle market and made eye contact with the policeman on patrol. For a few minutes, she watched him pace his route; she wanted to know how far away he might be if she needed help. Then she walked through the market to the park entrance.

She only waited a few minutes, not long enough for the cold to set in, before she saw him coming up the sidewalk. In his long, velvet coat, he looked like one of the park coachmen who'd lost his carriage. He'd even donned a top hat, which was collecting snow in a way that made it look even more elegant.

"That's close enough." Larisa's eyes scanned the walk behind him for cronies, but the park was empty. It was too cold for joggers. Too early for tourists. The homeless were still asleep in a tent shelter on the East Green.

Lucas stopped and gave her a little smile like he thought her precautions quaint. "I can smell him on you from here."

"What do you want?"

"I wanted to have drinks."

"I'm being watched."

"There wouldn't be anything to see."

"You make me a target." Larisa gritted her teeth. *Us. He's made us targets.*

Lucas stepped closer. "You've been crying."

Because of you, you fucking bastard.

"I only came here to tell you that your little stunt worked."

Even through the veil of snow, she saw Lucas's eyes glitter with interest. "If he can be upset that easily, he's not worth your time."

"Yeah, well." Larisa felt fresh tears welling up. She brushed them away impatiently. "No one else is you, are they?"

"My offer from this summer still stands. We could leave right now. Go wherever you want. I have zero expectations."

"I can't."

"You won't." He took another step forward. Larisa took a step back.

"You promised not to do this."

"I was worried."

"You weren't worried," she spat. "You wanted to check him out."

"And prove to you he's nothing."

"I'm allowed to figure that out on my own."

Lucas held up his hands in apology, though not the least apologetic sounding as he said, "I'll do my best not to interfere again. Unless necessary."

"No. No! I can't have you showing up when you decide I'm not living my life the way you think I should. You can't do that, Lucas."

"I want you with me."

"We've been through this."

"If I stepped away—"

"You won't."

He frowned as though trying to puzzle out what he could say that would give him a different result.

"I meant what I said last night. I have a phone number to a direct line at the CIA. They'd love to hear from me."

"The winery is irrelevant. You can't use it." He sighed. "But I will respect your wishes. Clearly you haven't changed."

"Neither have you."

Lucas gave a bow from the waist and, even though she was wearing pants, Larisa curtseyed in return. He turned to walk back down the path, then paused. "I don't mind you keeping him as a pet. He won't satisfy you for very long, but he's better than nothing."

She watched him fade into the snow. She was shivering. Maybe not just from the cold. She walked down Eighth Avenue until she found an open coffee shop. Even though she hated to do it, she sat there nursing a cup of black coffee she had no interest in drinking, until long after Quinn's first interview had started. The interview they were doing together began at eleven; afterward, she and Quinn would attend a closing lunch together for questions in a more informal environment. Then they would fly back to LA.

Sometime between now and then, she needed a plan. Actually, she needed two plans. One she would share with Quinn that explained why Lucas had shown up, and how he wasn't going to be a problem in the future. And the second, would be a secret plan of all the things she'd do to make sure this didn't happen again.

By the time she walked into the junket suite for her interview with Quinn, she had some semblance of the first, but nothing for the second. Because the things she'd used to threaten Lucas could burn her as equally as they'd free her. There was no way around the fact that Lucas could do whatever he wanted, whenever he wanted, and the only thing she could trust to keep him away was his respect for her. Clearly, that wasn't enough.

Quinn looked so relieved to see her she almost started crying again. *This isn't fair to him. Fuck.*

"Are you okay?"

"I just went for a walk. I'm sorry. I should've texted."

"Your phone is off." The way he said it, she realized he knew. Somehow, as though it was obvious, he knew where she'd been. *What does it mean for us that he'd assume I'd see Lucas in secret? Does he think so little of me?*

There was no anger in Quinn's face, only searching, uncertainty. Every other man she'd ever met would've been furious, wounded in that particularly American male sort of way that got so many people hurt. But she knew Quinn didn't feel the right to possess her. He had not claimed ownership. Maybe this was why they'd been struggling. Part of her wanted that, or at least expected that. She didn't know what to do with a man who had no interest in adding her to his collection of accomplishments.

"Larisa, hello. I'm Sarah Michelle from the *New York Times*."

Larisa pressed her welcome smile onto her face, then turned to greet the reporter. "Morning. I'm sorry I'm late. Could we just have a few minutes?"

"No problem."

Sarah Michelle withdrew to the chair where she'd be sitting and began to look through her notes. When Larisa felt sure she was distracted, she took Quinn's hands and held them in hers. "Do you believe I love you?"

"I do."

"I need you to follow my lead."

His mouth opened to ask a question, but the question never came. He nodded. "Alright."

Still checking to make sure Sarah Michelle was occupied, Larisa brushed a soft kiss against his lips, then withdrew.

Showtime.

As they crossed the room, she said, "I don't see how you can go through with this after last night."

Quinn stared at her, so startled she thought he wouldn't follow through even though he'd just agreed to it. "Our people expect it."

"Fine," said Larisa. "Then I'm telling the truth."

"Fine."

Larisa marched up to the couch where she and Quinn would sit. Sarah Michelle was still looking at her notes, but she'd gone still with that ear-burning posture of someone who'd just heard the best gossip and was ready for more. As Larisa and Quinn took seats on opposite ends of the sofa, she looked up and smiled.

"Larisa, Quinn. I'm so excited to be with you here today to discuss your truth."

"The truth is he doesn't love me," said Larisa.

"That's not true," said Quinn, genuinely flustered.

"It is. You're getting all this attention. Attention because of me no less. And you like it."

"What?"

"Were you at the reception last night, Sarah?"

"Unfortunately, I wasn't."

"He was flirting with one of the reporters. And I don't even know what you've got going on with Dansby Vaast." To Sarah, she said, "He doesn't want a real relationship. He just wants to feel like he's kind of the world."

"I admit I've been distracted," said Quinn.

"Whatever. I'm done. That's the truth of it, Sarah. All this harassment I'm getting in the press because of him, like I'm some sort of sexual predator. Well, I'm the one being hunted. Everywhere we go, he sneaks out to meet someone."

"Do you think your BDSM lifestyle has made fidelity more difficult?" asked Sarah.

The question was directed at Quinn. Larisa heard him make a small choking noise like he'd almost laughed.

"We're not in the lifestyle anymore," he said. "Parish ruined it for us."

"Case in point: the ex-girlfriend who won't go away." Larisa triumphantly swung her arm through the air. "Do you have any questions for a not-together couple, Sarah? Perhaps you harbor a secret desire to be whipped? I'd love to talk about how women don't need men to satisfy themselves." She glared at Quinn. "Because I'm certainly planning to get back to the club now that I don't have to deal with his baggage."

It was just that simple. So simple, it made her want to cry. Why was she so good at manipulating people? Why couldn't her life allow her to be a real person, to not always have to calculate and scheme and damage control for unknown situations? *Think about that later. You're not done yet.*

Larisa carried her rage through the luncheon. Pretended to get drunk and flirt with one of the waiters. Two hours later they were on their way back to the privacy of the suite.

"I feel like I'm in a soap opera," said Quinn, as soon as she closed the door.

"That's a reasonable comparison."

"So, we're dating in secret now?"

"Yep."

"Because of Lucas."

"Yep."

Quinn walked over to the divan and sat down sideways so he was facing the other end where he expected her to sit. "We should talk about this."

"Can I get a drink first?"

"I think we should do this sober," he said. "Or as sober as possible."

Larisa sank into the other end of the divan.

"I want you to tell me everything."

Everything isn't possible.

"You have no idea what it was like waking up without you this morning. I almost called the police. I thought he'd taken you."

At least he didn't think I'd left him. She studied Quinn's face and thought there was a part of him that had believed she'd left him, and that's why he hadn't called the police.

"If you're not going to tell me everything, then I at least deserve to know why. Because I don't like sharing you with a ghost. And I really don't like that ghost showing up at my event like he owns the place." Quinn took a breath to steady himself. "What happened this morning? Are you going back to him?"

"Absolutely not."

"Did he threaten you?"

"No."

"Did he threaten me?"

"Not exactly."

"Then what the fuck, Larisa?"

"He's interested."

Quinn processed this for a moment as he brought himself back down to his preternatural calm. "Interested in us."

"He doesn't have boundaries like regular people. I belong to him, so he feels he should be involved in anything I do. He believes there's no one for me but him, so he came to evaluate you."

"And?"

"I think he's decided you're not much of a catch."

"So then, why the breakup charade? After all we've worked for, you'd rather be single than deal with the fact that he showed up at the junket and flirted with me?"

"You don't understand."

"Well, you're not doing a great job explaining."

Larisa looked over at the dead fireplace, fresh tears threatening. *God, I'm such a wreck,* she thought. In contrast, Quinn was almost cold, as though each minute she resisted him, he withdrew from her, put up his old walls like a defeated army erecting barriers to cover their retreat.

"If we'd done that interview the way we'd planned, he would've known I lied to him this morning when I said you were just a distraction. He can't know..."

Something hard rose up and stopped Larisa's breath. She pressed the palm of her hand to the base of her throat and massaged it until the pressure died back. "He can't know what I'd do for you. How important you are to me."

She watched him swallow down pressure in his own throat. "You could file a restraining order," he said.

"It will only encourage him."

"Then he'll be arrested."

"It won't work."

"Why the hell not? He's not royalty, is he? Not some god come down to walk among mortals?"

"I can't tell you that."

"Tell me what?"

"Quinn. Let's just stop here, okay? There's a line I don't want to cross. I need you to trust me. Once you know . . ." She paused, remembering the day she'd understood Lucas's secret, how she'd known immediately that her life would never be the same. "Once you know, that's the end of life being easy."

He stared at her with that kind of incredulous stillness she recognized as Quinn holding back his temper. She thought this was probably the first time he'd really had to restrain himself with her. Quinn's temper was a thing enacted against smaller, simpler people who weren't self-aware enough to know when they were bothering him. Now, she'd become one of them.

Finally, he took a breath. "Larisa, I know there are things you want from me that I'm not ready for. And there's a lot we don't know about each other. But I am with you. I'm committed to family dinners with your parents, national holidays in Minnesota, house parties with your friends, scandal rag gossip, and even maybe learning to appreciate opera. And if what you're trying to tell me is that I have to add your old boyfriend to that list, then fine, I can do that. But I don't give a flying fuck what he thinks or what he might do because all that stuff I listed is just the stuff that's extra. I'm here for you, and you alone. And you don't get to shut me out of your decisions just because you're scared."

He paused to study her face. "What? Am I coming on too strong?"

"You're fine." She swallowed back more tears. He was absolutely perfect. Really, she didn't understand how she could've gotten so lucky. But nothing he'd said changed their fundamental situation. She either had to break his heart, or she had to tell him the truth and hope somehow it would be okay.

"Please talk to me," he said.

No, Larisa, don't.

Trust is a choice, said Dr. Bade.

"Lucas is an arms dealer. He supplies everything from ammunition, to training personnel, to nuclear missiles, to whoever pays. The CIA monitors my phone. They visit every so often to ask me to help them trap him. They'll probably find me in the next couple days to ask about what happened here."

"And you say no. Why?"

"I'd like to keep living."

For a long moment, Quinn stared at some space just above her hairline. Each second that ticked by, she regretted telling him. As if their relationship wasn't complicated enough, she'd thrown this into it. Of all the secrets they'd already kept from each other, there'd still been this. If her life was ever made into a movie, it would be considered implausible to have so many plot twists.

She didn't want to watch his face as the full weight of what she'd said sank in and leeched its truth into all the other things he'd believed. But she also couldn't stop looking at him and marveling at his existence, of the fact that he remained before her, those quiet, steady eyes, gray-blue in the sunlight that burst through the windows, as infinite as the sea.

Finally, he said, "Is there anything else you're hiding from me?"

She shook her head. It felt impossible to breathe. But somehow, she was still breathing. Somehow still alive after doing the thing she'd promised herself she'd never do to him.

Slowly, he unfolded himself from the divan. He stood and offered her his hand up. She took it. His arms drew her forward and enfolded her so that her chest pressed against his chest, her hips to his hips. He felt so good she wanted to fall asleep in his arms but be conscious while doing it so she could remember every moment. At the same time, she wanted to make love to him, slowly, softly, coaxing little fires of pleasure to life as he moaned beneath her.

"You're not alone anymore." He pulled back and looked into her eyes. "Say it."

"I'm not alone anymore."

"Promise you won't leave me again like you did this morning."

"I like it when you give orders," she said.

It wasn't the answer he wanted, but he seemed to recognize that she wasn't ready for promises.

"I think we have a plane to catch," he said.

She nodded. It was a relief to have something to do, a deadline, a direction.

All through packing, the drive to the airport, and take off, Quinn didn't speak. Sometimes, she caught him looking at her as though seeing her in a new light. The drink service came and went and, finally, she couldn't stand it anymore.

"Please tell me what you're thinking."

"I'm thinking . . . I'm glad you decided to stay at your parents."

"I was actually planning to move out this afternoon when we get back. My mother's going to make a stink about the interview, and I'm not ready to try and explain secret dating to her." The thought of Suzette made Larisa's head ache. She'd spent so much energy trying to make her mother happy. It never felt like enough.

"Then I'll stay with you at the apartment."

"And do what, Quinn?" Larisa kept her voice gentle even though her irritation was growing. "Lucas found us in New York. If he wants, he can find us in LA. The idea is to not be interesting enough that he bothers."

"What do you think he planned to do in New York if he'd decided I was worthy?"

Larisa shook her head. "There aren't answers to those questions."

"And you just live with that all the time?" he asked.

"You get used to it after a while. You train yourself to trust what you know. I know Lucas is restless, easily distracted, highly intelligent, and generally not malicious. I believe he respects me enough to stay away."

"Except he didn't." Quinn's voice sounded like disbelief instead of a critique; it sounded broken. So, instead of agreeing they had no guarantees at this point, she said, "I think we'll be okay for a while, as long as we stay away from cameras."

"What about the premiere? What about London?"

"I'll still go with you. But we'll have to pretend we're having problems or something."

"For how long?"

"What do you mean?"

"How long do you think we'll need to go out in public looking like we hate each other?"

"This is why I hadn't told you. There are no good answers. This isn't something we can fix. Believe me, I've tried."

"Tried how?"

Larisa swallowed down tears. "I was never going to keep you. That was the plan. I needed a fake boyfriend to get through Jaden's wedding and get my mother off my back so I could hold things together long enough to finish school. And I just . . . it's your fault for being so wonderful." She started to cry.

"Stop that. We'll figure it out."

"I don't want you to move in with me because you're scared. I want you to do it because you love me." The tears redoubled their pressure, coursing down her cheeks, sending snot to fill her nose. Quinn was still holding her, but it almost felt like a cheap trick in the wake of his silence. He still didn't know if he loved her.

Chapter 13

Together at Last

Quinn liked to think of himself as a dynamic person. Like a prize fighter, he rolled with life's punches. He didn't tend toward catastrophizing. So, he knew this was a particularly bad shock when he woke up in his own bed Sunday morning and felt like the world had ended without giving him all the foreshadowing. Yes, he'd known Larisa was keeping things back. But what person looked at his girlfriend keeping secrets and thought, *Oh, she must have dated a criminal, and that's why she can't talk about it.*

Not just a criminal, an arms dealer. Just like in the movies. He'd spent an entire day talking about the nuances of spy thrillers, and CIA consultants, and how it was impossible to trap international terrorists. And then, a real one had watched his movie, shook his hand, and probably would've tried to kiss him if Larisa hadn't arrived to interrupt.

I almost let him kiss me.

Sid was at the kitchen table where he'd spread a variety of magazines and newspaper clippings that had either covered *The Key* or spread the gossip about him and Larisa.

"I don't want the bad ones on the wall," said Quinn, as he helped himself to coffee.

"None of these are bad," said Sid. "How was the Big Apple?"

"Interesting."

"Yeah?"

"Larisa's ex came to the reception."

Sid dropped his scissors on the table. "What?"

"Yeah, he's a . . . a little territorial, I guess."

"How so?"

Quinn's mind failed to summon an answer. All he could think was, *I can't tell Sid.*

I can't tell Sid.

I can't tell Sid.

"Oh-kay, well, did you get out and see anything?"

"There wasn't any time."

"And you made it through the couple's interview?" Sid was trying too hard, his eyes wide with the effort of not circling back to the questions he really wanted to ask.

"Look, I've been talking for two days straight. Can we just . . ."

"Sure." Sid gave him a side-eye.

Quinn's phone vibrated, startling him so badly he jumped and knocked it off his lap.

The side-eye deepened.

> Larisa: That meeting I told you would happen is happening. If you want to come, I'll pick you up tomorrow at 5.

> Larisa: No Sid.

Quinn tucked his phone into the pocket of his pants like it contained incriminating evidence.

"So, I noticed you didn't check your emails while you were gone," said Sid. "FilmStreams wants another meeting, but at the studio this time. With the holiday and all, it has to be tomorrow or Tuesday."

"Tuesday."

"K. I think you've got something for *The Key*, but I'll get it worked out. I looked at a map, the FilmStreams office is close to the studio. Wednesday night, we've got pre-Thanksgiving dinner at Jaden's. And Thursday, my mom is expecting us no later than nine. Apparently either we manage the cooking this year or we don't eat."

Sid paused as though he'd asked a question that required an answer.

"That's fine," said Quinn.

"You doing any holiday stuff with Larisa?"

"We're going out tomorrow afternoon. I think she's going to her mom's family Thursday."

"You haven't talked about it?"

"Sid."

"Yep, I'll just ask her when we get there."

"There?"

"We're helping her move back to the apartment?" Sid blinked. "Do you think all her stuff will fit in the trunk? Or is there like a lot of stuff?"

Quinn had no memory of a plan to move Larisa into her apartment that afternoon. He wanted to see her but not with Sid, who would be even more suspicious once he saw the two of them were keeping something from him. Still, he couldn't help Larisa by himself, and Sid knew it.

The afternoon was an unending agony of avoiding eye contact and not being able to keep up with conversations. He kept waiting for Sid to burst out with a direct question that left them no choice but to answer. He never did. And Larisa, for her part, seemed mostly normal. It was Quinn who couldn't pretend, couldn't get over the chasm that had split down the middle of his mind as the hours ticked by and it became more and more clear that nothing was going to be the same for him. Everything he said to Sid now would be calculated, filtered through the possibility of too much honesty.

And with the shock so fresh, the realizations constantly materializing and piling on top of each other, the only thing Quinn could think about was Lucas and what he couldn't say.

They met the CIA at a hotel in Anaheim. Quinn thought this was a little excessive. But what did he know? That morning he'd done an interview for *Spy Magazine* talking about espionage in the modern thriller and what real-life instances had inspired the plot of *The Key*. He'd made up a lot of his answers on the spot. For one, he hadn't written the script, and two, he didn't know much about espionage except what he'd seen in the movies. After today, he would have personal experience.

"The low point was when I said the plot of *The Key* is plausible because it fits with what audiences know from other movies in the genre," said Quinn. He'd been talking since they'd left Santa Monica.

"You were probably great." Larisa peeked through the curtain of their room's window, looking just like a nervous suspect in a movie watching out for their government handler.

"Funny thing, when movies become life." Quinn clenched his jaw shut, resolved not to say anything else. It wasn't so much his words but the tone of them that bothered him, how rushed and needy they sounded. "Should we be doing this?"

"If I hadn't set this up, they would've come to the apartment and made a scene."

"I know, but its . . . I mean, I've never met a spy."

"Do you want a Xanax?"

"Would you just look at me for a second?"

She stepped back from the window and turned to face him. The lighting in the room was dim, probably to obscure the chips in the baseboards and the mismatched paint in the corner of the ceiling. This had been a nice hotel once. Now it looked like the scene of a murder, except it was too obvious.

Your life is not a movie, Quinn.

But it felt like one.

"Can they arrest us for not helping?" he asked.

"That wouldn't do them any good. And if I was arrested Lucas would be suspicious."

"If this were a movie, you being arrested would invite him to come save you."

"That's the plot of *your* movie." She leaned into him, playfully brushing her finger along his nose. He reached for her hand and caught it. New nails, the softest skin. When had she gotten a manicure? He might have complimented them, but he wasn't sure how long he'd failed to notice.

"And *Mission Impossible Two*."

"Your movie will be better than that one."

"Don't say that until you see it."

A knock sounded on the door. With it, Quinn's heartbeat raced as though to run through the door, away from this meeting, away from all of it.

Larisa pressed a kiss to the side of his head. "I've done this several times. It'll be okay."

Two agents entered the room, showed their badges, and gave their names. Quinn immediately forgot them. There was only one chair in the room. They both ignored it. One sat down on the side of the queen bed, the other took up a position standing slightly behind the first.

"What's he doing here?" asked the one on the bed.

"He's part of it now," said Larisa. "I think you should brief him."

"We're not an infomercial," said the one behind the bed.

"No, it's fine," said the first. He had an intense double chin and an old-fashioned crew cut that barely concealed a bald spot by his right temple. "You were the one Lucas approached in New York, right?"

Quinn thought about the choice of the word 'approach,' which sounded more neutral than what the actual experience had been. But, as it expanded into the space of being spoken, it became an accusation. As though Quinn had done something to invite attention.

"What did he say to you?"

"He talked about my film and the critics." Quinn hesitated a moment before adding, "He touched me."

"He does that. Very hands on, fancies himself a renaissance man. What was he wearing?"

"A red velvet coat, like a Victorian vampire."

"He loves red," said the agent behind the bed.

"We believe he wears red to mark certain occasions or intentions." The agent studied Quinn. "This is good. He tried to get to Larisa through you. Did you reject him?"

"We're not going down that road," said Larisa. "We're here today to remind you we're not criminals, and we want nothing to do with your case."

The agent on the bed was still studying Quinn as though he could see that Quinn wasn't so committed to a hands-off dismissal as Larisa.

"Did she tell you how bad this guy is?"

"She said he's an arms dealer."

The agent rolled his eyes and pulled a tablet out of his bag. "Lucas Onslow the Third is a British national from a family of bankers who think very highly of themselves. On paper, he's a mid-level lobbyist for the Kahnoli Group, a firm that specializes in representing international interests to the US government."

"Mostly imports inspection and taxes," said the second agent.

"But he's also Pasolini, a broker for illegal arms and munitions trading."

"Through the company?" asked Quinn.

"Most likely. These firms are so huge they can bury entire subsidiaries and no one would know about it unless they knew what they were looking for." The agent on the bed gave Larisa a dirty look Quinn didn't understand. It felt like they were old friends. Or rather, old enemies.

"More recently, Pasolini has been giving some clients special services by managing logistics for the items himself."

"We think he's moving toward building his own cache to cut down shipping times."

"I told you he wouldn't do that," said Larisa. "It's too risky. He's a public person."

"He's moving without detection. We didn't know he was in New York. And we didn't know he'd followed you to LA until this morning."

Larisa lurched forward. "What?"

"Our sources say he's come to clean house. One of his underlings misstepped."

There was a pause as the agents withheld information. They weren't as obvious as to look at each other and agree what they would or would not say, but the effect was the same. Quinn glanced around the hotel room and suddenly felt their drive to Anaheim had not been long enough to make them safe.

"There's still time, Larisa," said the agent behind the bed. "Give us something actionable. Help us save lives."

Quinn watched Larisa's expression harden into something he'd never seen before. Not the fear he expected, but rage so pure he shuddered.

"What makes you think Larisa can help you?" asked Quinn.

"She's the only one who's made it out."

"Lucas keeps a small village of followers around him, but they're all tied into his network. The few times he's become involved with an outsider—"

"A civilian."

"—they die when they learn too much."

The agent sitting on the bed widened his eyes dramatically. "It's usually a strategic death designed to draw attention to a rival or punish a bad business deal."

"Which is why we don't meet like this," said Larisa. "I'd like to stay alive."

"We believe she knows the name of the shell company he uses for invoicing and logistics. And the alias he uses for his other properties."

"One of which is most certainly a weapons cache."

Larisa erupted. "Really? This is absurd. You're just ejaculating bullshit. Anything I'd give you would have to be verified. You'd sit on it, you'd watch. And then you'd make a mistake, you'd move too early, or fail to get approval. And Lucas would know. And he'd come for me."

"It appears he's already come for you." The agent on the bed kept his eyes on Quinn, an audience of one, and Quinn didn't like it. He felt like he was in a movie playing the role of a shocked spouse learning about his wife's secret life. But he couldn't tell what kind of ending the scene was building toward. Was this the moment he realized he couldn't do it and he left her? Or the moment they say his life's in danger, and he has to go underground while she goes off to save the world? Or the moment someone says, 'she needs your help' and the civilian husband must decide to rise to the moment, learn how to shoot a giant black gun, fight in hand-to-hand combat, beat a polygraph.

Through the haze of adrenaline pumping anxiety through his body, Quinn thought the only good ending for him was the last one. That's what he wanted. For one of these men to break the impasse and say, 'she needs your help' and he would do whatever they asked to fix this, so Larisa would be free. So they could be free together.

But when he looked at her, a pillar of immovable determination cemented to her place beside the window, Quinn couldn't imagine what he could do that would help. The agent on the bed was listing off more information they felt Larisa knew: bank accounts, key business partners, secret government buyers. The longer the list went on, the more Quinn couldn't believe Lucas had let Larisa walk out of his life knowing those things, and the more Quinn felt the total entrapment of her position. To reveal anything she knew to the agents would have revealed her as their source. This was the agreement she'd made with Lucas. Keep his secrets and she was free. Reveal them and people died.

"If you had this information, you could stop him?" asked Quinn.

"Well, obviously that's the end goal. But we also need a better picture of his organization. Who protects him? How he finds his sources? Really, what we need is a spy who he trusts implicitly." The agent sitting on the bed cast yet another look in Larisa's direction as though her refusal to play his game was a betrayal.

Quinn felt the subtle shift of his body moving from panic to anger. "You're absolutely not sending her back to him. That would be too obvious."

"There are ways to make it less obvious. Of course, now that scenario is less plausible because of you."

"We wanted to place her this spring when everything went south. He was ready to rescue her."

Quinn thought back to that summer. As Larisa mourned the ruin of her professional and personal lives, these two men had pressured her to work for them. And where had Quinn been? On a beach in France finishing his movie, licking his wounds, hiding from her.

"I think we're done here," said Quinn.

The agent on the bed rolled his eyes. "Let's not be dramatic."

"You're the ones being dramatic," said Larisa. "If Lucas was really here, and if you really wanted to stop some expected attack, you'd ask me to text him and set up a meeting. But you're not asking me to do that because you know exactly where he is and you're not planning to stop him. Any information I give you costs me too much."

"You should know we can't guarantee her safety if she continues to resist," said the agent behind the bed.

"And then there's the fact that she's knowingly allowing terrorism to continue," said the other. "Possibly contributing to the deaths of thousands of people. If there's an attack in LA, people you love will die."

"Out!"

"You're not safe with her," said the agent on the bed, as he stood and followed his partner out the door. "You'll never be safe, Quinn."

Quinn slammed the door behind them.

"Fuck!"

Larisa came and set her hand on his back, applying a gentle pressure until he stopped hyperventilating, then pulled him in for a hug. "I'm sorry," she whispered at the same time as he said, "I'm sorry."

He pressed his head against the side of her head. "It isn't fair."

"I know."

And then it happened. He turned and set his hands on her waist because he was afraid of her pulling away, retreating back into the distance between them. With his hands on her waist, the pieces snapped into place. Here, in this one moment, the unforeseen climax of a scene that seemed like it would end so many other ways, he saw her.

In this moment, he didn't worry that she knew more about everything—including film—than he did. He didn't worry that she was embarrassed by his clothes, or his dubious hair hidden under an even more dubious beanie (he was willing to replace it if she bought him something more suitable that did the same thing). He didn't worry that the only way she turned him on was by commanding him to submit. He was holding her and, for the first time, she was a whole person in his mind.

"I love you."

"Now?" she laughed.

"Now. Because I just realized I would do anything for you. To make your life better, easier, to give you the freedom you want. I'd do anything, even if it meant you were better off without me."

Her laugh turned into a sob. She collapsed into him, tears running down the side of his neck as she cried. "I don't want to ruin you. I don't want him to be near you or ever know that you're more to me than he ever was."

Quinn felt his old instinct to argue, to doubt, to make sure that she was really talking about him and not some other guy she'd made up in her mind. But this wasn't a moment for doubt. He guided her over to the bed and gently maneuvered her down onto the comforter of vague cleanliness. He brushed her hair away from her face and gazed down at her.

"I just thought of something I should have said to that reporter this morning. *The Key* doesn't need to be plausible to be a good movie. Ultimately, what people care about is how far someone will go for love. We all want to find that person who'll rescue us even when it's dangerous, the one who'll stand on the line and say no one gets past them." Quinn caught sight of her collarbone rising up from the open triangle of her blouse and ducked down to kiss it. He couldn't help himself.

"We don't want plausible. We want delusional, messy, burn-down-our-world-for-one-person stories. That's what we're going to be." He bent down, found the other side of her collarbone, and stroked its long, hard line with his tongue.

"But I don't want that for you," she said. "I'm supposed to be the one who holds the line. I wanted to protect you."

He reached under her shirt, her ribs molding his hands as he pushed her more fully onto the bed. Shirt off, he filled his eyes with her, his Larisa, the body that was no longer alien. He saw it now, the Queen who was also a woman fighting too hard for what she wanted.

"We protect each other."

She stared up at him, eyes searching his face as though she couldn't believe him. "Say it again."

"I love you."

Fresh tears filled her eyes. "Okay."

He kissed her cheek to catch a tear. Then kissed the skin beneath her eyes, her forehead, her nose. At last, he brushed his lips against hers. A test run, almost a tease. She shivered beneath him.

"You're wearing too many clothes," she said.

"In a minute." Again, he brushed his lips against hers, used his tongue to toy with the opening of her mouth as he reached beneath her skirt.

"Quinn."

"Shhh. I'm busy."

When he'd been with the Queen, she'd been in charge, and he'd wanted it that way. But when he'd been apart from her, dreaming of her, his mind had expanded on the possibilities of what they could be together once he was worthy of her. Now, without a hint of the seemingly insurmountable insecurities that had been holding him back, Quinn brought one to life.

He tilted his hand so his thumb pressed against her center, softly sliding between her folds as the rest of his fingers curled around the luscious curve of her meaty ass. For a moment he lingered there, feeling her clench and release, then clench again around his thumb as she gasped. He moved two fingers into the damp heat between her ass cheeks, stroking up and up until they found the soft, taut slit of her second hole. She yelped once, a sound more excited than nervous. At once she began to move against him.

"Quinn!" she hissed.

"You're beautiful."

"Put your dick in me, or so help me."

So, he did. Only the head at first, which seemed more than enough. He wanted to remember every moment, press every transition into his mind so she would be with him always, his Larisa. "You're so soft."

She whimpered and, this time, Quinn felt the sound belonged to her, to both of them in their shared lust. He pulled out of her and massaged her folds, then dipped back in. She writhed beneath him, panting coarse, ragged breaths.

"I can't—" she gasped, fingers drawing mountains of bedding into her fists.

Again, he pulled out and massaged her. He hesitated for just a moment before dipping back in. To offer her that much of him, it was like feeding a baby bird, an offering, a protective gesture, as though she couldn't take all of him.

"Enough!"

Larisa's arms swept up, wrapped him, then toppled him, so he was on his back, and she was on top. She seized his head in her hands and brought their lips together, diving down to devour him until everything but her vanished from his mind.

Chapter 14

Negotiations

When Quinn made up his mind that he wanted something, and he wanted it just so, there was no talking him out of it. She'd thought there was nothing good that could come out of the CIA meeting. But now, it would be something she remembered forever. The look on his face when he'd known he loved her had looked like so many other things. She'd thought he was angry, crushed, ready to leave her, ready to murder someone. Who knew a look could hold so much meaning and still not reveal the truth of itself? And then he'd said the words she'd been waiting to hear, and it hadn't felt real.

But it was real. He'd proven it to her by putting her on that sketchy hotel bed and torturing her with his soft touches, with his refusal to speed up. That first time, she hadn't been able to stand it. She'd taken over. He'd been frustrated enough that she'd forced herself to let him have his way the second time, and the third. After so much time spent on the brink of orgasm, as he'd explored every nerve in her body, Larisa was having trouble coming back to earth.

> Kahleah: Are we all sure about this dinner? What if she scams us again?
>
> Rosa: Jaden wouldn't do that.
>
> Kahleah: I reserve the right to leave.

> Kahleah: We'll probably be late anyway.
> Cade's assistant messed up his calendar and
> put a meeting right before. Who doesn't know
> how to calculate drive times?
>
> Hannah: I'm getting in the holiday spirit. You?

A picture of the turkeys their great-grandmother had knitted appeared on Larisa's phone.

Larisa studied the latest text as though staring at it would help it make sense. *Hannah's so weird,* she thought.

Just after it, a text from Quinn arrived.

> Quinn: I'm sore.
>
> Larisa: 🍆💦😏😈😊
>
> Quinn: I know we need to talk, but I'm not thinking about talking.
>
> Larisa: Don't think about either. Focus on your meeting!!!
>
> Quinn: I'm going to fight them. I feel ready to fight everyone.

Larisa smiled to herself, though she couldn't help but wonder if Quinn's sudden gumption would serve him well going into this latest meeting with FilmStreams. *Real life today,* she thought bitterly. *Why can't we go back to yesterday?*

Quinn was right, they did need to talk. They hadn't had a conversation, just the two of them, since she'd dropped her bombshell confession in New York. But his body was in her mind, and the sounds he'd made as they rocked that cheap bed in the Anaheim hotel, echoed so loudly in her living memory that she kept glancing around to see if someone else heard them. She knew, even if they resolved to talk, as soon as they were together again, they'd be looking for a bed. Self-conscious, her hand went to her mouth, feeling the bruised swelling of her lips. He'd kissed them raw and still she wanted more.

"You're distracted today," said Teale.

They sat together on the couch in Larisa's childhood living room. Rockie sat in the far corner looking like she'd swallowed rocks. Larisa wasn't sure why she was present except that Suzette had invited her. They were gathered with Larisa's stylist, Jordan, to find a suitable dress for *The Key* premiere.

"This is really beautiful, but too flashy." Suzette held up a gown for Rockie to see. "What do you think?"

"What I think is irrelevant."

Suzette made a pouty face. "Don't be like that. Larisa made a mistake. The adults in the room know a junior manager isn't what she needs. No offence, Teale."

"I'm not setting up any more meetings for her. If Teale thinks she can get Oprah, fine. She takes on the risk of *her* client sabotaging her work."

"What are you talking about?" Suzette turned to Larisa. "What did she do?"

"The couple's interview in New York was a wash. Full of lies. I had to convince them not to print it."

"What?"

"Larisa told Sarah Michelle that she and Quinn were done. As there's been no official announcement, I assume Larisa decided she didn't need to take the interview seriously. The two of them played a *New York Times* journalist for laughs."

"Did you really do that?" whispered Teale.

"It's complicated," said Larisa.

"And she didn't even loop her new publicist in on the game." Rockie gave Larisa a sinister smile. "I say let her wear whatever she wants and let the wolves do what they will."

"That's what I was planning anyway," said Larisa. "I knew ten minutes ago none of those dresses were for me."

Jordan looked to Suzette, her mouth a bloodless line of repressed irritation.

"I think my work is done here. Can I go now?" Larisa stood and started for the door without waiting for permission. Teale hounded her footsteps.

"What the fuck?"

"Call Sarah Michelle and tell her to print the interview. Quinn and I broke up in New York."

"But you're picking out a dress for his movie."

"That's why it's complicated."

"And send out an announcement that we broke up. I should have told you Friday. It's just been rough."

"Rough, huh? Is that why you reek of sex?"

Larisa paused to smell her blouse. She'd spritzed herself in the downstairs bathroom before the meeting. Apparently, it hadn't been enough.

"Are you trying to fake people out again?"

"Not people." *One person.*

"It won't work. You're too visible now."

Larisa jogged down the stairs. Her phone vibrated. More texts from Hannah, who only thought of Larisa during the holidays.

"Did you at least read the book?" asked Teale.

"Almost done." This wasn't quite true. Larisa had no idea where the book was, or if it had even made it back into her suitcase when she'd packed to come home. It didn't matter. It was amazing how few things mattered. She threw open the front door and charged out into the sunshine.

"Teale, it's almost Thanksgiving. Do yourself a favor and slack off. We can talk about this next week."

"Are we really going to talk about it then?"

"I promise."

"You're going to see him right now, aren't you?"

Larisa slid into her Bentley and closed the door, blocking out whatever else Teale called out. Inside the car was peaceful, empty. Larisa spread her knees and stroked two fingers along her clit. The thin satin of her panties was damp. She hadn't showered yet that day. There hadn't been time after coming back from Anaheim.

Really, it was a miracle she'd managed to show up at this meeting at all. And now, she was certainly going to be punished for ruining it.

Whatever.

More incoming messages on her phone.

> Quinn: I'm going in now. I'll see you in a couple hours.

> Hannah: I've been thinking about the year you left.

Oh great.

> Larisa to Quinn: Don't let them bully you.

> Larisa to Hannah: Not my best look.

> Hannah: That's an understatement.

She hates me.

> Hannah: Anyway, are you bringing a plus one for Christmas? I think I've got a good candidate.

Larisa drove back to her apartment without replying. When she opened the door, Sabrina rushed her feet and began mewing as though the apocalypse had arrived.

"Can't I shower first?" asked Larisa.

The kitten drove her head into Larisa's shin.

"Alright."

First, distribution of wet cat food—beef and cheese because that was Sabrina's favorite, and she was not adjusting well to the apartment—then shower. Last, a complicated decision tree to assemble her wardrobe for the night.

"Is black lace too much?" she asked Sabrina. "I think he liked black leather, so . . . but it seems like we're not at that point. I think the pink halter with matching panties is good. And a skirt over, just in case he wants to talk for a bit. We do need to talk." Larisa paused as a sudden wave of dread swept over her. She grabbed her phone, certain something had gone terribly wrong. The only new messages were in the group chat, the sisters convincing Kahleah that Jaden's dinner the next night would be just the kind of holiday kick off she needed.

If something was really wrong, Quinn might not tell me.

Larisa considered calling. But then she might interrupt his meeting.

He's fine.

She went into the living room and turned on the news. No terrorist attacks, no fires, not even a mysterious, unidentified body in a drainage ditch. "They shouldn't have said that about Lucas being in town. It's like they want me to be afraid all the time no matter what I do."

Sabrina meowed in sympathy.

"I'm not going to think about it. Quinn's fine. Teale's going to send the announcement. Lucas is probably in DC, pretending he's a lobbyist. Let's plan dinner. Want to pick the mood?" Larisa's free hand tapped a comforting beat against her chest as she scrolled through her iPod playlists. Sabrina flounced her tail through the air as she went into the living room section of the apartment's central room and began to sniff around discontentedly for a sleeping spot.

"I know what you're feeling." Larisa plugged her iPod into the stereo. Madonna's "Material Girl" began to pour out of the speakers.

By the time Quinn arrived, Larisa had willed the feelings of doom and dread away. She was ready to greet him at the door with a brilliant smile, only to find Quinn was less than able to reciprocate.

"What's wrong?"

"I feel sick."

"Sick how?"

"It's just me. The stress's catching up."

"The meeting was bad?" She reached for him, then retracted as he staggered past her and collapsed in the fluffy white papasan chair beside the stereo.

"Not bad. Not good." He cupped his hands over his mouth and began to breathe through them like people in movies blew into paper bags.

"I'll make you tea." Larisa went to the kitchen and started her water boiler. The stereo had moved into the slower half of her late-eighties playlist. She hummed along as she watched Quinn count his breaths to keep himself from hyperventilating. Behind his hands, he watched her in that way that told her he was asking questions in his mind.

When he had more control of himself, he asked. "What song is this?"

Larisa paused. She'd been so focused on him she hadn't even been aware of the song. "It's from *Carousel*. 'You'll never Walk Alone.' This is the Gerry and the Pacemakers version. Huh. It shouldn't be on this list." She picked up her iPod. "Here, I'll play the original for you."

"That's okay. I'm really overstimulated right now."

Larisa brought out a mug, opened her tea cabinet, set the leaves to steep, and set the microwave timer for eight minutes. She started humming again, and when she caught herself at it, she felt guilty. *He's thinking about Lucas. He's thinking, 'I'm not a Broadway musical person.'*

Sabrina buzzed in from using her litter box, sprinted in a panicky circle around the room, then came over to sniff Quinn's legs.

"Hey, sweet thing." Quinn reached down to scratch her head. "Getting used to the new place?"

Sabrina rewarded his interest by jumping up on his lap and

setting about making biscuits on the blanket. He leaned forward so her narrow little back brushed against his chest. For a moment, it looked like she might curl up and sleep on his lap, but the microwave timer startled her. Quinn flinched as Sabrina dug her claws into his jeans and leapt from the chair over to her cat tower.

"Sorry," said Larisa.

"It's fine. I just—" he took a deep breath "—I think I've been running high since Thursday and didn't realize it until I crashed on the way over here."

"It's been a lot." Larisa let her fingers brush over his as she handed him the mug, then knelt on the floor beside him.

Quinn took a deep inhale of his tea. "This smells interesting."

"It's licorice. It should help with everything."

"Miracle tea, huh?" He took a sip. She watched the tension creep off his shoulders inch by inch. He leaned back in the chair. "How was the stylist meeting?"

"A waste of time."

"So, no dress yet?"

"I'll figure it out."

"Don't tell Sid. He's worried."

"Did the studio agree to your proposed changes?"

"They're willing to let me submit a revised budget and shooting schedule. No promises. I feel terrible about it. Like I'm delaying production on a whim."

"You're not."

"This is nice." Quinn took another sip of the tea. "Can I ask you something?"

"Of course." Larisa looked up at him, leaned into the edge of the chair, and tried to look open and trustworthy. *Whatever he asks, I'll tell him.*

Please don't let it be anything hard.

"What happened after the reception?"

A slow smile pulled at Larisa's mouth. She looked at his mouth and thought about how much she wanted to suck the film of licorice from his lips. "You mean the beating I gave you? Or the sex after I fed you dinner?"

Quinn peered at her over the rim of the mug. His eyes were soft with affection, something she still couldn't believe after so long with his cold uncertainty for company. With the lower part of his face hidden, his expression was incomplete. She couldn't tell what he was thinking. It seemed he wasn't going to give her any hints.

"I had a lot of negative energy after the reception. I felt if I didn't exert myself, I was going to go after Lucas and do something I would regret. I didn't want him to know he'd bothered me that much. So, I put it into giving you what you deserved." She paused as memories of that night came back to her. The marks she'd left on Quinn's full-moon ass cheeks. The way his eyes hadn't left hers as she'd set delicacies on his tongue. "I'd been holding myself back, so you'd have the space to figure things out. And that night I realized I was done waiting. I wanted you. And I knew as soon as the dust had settled everything between us would be different. I wanted that night for us. So, whatever happened after, at least we'd have that."

"Thank you." He finally lowered the mug. "I'm sorry I've been so slow."

"What else are you thinking about?"

"Was bondage something you learned together?"

"He'd already been involved with it for several years. We met at a sex party. I wandered into one of the rooms. Everything else was boring and I thought I'd just leave. But he was there, and he asked if I thought I could do it."

"Do what exactly?"

"Submit."

"To a complete stranger, just like that?"

"Don't judge me, Quinn. I was chasing a transformative experience. I wanted color in my life, and all I'd found was gray until him."

"You trusted him."

"I was willing to take the risk."

"He could've done whatever he wanted to you."

"He did."

Quinn flushed. "He did what?"

Larisa knew from the deepening sick expression on his face that she'd gone too far with her experiment in honesty. For now, she would spare him the details. "He made me feel alive."

"As a submissive."

"Yes."

"But now you're not."

"When I started going to Club D, I thought I'd be a sub. But no one could give me what I wanted." She saw him wanting to ask what exactly she had wanted that only Lucas could give her, so she rushed forward, not giving him space to interrupt. "One night, I switched, and I brought my partner to the best orgasm of their life. They begged me to meet them again."

Quinn stared down at his tea like he disliked the way this story was going. "Are you a domme because that's what other people wanted?"

"There's nothing wrong with taking care of people."

"Except that what you're saying is there's only one person who can really give you what you want."

"Four years ago, maybe that was true. But I'm different now. I'm not even sure I'm still interested in bondage." She said this last bit quieter than the rest, another secret that had slipped out and she was afraid of what he'd think. Larisa had never planned for Quinn to know so much about Lucas, so she'd never planned to have this conversation. "I think it's more like what you said. What I want out of it is you."

She watched him consider this, line her words up with the ones in his mind, revise his vision of their future. It felt like failure. The urge to take back what she'd said, to convince him she wanted what he wanted, itched across her skin. But she didn't take it back, if only so she'd be able to tell Dr. Bade she'd made this one step toward love, to make a space for herself within it.

Finally, Quinn said, "I like that I'm the only one you've been with like that. Something I don't have to share with his memory."

"He's not as omnipresent as you think."

"Oh really?" Quinn gave her a look, so incredulous it was almost comical. "I even look like him."

"No, you don't."

"Same stringy body, dark hair. He's warmer than I am, but you, my lady, have a type."

Larisa felt herself growing warm. "It's a coincidence."

"Your sisters knew at the wedding, didn't they? Everyone looked at me, and knew I was going to be kept around because I looked like him."

"I think we're getting into pop psychology territory here."

"And he saw it. That's why he came."

"He was just testing you."

"To see if I like complete strangers touching my face?"

"Did you?" she asked.

"Did I what?"

"Like it."

He stared at her. Larisa couldn't tell if he was horrified or just processing her question.

"I was just curious," she said. "You know I have very few boundaries, and I have a thing for public indecency."

"I'd like to stop talking about this."

She shrugged. "Shall we figure out holiday plans? Or are you feeling well enough I can drag you into the bedroom?"

Quinn took a final sip of his tea and then set it on the floor, too serious to be thinking about the holidays or sex. "So, two weeks ago when I said to you, 'by the way, I told a *Film Comment* reporter we were dating,' and you said, 'that's great.' Did you know there might be some kind of reaction from him?"

"There wasn't this spring."

"But you did think about what he might do when we decided to stage our relationship."

"I thought, 'I'm glad Quinn looks so boring on the outside, so Lucas won't see him as a threat.'"

She waited for Quinn to ask the obvious question, *A threat to what?* And when he didn't, she was relieved. She didn't know what answer she could give him. There was truth that could be spoken with words and truth that came from lived experience, from impressions, from instinct.

"How do you do it?"

"What?"

"Live like this."

"You get used to it." She tried to sound carefree, as though this one mistake of falling for Lucas didn't act like a giant diving bell around her life. "Humans are incredibly adaptable. We outright forget pain after it happens. And fear always comes in cycles. There's a chemical change sometimes, but consciously, we don't stay afraid all the time. We backchannel it from our awareness. It's like, I have these *Abbey Road* moments, and I have these Altamont moments. But most of it is just one foot in front of the other."

"You're going to have to translate that for me."

She laughed. "*Abbey Road* was the Beatles coming together to make an album like they used to, right? For those sessions, they dammed up all the ugly water under the bridge, and they believed everything they had was possible. And Altamont obviously was the day the sixties turned into a nightmare—music-wise, and in pop culture. People started looking behind the curtain into the darkness. The dream died."

"That's a really romantic view of the sixties."

"Well, it was an imperfect analogy, okay? It's just how I think about it. I'm not always thinking about him."

"Believe it or not, I have listened to *Abbey Road* multiple times. Sid went through a phase when all he'd listen to was the Beatles." Quinn shook his head, an almost smile on his lips. How she wanted to touch those lips, to end this conversation of words and start another with their bodies, which were true and pure and the only things they could trust.

She watched his face to see if he believed her, even though she didn't think it was possible. He was seeing Lucas in every part of her now, which wasn't fair. Nothing about this was fair to either of them.

"Quinn?"

"On the subject of holiday plans. I think it might be fun to pick out a Christmas tree."

Chapter 15

The Bigger the Better, Mostly

On Wednesday afternoon, Sid found Quinn in the walk-in closet of his bedroom surrounded by piles of books. Until that morning, when Quinn had begun working on the new budget for *Poseidon*, this closet had sat almost entirely forgotten, the holding zone of all the moving boxes of possessions Quinn wanted to keep but never used. He'd come here to look for a college textbook with a chapter and resource list on film budgeting. He hadn't found it yet, but he'd found other things: high school yearbooks, novels he'd annotated, scripts to Oscar-winning movies (also annotated), old textbooks, a photocollage made by Guilia during college, his story notebooks. They probably weren't as compelling as they seemed. But after the chaos of the past week, it felt good to drift from one found thing to the next, to remember old friends, and ideas, and his younger self.

"I didn't know you had so many books," said Sid. "Have you read all of them?"

"If I have, I don't remember." Quinn held up a ragged, spiral-bound subject book. "This is my story journal from freshman year of high school. I have almost ten of these." He fanned through the ink-covered pages. "Full of stories. Did you remember I wrote this much?"

"Uh yeah." Sid rolled his eyes. "But I thought you'd burned them or something when you, and Jen, and Guilia did your blood sacrifice to the gods of film or whatever. Is it any good?"

"I think so." Quinn wiggled his legs to get the blood flowing. For a moment nothing happened, and he panicked. What had seemed a normal activity became the sign of something dangerous. He was losing touch with his body again. But then the tingly feeling of blood pushing back where it was supposed to be pulsed through his toes. He shook off the premonition. *I'm fine. I'm handling it.*

"I should call Jen. She could work on *Poseidon.*"

"She's getting married."

"What?"

"To Guilia. The invite's on the fridge downstairs. I told you about it."

"I think I saw that."

"How long have you been sitting here?"

"What time is it?"

"Six-thirty."

Quinn looked up from a stack of magazines. "What?"

"Six-thirty. I'm here to drive you to the party."

"I told Larisa we would—"

"She called me when you failed to respond. She'll meet us there. We'll drive her home after. It's all handled."

"I'm sorry, Sid."

"Are you having another off day?"

"Another?"

"Since New York?"

Quinn nodded slowly, yes that was exactly it. Another off day. *Because a terrorist touched my face, and I can't tell you about it.* Lucas's voice rose up between his ears. The sharp tang of an invitation as much as a threat. *Bend you over a table and fuck you while she watches.*

"New York was a lot," said Quinn, avoiding eye contact as he got to his feet.

"And yet, no details."

"I'm not ready to talk about it."

Sid shrugged. "Well, come on then. We're going to be late."

Fifteen minutes later they were in the BMW, winding through the mountains to Jaden's house in the clouds. Sid had spent most of the ride channel-hopping on the radio and for once Quinn hadn't stopped him. Too many thoughts pressed the margins of his head to try to pretend with Sid. If he was going to lie, at least he would do this, allow it to be obvious. Sid would wonder, maybe even resent it, but eventually they'd adjust.

I don't know how to keep a secret from him.

Larisa has been doing this for years.

At least she told me.

Quinn massaged his knee, which had started aching during the drive. Maybe it had started before, but he hadn't noticed. He hadn't been able to notice, which was the kind of dissociation he was supposed to watch out for, stress signals.

The garish purple and orange Halloween inflatables had been replaced with less garish, but still extremely gauche, red and white ones. Inside the house was no better. A pair of stick trees outlined in red LED lights framed the atrium. Garlands of mass-produced silver tinsel mingled with string lights of little plastic baseball helmets. Every room had been stuffed to the ceiling with decorations, but nothing matched.

Jaden's little yappy dog slid into the atrium to greet them. It took an investigative sniff of Quinn's pant leg, then promptly turned and ran away.

"I'd never be able to sleep in this house," said Quinn.

"I would," said Sid. "Smell that?" He led the way to the kitchen. Larisa leaned against the wall beside the kitchen table where Rosa sat with her legs propped up, the two of them watching as Jaden and Krissy argued over the canapes plated on the island.

Seeing her, everything in him moved from low-level alert to full peace. There she was. His Larisa, watching her friends argue over sauce-covered appetizers. If this were her party, the debate would never have happened. Because she tolerated no divergence of opinion, no vision except her own.

In a month, Lucas won't matter, thought Quinn. *We'll have worn each other in, we'll be inseparable, on our way to something bigger.*

"Quinn, honey, the boys are in the den," said Jaden. "Do you need a drink?"

Larisa went to the fridge, found a bottle of sparkling water, and carried it over to him as Jaden screeched, "Why is this so fucking difficult?"

"I found him in the closet," Sid said to Larisa. "I think he'd been in there since breakfast."

To Larisa's questioning look, Quinn parodied defensiveness. "I was working on my budget."

"You haven't eaten?"

"I'm starving, by the way," said Sid.

"There's chips and dip in the den. They're watching the game."

"Point the way."

Larisa pointed, and Sid hurried off. With his departure Quinn relaxed even more. He hated himself for it, wanting to be away from his best friend, but he didn't see any other option.

"Sometimes I think he wishes I was a different kind of man," said Quinn.

"A more manly man?" teased Larisa, as she pressed into him, twining her fingers in his as though they'd been separated for days.

"I can infer that, at this time of year, when someone says 'the game' the event in question is most likely a football game, right?"

"Points to you." She laughed.

"The kids' table doesn't need a platter," said Rosa from her chair. "Just consolidate."

"That's what I'm doing,' said Jaden.

Larisa detached herself from him and went over to the island where she plucked two of the saucy things up onto a plate and absconded into the dining room.

Jaden yelled after her, "You just ruined the plating!"

"You already got your picture," Larisa called back.

The giant windows of the dining room's exterior wall overlooked the pool that overlooked half of LA. It reminded Quinn of an updated Stahl house, more comfortable but less character.

"Nice view," said Quinn, as he took a careful bite of the stolen food. An invasive thought soured the taste as the sauce coated his tongue. Had she tended to Lucas this way? *Is he also a man who forgets to take care of himself?*

"Would you live up here if you could?" asked Larisa.

"I'd spend half my time in a car trying to get somewhere. What about you?"

"I prefer being in the middle of things."

"Sorry about not picking you up."

"It's fine. Cade and Kahleah aren't here yet either." She smiled a smile with a question embedded in it. She looked at him as though trying to evaluate how he was doing. *How am I doing? I lost six hours today and didn't notice.* He'd read the very long Wikipedia entry of Lucas's family over breakfast and, afterward, everything had felt fuzzy, like he'd slipped into a dream.

They turned from the window. "The table is overdone," he observed.

"Agreed." She slipped her arm around his back, pressed her fingers against his side, hungry for him.

"And the colors."

"We already knew what Jaden does with colors." She led him into the front room with its vaulted ceiling and the Christmas tree that reached almost to the top.

"Now that's something."

"When I have my own house, the tree will only be seven feet tall and it will be tricolor," said Larisa. "Soft white lights, silver and red glass balls. Maybe a ribbon."

"I approve."

She swatted at him. "You'll probably look at it and tell me something has to move because of the way the light hits it at ten in the morning—" He caught her as she tried to move further into the room, pulled her against him. "Stop teasing me," he whispered.

"And then you'll come back that night and say it has to move again."

"I would only do that if we were taking pictures."

Around the far side of the tree, where there was a sliver of the front windows visible, they saw a black SUV pull up and Kahleah and Cade's two boys jump out with the older, more dignified, Chloe, stepping out behind them.

"What else?" he asked.

"What else what?" She nestled her face in his neck.

"What else do you want when this is your life?"

Her hair tickled his nose as she swayed against him, pretending to think hard. "A stereo system that can read my mind. Maybe more cats. A solarium larger than my parents'."

"But a smaller house overall. Your parents' house is too big."

"They like having big events at the house. I'd just rent a venue."

The boys burst through the front door. One chasing the other, as familiar as though they lived there. Jaden's dog came running in to greet them, ran in a circle around their feet, then chased them upstairs to the game room. Chloe came through the door, gave the stairway a tired look, as though she was too old for game rooms, then followed her brothers.

Cade walked in on his phone and flanked by an assistant in a sharp little business suit with a very short skirt. The pair of them took a right turn into a dark, empty room off the entryway. Kahleah came last, closing the front door. For a moment, she looked right, her gaze following her husband, then she looked left into the front room.

"We're late," she announced. "Where'd Cade go?"

Quinn pointed to the dark rectangle of the room off the front hall where there was just enough light to see two figures with their heads bent together in the glow of a tablet screen. Kahleah made a hissing sound.

"You're not late," said Larisa with a little too much brightness. "You're perfect. You should see the disaster in the kitchen." Larisa began to direct Kahleah toward the kitchen.

"Let's just . . . pause here." Kahleah glanced at Quinn, then at the tree, tilting her head up to see its distant angel topper. "We got the party's endorsement."

"Woo-hoo!" said Larisa. "That's great."

"Congrats," said Quinn, decidedly less enthusiastic. He thought this was one of the things that would define them, her over-the-top enthusiasm and desire to celebrate even small things, and him, restrained, moody, begrudging with his praise. A perfect balance.

"But it's not official because the mayor hasn't agreed not to run for reelection." Kahleah looked at Larisa. "I'm sorry to bring up a sore topic, but do you have an in at the Pacific Heights Clinic?"

Larisa blanched. Quinn wasn't even looking directly at her, and he felt it, a sudden movement as though she'd been struck by an invisible hand. The clinic clearly held some significance to her that Kahleah hadn't anticipated.

After several long moments, Larisa said, "Why do you ask?"

"There's a rumor the mayor's son is being treated there. I wondered, well, you know . . . a personal scandal might motivate him to stand down."

"Politics." Larisa had turned and was looking out the front window as though her mind had gotten up and walked out of the house, and she was watching it go.

"This is what we do for the good of the city," said Kahleah. "Or, I guess, what Francesca does." She glanced over her shoulder across the entryway to the dark room where her husband and his assistant had disappeared. "I'm just raising the children. And technically, the nanny's better at that than I am."

Whatever Larisa had been thinking passed. Quinn watched as she pulled her focus back to the room, roused herself as though from a dream, and slung her arm around Kahleah's shoulders.

"Well, you look fabulous. And points to you for giving Jaden a second chance."

"I deserve so many points."

"You do. And guess what? Tonight, you can cash them in for bottomless eggnog-flavored margaritas."

"Lead the way."

He hated Larisa leaving him, but he wasn't ready to go back to the chaos of the kitchen. The evening had barely begun, and he already wished it was over, or that he and Larisa were enjoying a quiet dinner somewhere. It'd be just the two of them, playing footsie under the table, making up absurd answers to even more absurd questions, talking so fast they didn't have time to think about what they weren't saying.

Quinn stayed alone looking at the tree. There was so much about Larisa he didn't know. Maybe he would never fully know her, but he was beginning to feel okay with it. He knew *the* thing now. Everything else was small by comparison.

The pitch of the women's voices in the kitchen rose to greet Kahleah. Quinn debated his options and decided to remain alone in the front room. The heavy solitude of the day lingered. Part of him wished he was still in the closet, alone with his thoughts, not worrying about explaining himself to anyone as he drifted from one thought to another, past blending with present, not actively accomplishing anything while also invisibly accomplishing so much.

FilmStreams will say yes. I'm going to make Poseidon. *It'll be the best gods-and-monsters movie ever.*

It occurred to him that, with all the focus on shooting locations and budget, he hadn't thought much about how one went about making the best gods-and-monsters movie ever. He thought about how Jaden and Adrian's Christmas tree lacked presence even though it was the largest tree he'd ever seen. Being large wasn't enough, which was a new idea to his impression of framing. *How did size translate on screen?* he wondered. *And how often was size different from majesty?* A god of the sea needed both.

The thought played in the back of his mind all through dinner, which was so fancy it was unidentifiable. He ate very little, but it was easy enough to sit beside Larisa, basking in her enigmatic shadow as the various parents boasted about their children, the children generally misbehaved, and Jaden told strange stories about being mistaken as a Malaysian aristocrat during their honeymoon in New Zealand. Meanwhile, behind the mask of his mildly attentive expression, Quinn measured the proportions of the room with his eyes. How high was the chandelier from the table? How large would a man need to be to stand on the table and break it? Would he reach the ceiling? How would he be lit, so that size felt like power?

After dinner, the children were excused to watch TV, and Quinn went with them. It wasn't hard to convince them to watch *Poseidon*. They had all seen it. They weren't at all surprised that an uncool adult, such as himself, had not.

But the movie was disappointing. The green screen translation was outdated and perhaps hadn't been high quality even for its time. The camera work lacked inspiration. And Steve Helston, despite his magnetic screen presence, looked more like a teen idol flirting with the camera than an all-powerful god.

Larisa found him splayed out on the chaise end of the sofa, abandoned by the children after they'd been given permission to go swimming.

"May I?"

He condensed himself so there was space for her to lay down next to him. The warm line of her body pressed in along his right side. His right arm rested on his waist, suddenly an awkward extra limb. After a moment, she took it and pulled it over to her chest, wrapped it up between her arms, and began to massage her fingers into his palm.

"Will you tell me a little about what you're thinking?"

"I'm thinking about *Poseidon*." He stopped there, unsure how much detail she wanted. "What about you?"

"I was imagining what kind of dinner parties we'd have when we finally have a house."

"I have a house."

She wrinkled her nose in a way that made her look a little like Sabrina. For a moment, he was distracted by one of those invasive thoughts he'd resolved not to indulge. *Did she give him that face. Did he ever think how adorable she looks when she's trying to decide if she should worry?*

"I know what you meant. A house for guests."

"Right. A hosting house. We'll have our core group of people who're never boring and are always trying new things. And maybe we'll have special, invited guests with particular expertise, who come and give us a peek into their world."

"That sounds complicated."

"Obviously, it's a long way down the road. Maybe we won't even be dinner party people." She pushed closer. "Do you think anyone would miss us if we snuck up to one of the guest bedrooms?"

"I don't want to do that." Quinn felt a rush to explain, then realized Larisa understood. Quinn liked his privacy.

"Or we could go home early." Her hand dropped to his groin, nimble fingers applying just the right pressure. She was so, so beautiful. And yet, even as he marveled at her, a dark fear lurked on the edge of his awareness, a thing he realized he'd been trying to keep back all day, and every hour of the days since Monday. *This isn't sustainable. I can't pretend the way she does.*

Spy Shit

"I'm still confused why you're here," said Larisa, arms crossed as though to bar Quinn and Sid from entering the nail salon.

"We were invited," said Sid with a grin that made her wonder how he was single.

"But how? And why?"

"Kahleah gave me her digits at the birthday." Sid flashed her his phone screen. "We're besties. And don't you think Quinn should have his nails ready for the red carpet?"

Larisa glanced at Quinn. He looked tense, like he hadn't slept well. She'd been away the entire weekend for Thanksgiving with her mother's family. She'd thought they'd communicated well long distance, but now she couldn't help but feel he'd been keeping things from her. *Neither of us is great at honesty,* she thought. Some part of her felt that this confirmed they were meant to be together, if at some point they did manage to learn to be more forthcoming.

"You missed a great Turkey Day, Risa," said Sid. "We set the stove on fire but not the turkey. Didn't know that was a thing, did you?"

"I didn't."

"He's exaggerating," said Quinn with one of his almost smiles that turned her insides molten. Four days and no sex. If she hadn't been so desperate to support Kahleah in her time of need, she'd have rescheduled this outing so she and Quinn could abscond to the apartment.

"Here I am." Kahleah rushed up the sidewalk in one of her now ubiquitous sweater sets, pearls, and low heels. "Traffic, I swear it gets worse every year. Hi, honey." She leaned in and gave Sid a smooch on the cheek while both Quinn and Larisa stared.

Larisa didn't remember Sid at Chloe's birthday party. There'd been the awkward political wives, Jaden's arrival, those tense minutes of worrying Kahleah wouldn't bend to forgiveness, a near disaster with the cake, a second near disaster with the firepit, and Quinn catching her watching from across the flames as he showed Jaden how to use her phone camera in low light. She loved seeing him do something technical. He acted like a person who didn't know anything, so when he did have a chance to demonstrate his expertise, it was just the sexiest thing.

"So, I saw the *Times*," said Kahleah, as they moved into the salon and followed the hostess into the private room at the back. "It called you two 'combustible with magnetic chemistry.'"

Quinn huffed out a soft laugh.

"Does it say we're single?" Larisa pulled out her phone.

She and Kahleah settled into the massage chairs for their pedicures while the men took seats at the manicure tables. A Vietnamese family owned the salon, which Rosa had found in college when she'd been trying to save money, and now they all came because it was quiet and off the celebrity track. It helped that Mr. and Mrs. Hu didn't seem particularly interested in their glamorous lives. They often carried on their own conversation while the girls chatted together. Today, the two oldest daughters had come in to do nails while their parents did the massages.

"It does not explicitly say we broke up." Larisa looked at Quinn, but he was sitting at the counter, his back to her.

"Did I miss something?" asked Kahleah.

"You and me too," muttered Sid.

"Is the temperature alright?" asked Mr. Hu.

"Great," said Larisa. She willed Quinn to turn around, or at least say something. This felt like failure. She'd worked so hard for this article. It was the thing that was supposed to save them.

Save us from what?

She couldn't answer the question, and yet the result felt vital, too large, almost insurmountable as her brain scrambled to redirect her strategy. "The premiere probably isn't a good idea."

At the nail counter, the Hu daughter working with Quinn said he had very nice hands. He thanked her for the compliment.

"Why is it not a good idea?" Sid had contorted himself so he could keep his hand where it was supposed to be and also look at Kahleah. "Is this making any sense to you?"

"Larisa has a complicated relationship with reality."

"Haven't you found a dress?" asked Sid, as though this could explain everything.

"Nothing that works," said Larisa.

"Risa, since when can you not find a dress?" Kahleah laughed. "I thought Jordan was meeting with you."

"She only brought the options my mother asked for."

"So, you're going to make him go alone?" asked Sid.

"You go with him."

"He can't take pictures with me," said Sid. "I'm the help."

The pictures, thought Larisa. Yes, that was the thing that must be avoided. Because any fool with a camera would be able to catch her looking at Quinn and know how she felt about him. And that picture would go out online and the whole world would see it. And then Lucas would . . .

They were here for Kahleah. She'd think about Lucas later.

"If it's that hard, I can loan you a dress." Kahleah held up the curio of nail polish colors. "I have one that would match this perfectly." She pointed to the color for Mrs. Hu. "We both want this one. Is it a gel?"

The color was a gentle, almost invisible pastel pink. Larisa remembered a time, not so long ago, when Kahleah led the way in extravagant nail design: tiger stripes, jewels, her glued on claws long and pointed. Now she was a gel girl who wanted barely-there pink. *Is this what Cade's done to you? Or have you changed?*

Larisa took a breath and decided not to point out that they hadn't been the same dress size since Kahleah's first pregnancy, and even then, they'd only comfortably shared tops not bottoms.

"I think we should talk about you," said Larisa. "Did you have a good Thanksgiving?"

"It was great. Cade stayed here. The kids and I went home. He didn't even try to call."

"Is that . . . I mean . . . did you like being away from him?"

"Sorry, can we just go back to the premiere thing?" Sid was glaring at Quinn, then at Larisa like he couldn't figure out who was more willing to give him answers. "WTF?"

"My publicist isn't sure I'm a good support for Quinn right now," said Larisa. "We thought the *Times* interview would help, but not being seen together might be best for a while."

Sid swiveled his gaze to Quinn. "Is this what you've been hiding from me? All this work to get a girlfriend, and she's going to leave you at the altar on the biggest night of your life?"

"It's not that simple," said Quinn.

"Thursday. It's on Thursday."

"Do you think it would help if I talked to Cade?" Larisa asked Kahleah. "Or maybe the three of us could—"

"I don't need an intervention. Really, if you want to help, I just need an in at that clinic. Something that isn't conspicuous."

Larisa had forgotten about Kahleah trying to get into the clinic. Did Quinn know Parish was there? Did he suspect she'd been visiting? *Why is this so hard? Life can't possibly be this hard for other people.*

Mrs. Hu said something to her husband in Vietnamese. At the counter, the daughter working on Sid's hand laughed and glanced covertly at her sister.

"Forget it," said Kahleah. "Obviously it makes you uncomfortable. Whatever. I've asked Lucas to do some consulting for us. He, at least, is willing to help."

Larisa watched a shiver travel up Quinn's spine, drawing his back together, somehow shrinking him into an even smaller frame than he already wore. He turned to look at Kahleah. "You asked Lucas to help with what exactly?" His voice was so low, so dangerously low, Kahleah sounded defensive when she said, "Lobbyist stuff. Campaign strategy."

For a moment, Quinn shifted his gaze to Larisa. He shook his head once, a side-to-side movement of disbelief that felt like judgement, as though this was her fault. *It is my fault.* Then he turned back to the counter and gave the Hu daughter his other hand.

One beat of silence, then another. Finally, Kahleah burst out, "This is just so typical, Larisa. You don't own Lucas. Just because you broke up doesn't mean I can't ask him for his professional opinion. My future depends on Cade winning this election. Don't you care about that?"

"I care," said Larisa softly. "You're right. Lucas is a great person to ask." Then, because she had to know, she said, "Did he ask about me and Quinn?"

"For fuck's sake." Kahleah clapped her hand over her mouth. "Now look, you've made me break my swearing sobriety. "No one cares if you're with Quinn or not, especially not the guy you dumped four years ago."

Larisa stared down at Mr. Hu's powerful hands working a salt mask into her feet and thought about how simple Kahleah's life was if she could say something like that. She'd married her high school sweetheart. She didn't have any experience with any kind of ex-boyfriend, let alone a man like Lucas.

"Kahleah," said Quinn, even softer than before. "Could you just answer the question?"

"No, we didn't talk about you. No, he didn't ask. He's dating someone new, and they sound very happy together."

"I don't want to go to therapy," said Quinn.

They were in Larisa's bed, naked, cooling off from an early morning shower because Quinn didn't like to lay in bed sticky after sex. They lay like two commas curled into each other, his head resting on the inside of her thigh, her head on a pillow on his hip. His fingers absently explored the shape of her ribcage below her breasts.

"I don't want to talk about my parents, or my self-worth, or any of that shrink stuff."

"You can tell him about Lucas."

"How? I don't even understand it for myself. There aren't words to describe what this is like." Quinn's mouth twisted at an unspoken thought, then he said, "Have you heard from him?"

"No."

"Do you think you will?"

"About the article? Maybe not. It was too polite." She reached out and stroked her fingers through his wet hair, sprinkling water droplets onto her leg. "I lie to my shrink. She doesn't even know Lucas's name. He's just the guy I dated in college."

"So you think I can lie to Sid? Wait, how does therapy help you if you can't talk about the biggest thing in your life?"

"You're the biggest thing in my life."

He looked up from her ribs, met her gaze with a soft knowing that tightened the already worn-out muscles deep within her.

"I want you with me at the premiere."

"How?"

"Maybe we just give up on hiding. What's the worst he'll do?"

Larisa considered that for a moment. She'd been thinking about it since she'd asked herself a similar question at the salon, but the answer still eluded her. It was a feeling in the back of her mind, an enemy ship in the shadows always evading her target lock.

"I don't know," she said. "Maybe if we acted like we hated each other. Or we were fighting."

Quinn laughed softly as he cupped his hand over her ribs. His touch was so gentle, so reverent. Even after all these days spent devouring each other's bodies, he was still looking at hers like it remained unmapped territory. "I'm already nervous about just being myself. You want to add a fake fight?"

"Maybe it would give you something to focus on, so you wouldn't be so nervous about the rest of it?"

"We're so weird. I mean, just listen to us, all wound up and contorting ourselves to make up this show for one man, and we can't even say why."

"But you feel it, don't you?"

He turned his face into her leg and kissed her thigh. "You want to pretend in front of Sid?"

"I think we have to. The further away he stays, the better. He can't know about Lucas."

Part of her wanted him to argue with her. Maybe he could present a reasonable counterargument, some alternative path where this secret didn't hang over them for the rest of their lives. But Quinn only said, "What time will you be back tonight?"

"Five or five-thirty."

"Too long," he sighed.

"You can text me every thought you have."

"Even the dirty ones?" He moved his head up her leg toward the tender pink lines of her engorged labia.

"Don't start something you can't finish."

"I'll call and cancel my appointment."

She pulled her leg out from under him, quickly turned herself around so she could lower herself down and pin him to the bed. He reached up and gathered her hair over her shoulder so he could see her face as she looked down at him.

"You need to go. Do better at therapy than I do. Find a way to say something that's close to the truth."

"I don't want to share you with him for the rest of my life," said Quinn. "That's the truth."

"Maybe he'll be assassinated." Larisa said it as a joke, but the idea bothered her. As soon as the words left her mouth, she felt they were a mistake, as though giving voice to them had awakened an old fear. The feeling, this nameless dread, stayed with her as she drove to Anastacia Sinitsina's house for their session, as she greeted the dogs, and the four of them took their usual places in the sunroom. She thought, *I don't want Lucas to die.* In itself, this wasn't an unreasonable thought. She didn't hate him. She just wished he was different. But the thought that followed disturbed her; it felt so much like the things she thought about Quinn. *I don't want to live in a world without him.*

Fuck.

Larisa fudged her way through the session, only half aware of the conversation. Anastacia said her usual things about how she wished she could fall in love with a robot because it would be easier to trust a robot than a person. She talked about her latest failed audition, and how it felt like everyone hated her for abandoning her marriage when, in fact, it'd been all her husband's fault.

As Larisa listened to Anastacia talk about her asshole husband, by now a familiar diatribe, Larisa heard it differently. Instead of Anastacia speaking from the logical space of a woman with legitimate grievances against a careless, flawed man, she heard loss. She heard longing for something to be different. It was the same feeling that echoed in her own heart. *If only Lucas had been just a little different, made one or two different choices . . .*

Larisa's phone vibrated noisily on the glass table where she'd left it screen-side up so she could watch the time.

Parish: THE BABY IS COMING.

"Let's just say I was going to try staying away from him," said Anastacia. "I'd have to go off to a convent or something. I mean, I've been trying to get a job, and I need to be here for that."

"It's an interesting challenge . . ." said Larisa, discreetly eying her phone as two more messages came in.

Parish: I'M DYING.

Parish: I DON'T WANT TO BE ALONE!!!

"But is avoiding Duck really going to change anything?"

"He might appreciate what he's missing."

Larisa thought back to Kahleah at the salon, adamant that Lucas had moved on. Hadn't some small voice in Larisa's head whispered about the power of avoidance? She felt their separation had made Lucas think about her more, not less. The idea that Kahleah could be right, and Larisa wrong, felt like a cosmic shift in the underpinnings of the universe. And yet, Larisa was sure Duck Turkin might not even notice his ex was avoiding him.

Lucas isn't other men, she thought.

"We're almost out of time," said Larisa. "I think you should try this out and see what it brings to your life." Larisa stood, pressed her phone screen against her hip so Anastacia wouldn't see it going off with more messages. "I'll see you after New Year's."

Anastacia waved her hand goodbye. "Tell your boyfriend good luck with his film. All the *men* in my life think he's got a hit coming."

Larisa wanted to say, 'There are good men out there, don't give up,' but she wasn't sure she believed this was true. Quinn was an anomaly, an untouched oasis of goodness somehow preserved over the first thirty years of his life just for her. And Lucas was the devil, who she couldn't help but love.

I don't actually love him.

Love, but not in love.

It took thirty regular minutes, and ten eternal minutes, to drive to the Pacific Heights Clinic. For the first half hour, Larisa believed

Parish was being her usual dramatic self, a woman who acted like a sixteen-year-old.

She didn't rush because she wasn't really in the mood for Parish's drama, and she knew babies took time to arrive. But then, as she sat at the light on Nichols Canyon turning onto Hollywood, Parish stopped typing in all caps. This somehow made the situation feel serious.

> Parish: I think theres something wrong
>
> Parish: They wont talk to me
>
> Larisa: What do you mean? What happened?

No response.

The next light. Nothing.

At the next light, a message from Krissy responding to Rosa's text that morning in the group chat, the last tendrils of a discussion about Krissy's family drama over the holiday.

> Larisa: Parish?

She tried to call. It went straight to a voice-mail box that hadn't been set up.

Then the eternal minutes began. Cars filled the road, the clock collected minute upon minute until they felt like compounding interest of lost time. Finally, she broke free of the traffic and gunned the engine as she tore up into the canyon. Larisa did a shoddy job parking and jogged into the clinic. She jogged instead of ran because she was in Louboutin's, and because some part of her was holding out hope this was a prank, Parish pulling Larisa's strings.

As soon as Larisa signed in at reception, a nurse materialized from behind the security door to escort her. This hadn't happened on her previous visits.

"You're the one Parish was texting?"

"What's the situation?"

"There isn't one. She was light-headed. Complained about some stomach pain after lunch. Her blood pressure elevated, but she's fine now. We gave her a sedative because she was anxious."

Larisa tried to read behind the lines. The clinical language was familiar, but it felt off. "Did you check the baby?"

"This isn't a hospital, Dr. de France-Kahn. Everything was normal at Parish's obstetrics appointment last week."

"She said something was being monitored. Blood work?"

"If that's true, I'm unaware of it."

They turned a corner and walked along the edge of one of the recreation common rooms. A woman rushing the other direction narrowly missed brushing Larisa's shoulder. A woman in a hat, sunglasses, and a wig. A woman who looked like—

"Kahleah?" Larisa laughed as the woman stopped short and made that hissing sound with her tongue against her teeth that was so familiar. "What are you doing here?"

Even Kahleah's giant sunglasses weren't enough to conceal the instinctual glance she cast over her shoulder at a table in the middle of the room where a group of patients wearing designer resort wear were playing dominos. Larisa recognized the fourth player, a teenager dressed in black industrially distressed jeans and a Death Head T-shirt, as the mayor's son. He was slightly less emaciated than the last time she'd seen him.

Oh.

"Really?"

"Don't judge me." Kahleah caught her breath. "What are *you* doing here?"

Before Larisa could formulate a plausible lie, an alarm began to sound. She looked to the nurse, but she was already running. Larisa ran too. They joined a flow of staff pouring out of various rooms, coming together in the hallway, then rushing to one particular room at the end of the hall. Someone called out a code thirty-seven.

Emergency transfer.

Larisa ran faster.

By the time she arrived, the doorway was blocked with rubberneckers. Being a tall person in four-inch heels made it easy to see over the crowd into the room. Parish, gripping the footboard railing of her bed, was bent over grabbing her stomach, sobbing. The crotch and inseams of her yoga pants were soaked in blood.

"She's gone," she cried. "I know she's gone."

Larisa wedged her arm into the gawkers and parted them enough that she could slip through. There were only two staffers in the room. One was going through the closet to get Parish new pants, the other was on the phone with EMS. Larisa came around Parish and held her from behind, wrapping one hand around Parish's belly. With her free hand, Larisa attempted to take Parish's pulse. She didn't know much about pregnancies, but it seemed like a lot of blood loss.

"It's going to be okay," said Larisa.

This only made Parish cry harder.

Later, after EMS had arrived and taken Parish away in an ambulance, Larisa found Kahleah out in the parking lot leaning against the hood of Larisa's Bentley. She was still wearing her disguise, still ducking to hide her face whenever someone went by.

"Is she going to be okay?" asked Kahleah.

"I think so."

"And the baby?"

"Unknown."

"I saw her earlier in the common room. I almost texted you about it. But then I would've had to explain why I was here. Should've figured you already knew where she was. Can we sit in your car?"

"I'm late for a meeting," said Larisa, a lie she didn't even bother dressing up. She felt hollowed out and distant. Kahleah was just a few feet to her left and the Bentley was close enough to touch, but they both felt far away.

"I can explain," said Kahleah.

"What you were doing is your business."

"I wouldn't have had to come if you'd told me the truth."

Now this is my fault?

It was all too much. Larisa felt the burning pressure rising up her throat of oncoming tears. She was so tired. Every day it felt like something new went wrong. How many times was she expected to absorb the blow, land on her feet, and keep going?

You're my friend, she thought. *How could you do this?*

Parish...

"You violated that kid's privacy and his health care coming here today," said Larisa.

"It's never going public. I wouldn't do that."

"Then why come? Why the desperation?"

"Last night, I talked to Lucas, and he thought it was worth checking. He knew the name of the clinic."

Larisa stared down at the pavement. The parking lot had recently been resurfaced. The dark-gray tar looked as smooth as ice. She thought, *Lucas knew the name of the clinic.* And then, *Maybe the baby is gone. I won't ever have to tell Quinn.*

"Larisa, believe me, this was just for a closed-door thing. Cade needs leverage."

Did anyone call Parish's parents?

I should go to the hospital.

I don't know where they took her.

"You don't know the pressure I'm under. This bid has to work. If Cade doesn't . . . there's no going back for us."

"Okay." Larisa moved toward the Bentley's driver's side door. It felt like there should've been more to say.

"Does Quinn know Parish is pregnant?" asked Kahleah.

"I'm going to go," she said. "Good luck with your campaign for Cade."

"Fine. Go. I'll keep your secret as long as you keep mine."

Larisa stopped with her door partially open. Driving was going to be difficult. Speaking was difficult. *Do you really think sneaking in to spy on the mayor's son and me hiding Quinn's baby are the same kind of thing?* For a moment, she imagined Kahleah calling Quinn, making a dramatic declaration. It would be purposefully vague, just enough to make him doubt. Whatever fragile trust they'd established would be ruined. And that didn't even consider the emotional fallout of learning he had almost been a father.

"My name's on the visitor list. If this ever goes to court, I'll be called to testify." Larisa took a breath. "So make sure it never gets that far."

"It won't."

"You should get a therapist."

"What would a therapist tell me?"

"She'd tell you this is a red flag, and if Cade asked you to do this, you should leave him."

Kahleah shifted her weight in a way that made Larisa think Cade had probably known, if not encouraged, her plan.

"And if he didn't?"

"Then you need someone to talk to who can help you sort through your next steps."

"I'm supporting my husband."

Larisa thought back to the night of Jaden's party, Kahleah's belated arrival. Cade on his phone, his assistant with the short skirt.

As though Kahleah knew what Larisa was thinking, she added, "I'm going to be a mayor's wife." She said it with a finality that carried its own kind of truth, finality that ended conversations.

A better friend would've gone back around the door and pulled Kahleah in for a hug. For a moment, this seemed like a thing Larisa was able to do. But then she thought, *Just once, I want to be the one someone takes care of.* She wanted to look at Kahleah and say, *I've been trying to help you, and you've blocked me out. You have no idea what's happening in my life.*

The last thought made her feel guilty, a violation of her belief that she should always give help and support when she saw the need for it. But along the way to being that kind of friend, she'd never figured out how to ask for help herself. The idea that, in this moment, Kahleah would look at Larisa and see how much she was in pain and be the one to reach for her was like the plot twist in a science fiction film, as unlikely as it was implausible.

She climbed into her car and closed the door after her, then looked at her phone. Three missed messages from Quinn.

> Quinn: I've been called into the studio for a last-minute panic session.

> Quinn: I think they want to make sure I'm not going to embarrass them.

> Quinn: I found you a dress. Did you know famous people can wear dresses without paying for them? You probably knew that. Anyway. It should be dropped off in the morning.

> Quinn: I love you.

And then, other messages, still in the process of coming in.

> Lucas: Exciting day.

> Lucas: Lucky for you.

> Lucas: You hadn't told him, had you?

Larisa's head swiveled to trace movement in her peripheral vision, Kahleah finally walking over to climb into her car. The visitor parking lot was empty, and yet Larisa felt eyes on her, watching. She felt the need to keep her face neutral as she composed her responses.

Larisa: Did you do it?

Lucas: I thought about it. For you.

Not quite an answer, but Larisa thought Lucas wouldn't feel guilt if he'd interfered with Parish's baby. He would own it.

Lucas: You're welcome.

Larisa: You shouldn't have done that to K.

Lucas: She needs someone to keep her honest.

Lucas: So do you.

Larisa let her head fall back against the headrest. The idea of driving all the way home felt too large. If she could just take a nap, when she woke up, the sharp edges of the day might have worn down.

Larisa: Compulsive honesty blows up people's lives.

Larisa: Are you trying to blow up my life?

Lucas: You have something you want to hang on to?

A bait question if ever there was one. Did he think she would fall for it?

Larisa: I'm going to write a blog series on a romance novel.

Lucas: I won't get in the way of that.

She took a breath. Relief didn't come. She looked out the windshield half expecting to see a figure in a long coat striding across the cement toward her.

Red Carpet

"Think of it this way, the hard part's already done," said Sid. "This is the celebration." He stood with his arms out like hangers, Quinn's shoes hooked on two fingers of his left hand, Quinn's suit coat on a single finger of his right.

"Did you see *The Post's* review?" asked Quinn, halfway relieved they could talk about the film instead of Larisa and the still unfinished conversation from the salon. "They hated it. Called it warmed-over nineties." Quinn stood in front of a floor-length mirror Sid had purchased from Target and leaned against the wall. The dress shirt Larisa had found for him was slippery even with the undershirt. Every time he moved it felt like it would come untucked.

"Everyone knows the nineties was a great decade for thrillers," said Sid.

"It's unoriginal."

"Even if that were true, we're in an industry that likes to remake things." Sid moved forward and set the shoes on the floor. "You're stalling."

"I haven't heard anything from Larisa." Quinn staged a strategic pause. He'd been dreading this all day. *You're doing it for him.* "It's been weird since New York."

"No kidding," said Sid. "She told me she's coming. Don't worry about it."

Quinn pulled out his phone and glared at it. No messages

from Larisa. He'd hoped for at least one even though she'd said radio silence was part of the fake fight they were now having.

"I think we should practice smiling."

"I'm a moody artist, Sid."

"But we don't want people to think you're difficult."

"Why did she tell you and not me?"

"Because she knows you're distracted. You want to wear the jacket in the limo?"

"I feel sick."

"I'll carry it." Sid turned and walked out the bedroom door. He waited at the top of the stairs for Quinn to join him.

The limo from the studio was already waiting outside. Seeing it, Quinn felt a wave of vertigo. *Are we really going to do this?* "Maybe we should wait a few minutes in case I have to—"

Sid gave Quinn a gentle push toward the limo.

Inside, Quinn sat on the seat facing forward. Sid laid the jacket out on the bench beside him. "Let's go over the plan Larisa sent. There's an hour on the carpet. You have five picture-staging spots, then mingling with people you already know. People who like you."

"No one likes me."

"You'll wave at fans and be jealous of Dansby signing autographs. But also glad because you don't have to get that close to the barricades. Then we all go inside the theater. You say a few words about how thankful you are to the studio, and Eddie, and how happy you are that everyone can be with you tonight, ex cetera, ex cetera. And then we watch *The Key*. It ends. Everyone gives you a standing ovation. Minimum presence at the after-party is forty minutes. We go home. Or you go home, I stay and party all night and tell people embarrassing stories from your adolescence when I get drunk."

"I didn't write a speech."

"It's not a speech. It's a spontaneous burst of pleasure and rejoicing."

Quinn turned his gaze from the window just long enough to

give Sid a look. Not once in his life had Quinn experienced a spontaneous burst of pleasure and rejoicing. It certainly wasn't happening tonight.

"Do you want to script it now? I could feed you some lines."

"Too late."

They'd arrived at Larisa's gate. Quinn pulled out his phone to call her, but there she was, already walking across the courtyard.

The dress he'd chosen was mudwash-pink, a hideous name for a color that looked more like a rosé. Not a color Larisa usually wore, but he thought it would suit her. He'd been right.

As she walked around to the limo door, the gathered folds of the dress sashayed at her hips, accentuating her movement, making her look even taller than she was. The top of the dress draped in a classical style reminiscent of an ancient Greek goddess with silver buckles at the top of the sleeves, which were cut open to drift in chiffon billows along her arms until they came together again at her wrists.

It hung open almost a foot down her back, exposing the corners of her shoulder blades. As he'd hoped, she'd worn her hair up off her neck. He would stand behind her as much as possible and fill his eyes with the strong line of her spine from her hairline down to the small of her back.

"Hello, Sid." The stiffness in her voice sent tingles down Quinn's spine. He wanted her to speak to him like that, as though he was dirt under her shoes.

"Larisa. You look ready to party."

She chose to sit opposite Sid on the unoccupied bench. "Are we pregaming?"

"Most definitely." Sid opened the minifridge built into the wall of the limo and pulled out two canned vodka martinis. He handed one to Larisa. They clicked the cans together in a silent toast.

"Thank you for coming," said Quinn. He made it sound like resentment instead of gratitude. She hadn't said hello, hadn't even looked at him. When they'd made this plan last night, he'd underestimated how hard it would be to not touch her.

"Well, you found me a dress, so I didn't have much choice, right?" Her voice matched his acid tone. "I mean, it's not a dress I would've chosen. Not sure how you managed to find something so old-fashioned." She laughed. "This color, or lack thereof, makes me look washed out. But hey, it's your party. I don't care one way or the other."

"If you hate it, why did you wear it?" he snapped.

"I wanted to make you happy. Aren't you happy?" She turned hard eyes on him. They looked red. For a moment, he thought she'd been crying. *Something's happened.* He wanted to ask her, to reach out and take her hand, to attach himself and not ever let go. As though she knew what he was thinking, her look darkened with warning. He struggled to pull himself back into the charade.

"You dress me, why wouldn't I dress you?"

Her laughter fell across the floor of the limo like a landslide of shattering ice. "Because you don't have a clue."

"Guys," said Sid. "I think we should take a time out and uh—"

"No one asked you," said Quinn. He'd never spoken to Sid that way. It felt too real. He saw his own horror reflected in Sid's shocked expression. The concern was almost worse than the look of betrayal.

All of this for Lucas, thought Quinn. And they'd never even know if it was worth it. The lack of some unknown terrible thing happening wouldn't be enough to justify what he was doing to Sid.

They pulled up to the staging area of the red carpet that would lead down to the El Capitan Theatre.

"I don't need you to do me favors. We're not faking it anymore. Stay here if you want. I don't care." Quinn opened the door before the driver had the chance to come around. He stumbled out, disoriented. The lighting was too bright in some places, and not bright enough in others. The noise of hundreds of people talking surrounded him, yet he saw only a handful of professional handlers in black suits wearing lanyard badges. Beyond them, a wall of billowing curtain barriers and a hedge of green plastic, slightly resembling foliage embossed with the falling comet logo of Discovery Studios.

Sid stepped up behind him, gave a low whistle. "Just like on *E!*" he said.

One of the handlers came forward wearing a winning smile. Her badge said Abby. She looked like she was fifteen. Her teeth were whiter than Quinn's. Too white. They looked fake.

"Mr. VanderVeer, so honored to meet you. I'm Abby. I'll be walking you through tonight. Have you done one of these before?"

Quinn glanced back to the limo. The door stood open, Larisa nowhere in sight. He forced himself to turn away. *You can do this.*

"I haven't."

"It's very simple. Just think of me as your tour guide. We'll make five stops for photos. We'll pose you, then I'll step back. Everyone will look at you, take their pictures, then we'll move on. Sometimes they yell questions. You can engage with them as little or as much as you want, as long as we keep moving."

Sid held out Quinn's jacket. He slid his arms in, then pulled at his shirt, which felt like it was coming untucked again. "Good?" he asked. Sid looked him up and down and nodded.

"The shirt?"

"It looks fine."

Fine wasn't what Quinn needed, but it was all he had. He cast one last look back at the limo, then followed Abby down the carpet and around the corner. *You only have to survive a few minutes alone.*

As they turned the corner, the sound of the crowd went from a din to a roar. A narrow corridor lay before him with a line of red down the middle. On one side, the walls were printed with the studio name and framed by *The Key* promotional images. On the other side, was a frighteningly flimsy barricade with a press of photographers crammed against it, their faces and bodies obscured by the strobing lights of their cameras. On risers behind them, and on more risers down at the end of the line, the fans. Maybe three hundred people. All of them seemed to be screaming like Rihanna had come to town. But it was only Dansby.

"Look at him go," said Sid with a chuckle.

"Sex sells," muttered Quinn.

"Sid," said Abby. "If you turn there, you can walk down without bothering the cameras and meet Quinn on the other side."

"Got to keep the help invisible, right?" Sid gave a salute and disappeared behind the plastic greenery. Quinn followed Abby up to the first mark.

You will survive this, he told himself. *They're just cameras. They're part of getting what you want.*

"Hands out of pockets," she said. "Would you mind putting your weight forward? Yeah, kind of like that. Hmm."

Cameras were starting to stutter with their staccato exposures. Someone yelled. Abby skidded out of the way. The flashes left colored squares fading through Quinn's vision. He did his best to keep his chin up, to look straight ahead. He knew how to take pictures. He'd just never taken them with the stakes so high. His film, his press tour, his career. People were watching now. The critics would decide if he was a worthy director, but the paparazzi would decide if he was a worthy celebrity.

The feeling of all those people staring at him, hidden behind their wall of lights, made him itch with discomfort. He shifted his weight. He put his hands in his trouser pockets even though Abby had said not to. He felt he should have unbuttoned the jacket.

"Quinn, where's your lady doctor?"

"Quinn, what's it like playing with the big boys?"

"Having some trouble at home?"

"How did you discover Dansby Vaast?"

For a moment, Quinn thought this last question had come

from Lucas. A deep-accented voice full of gravitas. But no specter wearing a long coat and top hat had materialized out of the wash of flashbulbs. He stared into the white void pockmarked with residual flares blinking across his vision.

Calm down.

Abby stepped in and waved him forward to the next mark. He'd locked his legs without realizing it and all the feeling had gone out of his feet. He tripped over the toe of his shoe and almost fell. The left side of his shirt came untucked under his jacket.

"This time could you just . . ." Abby pulled her mouth to one side as she looked at him, the problem obvious but the solution eluding her.

Quinn shifted his weight. He turned sideways, doing everything he could to look like he belonged. Then he felt a disturbance of the air at his back and saw Abby break into a relieved smile. He caught the whiff of perfume that was both familiar and unnamable, then Larisa was pulling his hand from his pocket, lacing her fingers through his, leaning into him, and resting her chin on the edge of his shoulder. He turned to look at her.

"Hold that," she whispered.

He saw what he hadn't been able to see in the limo. She'd done something to her lips. They looked bigger than normal, a lush frame for the thin, dark slit of her mouth. He stared at it, his mind full of all the things he wanted to slip through it. His groin began to tighten. Amazing that he still had the energy to get it up after being with her so much. Twice that morning, the night before, Tuesday morning, and everything before Thanksgiving. *I'm addicted,* he wanted to say. *I can't get enough of you.*

When she straightened, he turned his shoulders so he faced her properly, their sides to the cameras. She swung his hand in the air between them, no smile, and an almost aggressive look that said, *Play this game with me or else.*

He glared back at her. *Do you have any idea what you've done to me?*

At the third mark, people called out for Larisa to solo. Quinn stood back and got that view of her back he'd wanted. *Perfect dress. Perfect woman.*

She motioned him back to her, pulled his arm around the back of her waist, and set his hand to rest on the curve of her hip. "And hold," she whispered.

Someone shouted, "Kiss her!"

Quinn froze. That deep voice with the accent had followed him from the top of the carpet. If Larisa recognized the voice, she didn't show it.

A second shout, "Show us the real thing, Larisa!"

Others took up the call.

She turned and looked at him, that smile still dazzling but unreadable as he searched for direction. He pecked her cheek on the non-camera side, hiding himself as he whispered, "I need more."

"You're doing fine."

Mark four was easier. There was a commotion at the top of the carpet. Steve Helston and his wife Riley had arrived and were putting on a show for the cameras. They moved down the line much faster than Quinn had. By the time he and Larisa were at mark five, Steve and Riley had already made it to mark four. Steve broke away to rush toward Larisa. He fell down on one knee and opened his arms toward her.

"Larisa. Larisa. Grant your grace to this mortal."

Quinn watched, his mouth dropping open as Larisa fluttered her arms in the air as though flying, leaned down, and kissed Steve's hairline. "You are blessed, but you are mortal only until you reveal yourself."

"I'm excellent at revealing myself." Steve jumped to his feet and winked at the delighted reporters. "Let's give a round of applause for Larisa de France-Kahn to show how much we've missed her."

Quinn laughed. He'd known Steve was a clown, but seriously, did he really expect the faceless horde of paparazzi to—

But they were. The applause and cheers were almost as loud as the screaming for Dansby.

Larisa gave a bow then sidled up to Quinn, using her forefinger to press his chin up to close his mouth. "Jealousy looks good on you."

"I'm not jealous." His face burned.

"Will you punish me for jealousy?"

She arched a coy eyebrow, her eyes smoldering with something much deeper than her put-on rage. "We shall see."

They reached the end of the red carpet and arrived at an open area with bleachers for fans on one end. Dansby and the rest of the cast were signing autographs and taking pictures. The crew mingled, taking pictures together unbothered by fans. Sid was there playing the role of photographer. Quinn saw the gaffer he'd almost fired for being careless, the set decorator who Quinn thought was color-blind, Lane the DP who hated him, and Tish who would've taken over his movie if Eddie had asked her.

And there, grinning with self-satisfaction, was Eddie himself. They'd seen each other just the day before in a series of last-minute, wholly unnecessary meetings, but this felt different. They had no purpose to speak to each other, no business to settle. Quinn didn't know what to say. But that's why he had Larisa. She glided up to Eddie and gave him the Hollywood shoulder hug and air kisses.

"Eddie."

"Larisa, good to see you out of the house and as beautiful as ever."

"You say that like you expected me to wither away."

He shrugged. "It happens."

"How's Parish?"

Eddie glanced at Quinn. Months of working together almost every day and they hadn't spoken of Parish or the events she'd orchestrated that spring.

"She's doing better. I don't hear much."

"A good sign probably."

Larisa fell strangely silent. Eddie glanced around as though trapped.

Say something before people notice and take a picture of this, thought Quinn. *Or is she doing this so someone will take a picture?* His mind was cluttered with hyperawareness of those other people who were surely watching out of the corners of their eyes, waiting for him to slip up just as they'd watched him on set. And now, someone else was wondering. Lucas.

They were performing for him as though their lives were truly a stage play for an audience's entertainment.

Don't think about him.

The silence lasted an eternity of less than a minute. Steve finished with the cameras and came bounding into the open area. "So, Quinn—wow that's such a formal name." He rolled his eyes at Riley, who shrugged him off like he was ridiculous. "Do you ever go by Quinnie? Or Vandy? That sounds cool, right? Vandy. I heard you're being difficult with Kyle. Obviously, I agree location shooting is the best. But it's just not practical. Eddie will tell you the executives don't like the risk. They don't like shipping an entire operation overseas."

"Very true," said Eddie. "Is this *Poseidon* you're talking about?"

"Vandy has great ideas," said Steve. "But now there's this new budget being considered. Production might be delayed." Steve drew his lips into a pout. "Maybe this isn't a good project for you."

Quinn felt blood rushing from his swollen groin to fill his limbs as he prepared for a fight. In his peripheral vision, Larisa was giving him a warning look, but it was unnecessary. He knew how to handle someone like Steve.

"It might not be," said Quinn. "If I did sign on, I'd want more from you than what you've given to the role in the past. A character like Poseidon can only hold attention if he's more than an all-powerful god."

"The movies sell," said Steve with a flush on his cheeks like he was also working up to a fight.

"To kids, sure. But he could be so much more." Quinn shrugged. "And a realistic environment really helps with that. The god of the sea should be in the sea. Something to think about." Quinn took Larisa's hand and walked toward the theater entrance. When they were far enough away, she squeezed his hand with approval.

But Quinn's anger didn't diminish. There was so much more he wanted to say to Steve, to Eddie, to the reporters who'd been asking him waste-of-time questions for the past month. He stewed as they met the sound technician who gave Quinn a hand-held mic. He stewed as he watched Larisa thread her way through the seats to say hello to Tish and her wife. He stewed as Sid jogged down the aisle and paused to snap a picture of Quinn standing to the side of the screen.

By the time everyone had come in and taken their seats, he knew what he wanted to say.

"Thank you for coming tonight. All of you should know that without your dedication to your work, this film wouldn't be what it is." He paused. "A work of art. That's what we're about here. We're artists. It's a privilege to be part of this kind of production, where money flows in the streets and, if we're clever with the accounting, we can bring our imaginations to life. I will say that I'm not especially satisfied with my part of it. If I'd been braver, wiser, more confident, *The Key* would be a better film. You were my unwilling test subjects in this experiment of 'can VanderVeer make it in the big leagues.' It's possible the answer is no. But I just want you to hear from me, I've learned from you, and I appreciate you. And if I ever get another job, I'm going to do better." Another pause. "I think I'm supposed to remind everyone that the after-party is at Marquee on Fifth, which will be just through the doors at the far side of the lobby. Thank you."

He surrendered the mic to the technician as people clapped, not loudly, or with any certainty, but it was better than the silence he felt he deserved. Quinn slid into his seat beside Larisa who shook her head at him with a knowing smile.

"Feel better?" she asked.

"A little."

"He's watching."

For a moment Quinn tensed, certain she meant Lucas and that he'd somehow snuck into the theater. But then he followed her gaze to Steve sitting at the end of the row.

"Good," said Quinn. "He can go back and tell Kyle that I'm only doing work I believe in from now on." He noticed the satisfied look on Larisa's face. "Did you invite him?"

"I mentioned him to Sid, he put him on the list. And maybe I gave him a bit of encouragement."

"I don't know how you do it, everything in that head, always so busy, but so organized."

She laughed.

The lights were dimming. Quinn realized Larisa was about to watch his film. A moment he'd been anticipating for months, but it had arrived almost without notice. "It's alright if you hate this tonight."

"I'm not going to hate it," she said.

"But if you do, it's okay. Lots of people hate my other movies. The music isn't going to be what you want."

She laid her hand on his arm to silence him.

All through *The Key*, Larisa's hand remained on his, a warm, dead weight. Her expression did reflect reactions during the film, Quinn just wasn't sure what they meant. At times she seemed interested, surprised, even pleased. But what did he know about her actual thoughts? She certainly noticed the failure of lighting in the first prison scene, the sloppy transition at the grocery store. Dansby, and his stilted delivery. This was Quinn's umpteenth time seeing the film in a theater. He knew every beat, every false note, every moment he should've done differently. Even more maddening, he remembered when he'd been storyboarding, putting some of those things into his plans, but when the time came, they hadn't happened. Either he'd felt they were too risky, too costly, or he hadn't wanted to fight with whatever members of his crew were going to make it happen.

As Larisa had predicted, everyone in the theater stood and cheered at the credits. He took a bow that felt unearned, then sat back down. Sweat had his shirt sticking to his back. His face felt too hot. People began to file out. Larisa still hadn't said anything.

"Well?"

"I liked it."

"That's it?"

"The music was a surprise."

He relaxed with relief. Quinn had worked so hard on that music. The composer had threatened to quit. Tish had gotten involved. Quinn still thought it was too much, but he could let it go if Larisa approved. "Someone I trust told me that music's the most important thing."

"The music works." She stood and pulled him to his feet. "I think the more important question is why don't you like it?"

"It's imperfect."

"Did you feel that about your last film?"

"No."

She gave him a look like she didn't believe him.

"I mean, yes. But it didn't feel as obviously flawed as this. I used everything I had, as well as it could be used. This just feels amateur." He glanced around. The theater was nearly empty. The only stragglers stood in the opposite aisle, absorbed in their own conversation. "I watch it, and all I can think about is principal photography. I was a wreck the whole time. I hated almost every day."

Larisa linked her arm through his and pulled him close as they walked up the aisle to the lobby. "That's a reasonable thing to feel. But it doesn't have to be the only thing. What do you like the best?"

They crossed the lobby, moving toward the wall of doors that opened into the Marquee nightclub.

"I liked the lighting at the end of the prison sequence, when Dansby's rescued."

"He was the most beautiful, captured spy there's ever been."

"You're mocking me."

"I promise I'm not."

They stopped at the door to take in the room. Dansby stood at the bar surrounded by a small crowd of mostly women. Steve was making his way toward the bar, drawing attention to himself. The established star and the debutant, waging an impromptu competition for public adoration.

"He's signed on to three productions this year," said Quinn with a shake of his head. "How long do you think it'll take before they realize he can't act?"

"I think there are plenty of beautiful people in this town who can't act. Dansby is the nicest one I've ever met."

"He's having trouble with all of it. Did you see him on *Letterman*? Sounded like he was drunk."

"Maybe I'll go talk to him." Larisa briefly leaned into him, a soft reassuring pressure of her shoulder into his. "We should separate now. If anyone asks you about me, make it seem bad, okay?"

"I hate fighting with you, even when its fake."

"It'll be over in forty minutes."

"Thirty minutes," he said.

"Thirty-five, or else."

"Or else what?"

"I love you," she whispered. She gave him the saddest smile as she backed out of his reach, then turned to leave him.

He admired the long line of her back until the crowd swallowed her. Perhaps it was truer to say the crowd drew in around Quinn. Tish came up to ask how Sabrina was doing. Quinn made a joke about how she could always be his AD if she wanted. Only after she walked away laughing, did he realize he meant it.

Other people came and went. Some names he remembered, others not. A cloud of Discovery Studios executives closed in and gave him their hollow-eyed congratulations. One of them complained that his date had gone off to flirt with the talent. Quinn learned that the high number of young women drifting around the room, who he didn't recognize, had been invited by the studio to make the party more 'fun.'

Another executive made noise about Quinn's contract, and what his next project for the studio would be. He listened with half an ear as they discussed properties with titles they barely remembered, all of them tagged with significance by what stars had signed on to them, or how much they were like other successful films. Quinn had already seen the studio's slate for the next five years. He'd read a few scripts and found nothing of interest.

Across the room, Larisa had reached Dansby. Even from a distance they stood out as people of significance. Both of them in possession of not just natural beauty, but an effortless ease with the world. They were the gilded fronds of a lily, swaying with the wind. Quinn was a rock forcing everything to go around him.

"She's beautiful," said a voice to his right. Quinn turned to meet the petite blonde who'd come up to his side. The woman wrapped her fingers around Quinn's arm and drew him away from the executives. "Aren't you upset she's over there talking to another man?"

The woman spoke with an accent that he thought was continental European, German maybe. It might even have been Slavic, but she was trying to disguise it so he couldn't tell for certain.

"I'm not looking for company," said Quinn.

"That's only because you don't know what kind of company I provide."

She moved in front of him and put her arms around his neck, drawing his gaze down to the perfect orbs of her breasts pushing up past the top of her shrink-wrap dress. A dress that had been in style in movies when he'd been younger. A dress that looked more like what he'd had Parish wear for her role as a Russian hooker in *The Key* than what anyone else in the room was wearing, including the women brought in by the executives.

This woman didn't fit the scene.

Quinn turned his head and set his nose against her forearm, inhaled. No perfume, just soap, but not a familiar soap smell.

Across the room, Larisa had noticed them. In a moment, she would come save him. They would leave. In the limo they would laugh about this. But then he imagined what he would say, *this woman was coming onto me like I was Dansby.*

And it wouldn't be something to laugh about. Because he wasn't Dansby. And when Quinn described what he'd noticed about this woman to Larisa he knew what she'd think.

The woman pressed him up against the wall and began to grind her hips against his crotch. He'd spent most of the night halfway aroused, halfway dreaming of Larisa and her bed, Larisa and her voice, and what she might do to him if he managed to disappoint her. He knew he needed to get away from this woman, but his body had locked on to hers and was dangerously ready for whatever she wanted to do to him.

Over the woman's head, he watched Larisa. She seemed as frozen as he was, though obviously for a different reason. Now Dansby had noticed and was talking to her, had his hand on her arm like he was worried.

"I have a room across the street," said the woman.

"That would be nice sometime," said Quinn. "But I've had a long day."

"Had some sad news that wore you down?"

Quinn managed to reach up and pull the woman's arms off his neck. "Why would you ask that?"

She looked up at him with heavy-lidded, knowing eyes. "You've had a fight with your lover. She's been keeping secrets from you."

The sweat rolling down Quinn's back turned cold. His erection stalled, but did not wither, as though he was as needy as a fourteen-year-old boy.

Across the room, Larisa raised her hand above her head and pointed toward the theater-side exit.

"A waste for you to sleep alone," she said. "I can tell you're lonely." Her hand moved toward his waistband.

With a jerk and a shove off the wall, Quinn pushed past her. Walking was painful, the bulge in his pants embarrassingly obvious even with his jacket to help conceal it. No one stopped him. In this at least, the natural meanness in his face gave him an advantage. At the doors into the theater, he looked back. The woman was gone.

"Tell me," said Larisa. Heat radiated off her skin, her entire body fairly vibrated with energy. She was furious, but not at him.

When Quinn didn't answer right away, she grabbed him by the shoulders and turned him to face her. "What did she say?"

Quinn blinked. He couldn't think. *Did that really just— And I let her?* He was so cold.

"Quinn."

"She thought we were fighting. That you're keeping secrets from me."

"That's all?"

"Should there be more?" He stared at her. "What the fuck, Larisa?"

"She was just an observer. Harmless." The corners of her mouth turned up. "You're hard."

Was she changing the subject? He opened his mouth to speak and realized he was breathless, close to hyperventilating.

"Let's go," said Larisa.

She should have walked beside him, held his hand, or at least his arm. But they were apparently still having their fake fight. They walked back down the red carpet to the waiting line of limos, Larisa ahead, Quinn lagging alone. Half of him felt numb, the other half tingled with a rage of adrenaline that buzzed through his blood. Some too-large fraction of that buzzed part of him remained horny and was mortified by it. The entire night had become a conspiracy against him, and all the good he'd managed to claim for himself.

"Are we going to talk about this?" he asked loudly enough

that the security guard glanced his way.

"I expected it."

Quinn fell onto the limo bench, breathless. "You expected he'd have a spy at my movie?"

Larisa took a breath. "Are you alright?"

"What? No." He pulled at the front of his pants. "I'm not in any way alright." The limo door closed them in a cave of almost privacy. He realized he didn't want to talk about it. He just wanted her to look at him, take him in her arms and ruin him until the only thing in his mind was her.

But Larisa was digging in her purse. "I'll fix it. Hang on."

Fix how?

Larisa stopped with her purse, rolled down the window to the driver. She asked if he'd be okay driving around the city for the next few hours, and did he have a transmitter so her iPod would play through the speakers?

It was impossible not to stare at her. Their escape from the theater had left her with a fine blush of blood in her cheeks and a sheen of sweat sticking the frills of hair around her hairline to her forehead. The low light of the limo cabin drew shadows across her face, accentuating her bone structure.

Low jazz began to wind softly from the limo speakers. Larisa closed the partition window, a sly smile toying across her lips.

"You planned this?" he asked.

"I thought that after a night of hearing how amazing you are, you might need a little course correction." Larisa pulled a pair of leather handcuffs from her bag. "I didn't plan on you letting some blonde slut feel you up."

"She wasn't—"

Larisa pressed a finger against his lips as she shook her head. "You don't get to talk until you've earned it. I'm making the rules, and I say you have some work to do. If you come before I say, you'll be punished." She slid his suit coat off his arms and pushed it aside. Next came the shirt and the undershirt. She moved quickly but without rushing. Each movement confident with purpose. Each layer of discarded clothing bringing them closer together.

With Quinn's trousers and briefs pooled around his ankles, she cuffed his wrists behind his back, then withdrew to the far bench. "Present yourself."

Her purse was too small for a flogger, and even if Larisa had one hidden somewhere, the limo didn't give her enough space to use it. Unsure what was coming, but desperate to find out, Quinn slid off the bench onto the floor. He turned and knelt, lowered his chest down so his ass was in the air facing her. Any other place, with any other person, he would've been mortified, but this felt like an offering. It felt like the most delicious promise. The air around him stilled. The limo tires rolled over seams in the asphalt almost in time with the music as he waited for her to touch him, waited for the pain to come.

Still, when it came, he jumped with surprise. She'd struck the side of his ass with the flat of her hand as hard as she could. He heard the soft hiss of Larisa swearing under her breath, herself surprised by the pain. She struck him on the other side. His breath caught, a hot, tight feeling in his chest mirrored the heat in his groin. He wouldn't last long.

As though sensing this, Larisa reached between his legs and traced the line of his shaft with her nail.

"Oh God." He couldn't help but say it, even though she hadn't given him permission. He braced himself for even stronger blows to avenge his failure to keep silent. Instead, she said, "Get me ready."

Quinn turned and found she'd pulled the skirt of her dress up to her waist and slouched forward so her ass rested on the edge of the bench, knees open wide, her entrance a dark slit before him.

"What are you waiting for?" Her voice rang out, imperious and beautiful. He wanted to say how much he loved her. How he loved that she had planned this, knowing he'd need some recovery after a night of meditating on his failures. How perfect it was that she'd given him this, a chance to make himself feel worthy.

He lowered his mouth to her slit and thrust his tongue inside. She arched against him, much more ready than she'd seemed. He'd barely set to his work when she began to breathe heavily. Her hands clawed the air to find his shoulders, to pull his head up so that they could come together. She bit down on his shoulder as his swollen tip probed her entrance. A moan escaped that the driver certainly heard. Later, Quinn would care. But in that moment, it felt as though they were the only two people in the city. It felt like an eternity since he'd been inside her. It felt like the first time.

The second time, she'd laid down and he'd straddled her while she squeezed his ass, moving him exactly how she wanted until she came, one orgasm on top of another. He'd already felt empty by then, but when she'd told him to come, he had. After that, she'd released the handcuffs and allowed him to touch her, move her, sample her as he wanted.

They stopped to watch the sunrise on a bench at the Mulholland Scenic Overlook. Here, he couldn't resist composing the scene. Him, sitting in his disheveled trousers, no belt, half-buttoned shirt. Larisa, laying with her head in his lap, his suit coat draped over her waist, ineffectual for true warmth, but just the right look. He wasn't about to hide her beautiful arms. The only thing missing was a DP to capture the shot from just the right angle. *Slightly to the left*, thought Quinn. *And then a closeup of her looking up at me. And then from behind as we look out on the city.*

"It's tomorrow," said Larisa. She yawned like a contented cat. "Ten days until Christmas."

"Are we doing our own celebration before or after Minnesota?"

"After, I think."

"Agreed." He reached down and trailed his thumb along her

arm, enjoyed watching the rise of goosebumps as her nerves came to attention. "Can I say something without ruining this?"

She nodded.

"Did that woman at the club know something about you that I don't? Not the old you from when you were with him. The you now."

He felt her mouth moving against his leg, maybe chewing on the side of her cheek or griding her teeth. He tried not to be afraid of what she was going to say. He resolved not to be angry if she chose to lie to him. They were both too complicated to always be honest with each other.

"I've been going to see Parish at the in-patient clinic where she's serving her sentence."

Of all the things he'd imagined, Quinn hadn't expected that. It surprised him, but it was a surprise without thorns.

"Why?"

"I didn't want to hate her," said Larisa. "I thought it would help me process what she did if I reminded myself she was human."

"Has it?"

"Sometimes. Is that okay?"

"Yeah. I mean, it's an interesting idea. I don't think I could do it."

She reached up and locked her fingers between his. "Do you know this will be my first Minnesota Christmas in four years? Working over the holiday felt it was a penance I had to pay for having so much privilege. If not for Parish, I'd be working again this year. And I'd be filling every hour I didn't work studying for my licensure exam. You'd never have seen me."

"Are you saying I should thank her?"

"I guess I'm saying a year ago my life was clearly one thing. And now it's clearly something else."

"This isn't what you wanted."

"Maybe I wasn't ever going to feel like I fit in in medicine. I'd have had an entire career looking over my shoulder, afraid someone was laughing at my manicure, or not being taken seriously because of my name."

"And you'd have been fighting with your mother."

"Well, that hasn't changed. Now we just fight about things that are easier for me to deal with. And it's not all lost. Once I get enough clients to build a practice, I can do some volunteering at the community clinics. I might set up my own office and take on fee-free clients. Most of what I wanted to do with emergency medicine, I can still do if I get my counseling license. I have all this knowledge. I know how the system works. I can give that to people. The main difference is I'll have to go out and find them."

"What did Dansby say about working with you?"

"He asked if we could meet like we did during *The Key*. We'll start after New Year's. Apparently, he's going to seven holiday parties. But I think you're right, he's struggling."

"Make sure you charge him. He's going to blow past six figures this year. He'll get his SAG card. He can afford you."

"You're ruthless."

"But you love me."

"Hmm." She smiled a sun-painted smile. "I do. Remind me that you need a winter coat tomorrow."

"You think I'm going to remember that?"

Larisa felt around for her phone, found it on the ground beside Quinn's feet. He watched her face light up with the glow as she unlocked the screen, then draw together with worry at whatever she found there.

"Something wrong?"

"Kahleah is, uh . . . it looks like she's drunk."

"She realized Cade's sleeping with his assistant?"

"Looks like it."

Quinn clicked his tongue. "Small people."

"Why do you say it like that? It's perfectly reasonable to be devastated when you realize your husband prefers another woman."

"If they'd really set up a good marriage, as soon as the affair had started, she should've brought herself into it. Because if that's what he needs right now, then she should find a way to be a part of it. They're small people because they think love's about claiming someone as a possession."

"If that's what he needs, he could have asked her. It's not her responsibility to conform to what he wants."

"Ideally, sure, but sometimes people just get distracted. They chase an idea or a feeling. It doesn't have anything to do with their spouse."

"You'd share me with someone else?"

"If that was something you wanted." He smiled down at her. "I thought we already talked about this."

"And you expect me to share you?"

"You wouldn't?"

"I feel like the two of us is already kind of a lot."

"Tonight, when you saw me with that woman, what did you think?"

"I thought, she's one of Lucas's spies, and you better say the right thing."

"And what else did you think?"

Larisa opened her mouth and closed it. Color rose on her cheeks. He freed his hand from her hand and reached down to stroke his fingers across her lips.

"You didn't come rescue me," he said.

"That would've been obvious."

"And?"

The color deepened. "I would have watched to the end. But that's not the same situation. Cade could fall in love with the assistant. It could leak. He could ruin his life, and Kahleah's."

"Do you need to call her?"

"No."

"Then can we go home? I'm dead on my feet, and I want to fall asleep staring at you in bed while our cat watches."

Chapter 18

Well-Dressed Fish Out of Water

> Kahleah: I sent Parish flowers. The baby died.
>
> Kahleah: It's terrible to lose a baby.
>
> Kahleah: I saw Rosa yesterday and she said she was having this pain and I just thought, what if? You should see Tate. He's so sweet with her even though this is their fourth.
>
> Kahleah: It means more than we think for the men. You don't have kids, you don't understand. Quinn deserves to know. If you don't tell him, you'll regret it.

No messages from Lucas. But maybe that didn't matter. He'd sent two messages that spoke louder than any text message. He had spies in LA. They were close enough they'd known about Parish's stillbirth in real time. And they'd gotten to Quinn. There wasn't any reason to pretend. Lucas had made up his mind. He wanted Larisa to know he could step in and make her life with Quinn complicated whenever he felt like it.

Which meant he would—it was only a question of when.

Larisa and Quinn ensconced themselves in her apartment like newlyweds. It should've been her best life, but all three mornings after the premiere, Larisa woke from forgotten nightmares. Restless and too wakeful, she held a pillow against her chest and watched Quinn sleeping and thought, *I have to tell him about the baby.*

Always followed by her second thought, *I can't tell him.*

She would stare at him sleeping until she felt able to breathe again and then she marveled at the miracle of him in her bed. And when she couldn't keep to herself any longer, she moved herself into him, matching legs with legs, waists to waists, winding herself around him, waking him with her touch. Morning sex was soft and quiet and led to falling back asleep.

Over breakfast, she tortured him by reading reviews of *The Key* out loud, embellishing them with her own commentary. They went for long afternoon walks. At night they drove around the surrounding neighborhoods and looked at Christmas lights. They spoke of nothing important. Their minds remained independent domains cut through with the ravines of old habit.

On Monday, Suzette's assistant brought the family gift box to the apartment and Larisa set about the project of wrapping the gifts that would travel to Minnesota for her father's family: fifty-seven gift cards. Quinn said he didn't have an opinion about Christmas music—of course, he didn't—so Larisa started her iPod with Bing Crosby and tested out Quinn's knowledge of the classics as she worked.

Quinn's knowledge of the classics was worse than she expected. He'd never seen *White Christmas* or *Holiday Inn* and was surprised to learn the top-hits radio that had played at his old warehouse had included songs recorded in the 1950s. When he called her a liar after she explained that Judy Garland originally sang "Have Yourself a Merry Little Christmas," Larisa gave up.

"Have you always cared so much about where things come from?" Quinn was buried in her papasan with Sabrina in his lap and a worn, three-subject spiral notebook resting open on her back.

Larisa sat on the floor surrounded by dozens of small boxes, four types of wrapping paper, and ribbons. Sabrina had already been banished from the floor twice for getting in the way. Now her small face peered out with watchful interest from the fluff of Larisa's Santa blanket and the roof made over her head by the spiral notebook.

"Why is it so weird to want to know where things come from?" she asked. "It's history."

"Knowing where a song started isn't going to change my life."

"But it could enrich it. I watch *Meet Me in St. Louis* every year. And I always think, before this movie the world existed without this song. There was a before and after, and it's this moment."

"But you don't care about film like that." Quinn was getting adorably exasperated. "Or food, or when nail salons first became a thing."

Larisa zipped the blunt side of her scissors along a strand of ribbon to curl it. *He's thinking about Lucas.* "What are you saying, Quinn?"

"I just think it's interesting."

"You'd rather be ignorant?"

Quinn turned the page of his notebook. Larisa realized she didn't know what he was reading. A whole stack of old notebooks had arrived with Sid the night before, no explanation attached. She zipped another ribbon, but her angle was off, and it snapped under the pressure.

"Why don't you just say what you're thinking?"

He looked at her from beneath his eyebrows, a long look, intensely focused as though he was searching her face for something he couldn't find. Those eyes made her want to abandon gift wrapping and snuggle into the chair beside him.

"I guess I'm trying to figure out what's you and what's him."

She flushed red with a sudden heat. "This is all me. What?

You think I'm pretending to be a person who cares about history?"

"Forget it."

"No, I want to know."

"Relationships leave a residue. There's nothing wrong with it."

"But you're saying I'm not really me."

"I'm saying it's interesting you care about the history of some things and not others."

"I've always liked history. I wrote a history of the miniskirt for a research paper my freshman year of high school."

"Why are we arguing about this?"

"We're arguing because I feel judged." She picked up a bow and threw it at him. Sabrina lifted her head with a new level of interest.

"You're not judged. I just thought you were like me, adaptable. The things we know are from times when we've needed to know them, in order to fit in. We aren't the kind of curious people who ask big questions, or hang out at libraries, or are driven to find answers."

"I feel like I should be offended by that."

"It's a compliment."

Larisa reached for her mother's list of which gift card was going to which person. Using it as a guide, she lined up a set of boxes and began to set the cards inside.

"I don't understand why you're wrapping them," said Quinn.

"It's boring to hand out envelopes."

"But everyone knows they're getting a gift card, right?"

"Right."

"Does everyone else wrap them like this?"

"Not everyone. But my aunt likes to have gifts under the tree. Dad's family has been decorating the tree at the farm the same way since 1892."

"Like with candles and popcorn?"

"Obviously not candles anymore."

Quinn frowned, which made her laugh.

"You'll see when we get there," she said.

"You could take them to a mall and have a professional wrap them."

"That's what Mom did last year—not the mall, her interior designer has a gift wrapping and sundries business on the side—but I guess people complained that the gifts were too extravagant. So, even though I'm not good at crafts, I'm going to do them. And maybe my mother will finally forgive me about fashion week."

There they were again, back to Lucas. *Maybe Quinn's right to assume he's everywhere,* thought Larisa.

"If you have paper leftover, can I use it to wrap a gift?"

"You have a gift?"

Quinn was looking down at his notebook, not reading, but hiding from her as a secretive smile toyed with his mouth.

"You bought me a gift!"

"Nothing special."

"What did you get me?"

"Would you calm down?"

"This is a big deal. I didn't expect a gift." She crawled over to the papasan and peered up at him with big eyes. "Give me a hint."

"You're obnoxious when you're happy."

She laughed, ready to wave him off. But then she thought maybe it was true. She was happy. She was happy because, for the first time, it felt like they were walking down the same path in the same direction and there was nothing standing in their way. Somehow, she'd tricked herself into forgetting. It was an *Abbey Road* day.

"I'd given up thinking someone like you existed for me. Now I've found you, I'm going to keep you forever."

He looked down at her, his gaze soft as though seeing her was as much of a marvel as when she looked at him. Then he shook his head and nudged her away. "Go wrap your gifts. I'm reading."

Larisa had promised that her Minnesota family were 'normal' people, so Quinn packed his regular clothes and decided not to worry that Larisa perhaps didn't operate from the same definition of 'normal' he did. Five minutes in, Quinn realized he should have listened to his gut.

Flying to a Christmas celebration on a private jet as the special guest of Gunter Kahn was not normal. As soon as Quinn boarded the plane, he wished he'd dressed better. Yes, Gunter was wearing a hooded sweatshirt, the same as Quinn, but his sweatshirt looked like it'd been handmade with fabric so soft it could've been pajamas. It had a sense of its own style. Quinn's hoodie was from Walmart and was so old the cuffs were beginning to sprout tiny holes. This was to say nothing of Suzette, who was wearing Chanel slipper socks and a sleek mauve bodysuit under an oversized fur coat as she called loudly to the staff at the other end of the plane, explaining she wanted her champagne to be served at altitude, not at takeoff.

Quinn said the requisite hellos, then hid himself in the back of the jet with his notebooks. He'd brought three of what he thought were the most interesting. Maybe, if a moment presented itself, he'd share them with Larisa. Or perhaps he'd wait until he'd decided what to do with them. She hadn't asked about them yet, although he'd felt her curiosity. She sat across from him with a legal pad and a handful of colorful markers, which she used to make notes for the column she was going to write about the bondage romance novel Teale thought would solve Larisa's PR problems.

The possibility of doing any serious reading diminished by decibels as Larisa's feet reached out and played with his. She wore knee-high boots with leggings, a downy-looking shirt, and a quilted bohemian coat over it. It was strange to see her wearing so much clothing, almost as much as was standard for him, all skin covered, tucked into layers. *It's a good look,* he thought. *Extremely petable.* He leaned over and stole one of her pens to make a note in a margin. *Woman in extremely petable coat.*

"You're distracting me."

"Says the woman playing footsies."

She smiled at him. Quinn shook his head. "All I'm thinking about is petting you." It came out without thought, much too loud, and too obviously besotted, just as Suzette paced toward them. *Oh God,* thought Quinn. But she was on her phone, so maybe she hadn't heard. The phone call was an intense debate, something to do with Suzette's New Year's gala. Most likely she hadn't heard.

Across from him, Larisa watched his discomfort with a smug smile, as though seeing him embarrassed brought her joy. "You have no idea what it's like," he said.

"You're right. Can't think of the last time I've blushed. But it looks very cute on you."

"Thanks a lot."

Suzette placed one foot in front of the other in a distracted balance challenge as she listened, then told whoever was on the other line that everything they'd said was wrong. One side of her coat slipped off her shoulder as she turned to walk back down the way she'd come. Quinn leaned his head into the aisle and played the role of voyeuristic interloper as Suzette rested her hand on the back of Gunter's chair, then continued walking all the way to the cockpit door.

Gunter had his lounge chair rotated into the aisle to stretch out his legs. He turned to the side to let Suzette pass, then turned back. He was also on the phone. No sooner had he resettled himself than he waved his hand through the air as though to illustrate his exasperation.

"You gave him two million to make a picture about a baroque garden," he said. "What did you think would happen?"

Before he knew what he was doing, Quinn's mind drifted from his reading, from Larisa. He imagined how he would film this scene to imply Suzette was pacing to draw Quinn's attention. The camera would start at her feet and travel up from behind, its gaze caressing her body until it turned in one smooth motion, capturing the falling coat sleeve as it moved in front of her, then went ahead of her back down the aisle. The shot would expand to follow her hand as it rested on Gunter's seat while also keeping her face in frame. It would widen further to include Gunter's face, their silent exchange, their intimacy. In the context of the frame, it would signal some conspiracy. Quinn was their mark. She was telling Gunter everything was going according to plan.

Larisa's foot play became more insistent. "What are you smiling at?"

"Your parents. They're perfect."

"That's not remotely true."

"They just seem so well-worn in. Symbiotic."

"We've been over this. They haven't had sex since Reagan was in office."

"There are other things to love than sex. Just now, she checked in with him. They told each other how their calls were going with their eyes."

"I'm going to remind you about this when we're flying home. I bet you'll have changed your answer."

"Deal."

"How's your reading?"

"Weird. A little nostalgic. Often embarrassing."

Larisa folded her hands over her legal pad and sat straighter in her chair, a posture Quinn felt certain she used when she was working with clients.

"When you're done with whatever that is, can we go over Kahn-family logistics?"

Gunter's older brother Hans and his wife Alison had three children. One was married with two children of his own. One was a lesbian, though not out yet, so Quinn wasn't supposed to draw attention even if she brought a woman as her date. And one was Hannah, the cousin Larisa had lived with during medical school.

Yes, it was a real farm.

Yes, there would be a smell.

Gunter was the second child. After him, there were three sisters all married with children of their own. Larisa didn't expect Quinn to remember the names of all the cousins. What he needed to know was the oldest sister Bet didn't speak to Hans, and thus wasn't coming to the 'Big Christmas Day Event at the Farm.' So, as soon as the jet landed, the four of them would be headed to a Christmas Eve cocktail party Bet was hosting for her husband's family and friends. Many of them were middle management at 3M. It was important that Quinn not admit he'd never heard of it. People would think he didn't get out much. Yes, the whole thing would probably be a little weird. No, it wasn't a formal event. They weren't going to change clothes beforehand. Yes, he could go hide in an upstairs bedroom if he started to feel anxious.

Bet and her husband Greg lived in Mapleton in a Prairie School mansion with warm wood accents and stained glass. Quinn had never seen stained glass outside of a religious setting. The sight of the house all lit up with warm-colored light pouring through the windows out into the frosty night stopped him short, making Larisa bump into him when she got out of the car.

"Beautiful," he said.

"What?"

"The scene." He waved his arm at the bare trees with globs of snow trapped in the elbows of their branches, at the cloudy moonlight, at the house, which was the softest, most inviting composition of hard lines and right angles he'd ever seen.

Larisa's parents had already climbed the front walk and were walking in the door without knocking.

"You okay?" asked Larisa.

"Very okay." Quinn laughed. Not that he was super excited to spend the evening in a house full of strangers, but his usual social anxiety felt almost irrelevant. He was in Minnesota, in the winter, with Larisa. "I love it here."

"We landed an hour ago. All you've seen is interstate."

He reached for her hand and began to pull her up the stairs. "But look at this house."

Bet greeted them at the door with hugs. She was a short, midsized person with thick hair streaked with natural gray, a species of woman almost entirely unknown in LA.

"You have a beautiful house," said Quinn before Gunter had a chance to do introductions.

"Thank you, we really love it." Bet gave him a studied look, then focused on her brother. "How was the flight? Isn't it terrible flying this time of year? Everyone's coughing. You're certain to catch a plague."

Gunter opened his mouth but Bet saw her error and corrected before he could speak. "Oh, I suppose you came in the jet. We chartered a jet down to Cancun this year. Expensive, aren't they?"

"Very," said Gunter. "But convenient."

"Well, I'm glad you're here giving some dignity to my exile. Even if you have a terrible time, you'll make sure and talk it up tomorrow?"

Suzette's smile turned slightly plastic.

"You could come with us," said Gunter.

"I appreciate the offer. But I don't really want to. And you're bringing enough chaos with you." Bet's eyes flicked over to Quinn who'd been half-listening, half-eyeing the decorative glass set into the wall above the archway into the living room. Stained glass tulips in a black-lined grid of pink and orange geometric squares. He wondered what it would look like on camera.

"Chaos?" asked Larisa.

"Hannah said . . . well, I'm sure she was wrong. You know how she likes to follow Hollywood gossip. Very nice to meet you, Quinn. Is this your first time in Minneapolis?"

"First time in the Midwest."

"One of those true coasters, eh? Well, we're very friendly here. Let me know whatever you need."

It was a strange offer. As they moved into the house, through not one, but two rooms with TVs and purple-and-yellow clad people cheering at a football game, and a dining room with a table almost buckling under the weight of the buffet, he couldn't imagine what was missing that he might need.

"Does she think I'm fussy?" Quinn found the idea humorous, even though it should've been embarrassing. Here he was, a normal person, being treated by normal people like a needy celebrity.

"Who knows what Hannah has said." Larisa sounded stressed, which made Quinn feel like he'd missed something.

"They don't have any sparkling water," said Larisa.

"I'm fine."

"Flying is dehydrating."

He laughed. They were out of LA, away from spying eyes. He felt so free. Why was she worried? He gave her a second look and decided she was, in fact, worried and not about dehydration. Across the dining room, Gunter and Suzette had backed themselves into a corner, looking distinctly uncomfortable. Several people filtered in from the adjacent TV room to fill their plates. Each one, in turn, glanced at Gunter and Suzette, then turned their backs on them and glanced across the table at Larisa. He saw two people give each other a glance of exaggerated eye rolls as they forked what looked like French fries with gravy and cubed cheese onto their plates.

"What's wrong?" he whispered.

"Nothing." Larisa smiled. "That's poutine they're eating. Canadian, I think. We're practically in Canada up here."

Two more people came in as three went out. Both men. One wore a purple polo shirt with a Minnesota Vikings football mascot embroidered on the left chest. The other wore a jersey with spirit beads around his neck. He caught Suzette's eye, hesitated, then broke into a big welcoming grin. "You're Bet's relatives from Cali, aren't you? Welcome to Minnesota! You get drinks yet? There's still Heineken, I think. Brad, you want another?"

Brad gave his friend a thumbs up. He began to work his way around the table filling his plate. "It's Gunter, right? Bet said you're in movies?"

"I was a producer until I retired."

"Cool. Cool. That's like one of those jobs where you just do everything that people tell you to do, right?"

"Something like that."

"Cool. You know we're related? I mean, by marriage. I'm Greg's cousin. I'm a plant manager. People tell me what to do a lot too."

Gunter nodded.

Larisa turned to face the wall so her voice would be muffled as she whispered into Quinn's ear. "It's like this every time here. These people."

The friend returned from the kitchen. "Got the last four!"

"Come join us in the den," said Brad. "The game's a little more back and forth than I'd like, but that makes it good, right? Sam, this is Gunter and—I'm sorry, I don't remember—"

"Suzette."

"Gunter and Suzette. You can tell us about all that amazing Cali weather."

Quinn watched in amazement as Gunter and Suzette allowed themselves to be shown into the den.

"This is fun," he said.

"It gets old."

"Because no one knows how important you are?"

She shrugged. "I feel like a specimen."

"If you mingled more, people might not stare."

As he spoke, a mother and her young son came in and glanced over. The woman broke into a wide smile like her life had just been made better by Larisa's presence. "Hi. I'm Bethany. We met at Bet's baby shower a few years back. Melissa?"

"Larisa."

"Right. I suppose you're a doctor by now."

"Something like that."

"Well, congratulations. It's always useful to have a doctor in the family." Bethany turned her gaze expectantly to Quinn.

"This is Quinn," said Larisa.

"Hi, Quinn. Are you also a doctor?"

"I'm in film."

"Ah, with Larisa's father, right, right." Bethany beamed. "Great to meet you." Bethany and her son began a slow circuit around the table. The air thickened. Quinn was used to playing the silent role. Larisa always did so well keeping a conversation going. But here, for the second time in a week, she was noticeably silent. He couldn't remember what had caused her to lose her poise before. Now it seemed there was a lot going on in her head that he could only guess at. She was uncomfortable in this 'normal' people environment. Her aunt had said something when they arrived that bothered her. Was it still bothering her? Hard to say because it was clear she didn't want to talk to Bethany, but she also didn't want to leave the room to avoid her. So, on all levels Larisa was in need of saving. He could do that.

Quinn drifted up to the table, began to follow Bethany around it as he looked over the food. "What do you do, Bethany?"

"Oh, I'm just at home with the kids."

Quinn plucked a slice of cheese from a platter. Plain old American cheddar like he'd eaten as a kid, thick cut, from a plain old grocery store. He folded it in half, felt the familiar texture in his hand when the fold broke and crumbled. As he lifted half to his mouth, he also lifted his eyes to Larisa's, gave her a small, knowing smile as he slowly, slowly, slowly pressed the cheese between his teeth and chewed.

When he'd swallowed, he asked Bethany, "How many kids do you have?"

"Three. Which is plenty. Isn't that right?" Bethany grabbed

her son's hand before he pulled an entire plate of cream cheese tortilla rolls off the table.

Quinn massaged the second half of cheese through his fingers then raised it to his mouth. Across the table, Larisa's tongue snaked out and licked her lips.

"How about you, any kids?"

In his peripheral vision, Quinn saw Larisa flinch. "Nope," he said.

Bethany glanced at him, maybe surprised by the finality of his answer. "Well, I'm sure you're both very busy and important." She glanced at Larisa. "Larisa doesn't really date father types."

A strange thing to say, but Quinn let it pass. Bethany was on her way out of the room, and he was enjoying his little display too much to be bothered by whatever was going on there. He plucked a candied almond from its bowl and distractedly rubbed it along his bottom lip as he continued to study the food.

"Stop it," laughed Larisa.

He pretended not to hear her.

Someone had made chocolate truffles. He picked one up, held it to his nose, waited, milking the anticipation for all it was worth, then he opened his mouth, pulled back his lips to show his teeth, and bit down.

"For fuck's sake," hissed Larisa. "You're R-rated tonight."

"You like me."

He walked over and held the second half of the truffle to her lips. She opened her mouth and took it.

In the adjacent room, a child screeched with joy.

Larisa closed her lips around his fingers. He slowly drew them out, leaving behind a stain of the chocolate that had melted onto them. "I'm wet," she whispered.

"Is there a place we can take care of that?"

"I thought you didn't do sex in public," she whispered.

"This is different." He leaned into her, standing close enough it wouldn't be immediately obvious that he'd brought his hand down to cup between her legs.

"God, Quinn. Stop."

"You don't want me to stop."

"You should."

"I think you hate it here. You're bored already."

She laughed.

"Take me somewhere and ruin me before I do something to make these people remember us forever."

"Fine. *Fine.*" She turned him and marched him out of the room, along the back wall of the den where Suzette had been smashed into a sectional couch between two sweaty, red-faced men, and Gunter stood uncertainly by a potted plant frowning at the television as though football was a foreign language he was trying to parse.

Around the corner, they climbed an elegant, dark wood staircase with a plush carpet runner. The second floor was empty except for the distant sound of children playing in the attic. Larisa led the way into a bedroom with pastel-blue walls and a gas fireplace. Quinn supposed a nice house in Minnesota needed fireplaces on every floor, though it seemed like a bit much to him. He wasn't remotely cold.

Larisa led the way to the bed in the center of the room, but Quinn diverted her to the window seat lined with five stained glass windowpanes all featuring their own long-stemmed tulip. There was no streetlamp outside and the sky clouded the moon, but there was just enough light to see the outlines of trees beyond the house.

"I'll break my back on that," said Larisa.

Quinn rearranged the pillows. Then, when he was satisfied, he hooked his fingers into the waistband of her leggings and began to slowly roll them down.

"We're not breaking anything tonight," he said. "We're going to go so slowly, and so quietly, no one will ever know we were here."

"Speak for your—"

He cupped his palm over her mouth. "Silence." He felt her

wanting to argue so he pushed his hand down between her legs and began to stroke her, a soft tease. She took his other hand into her mouth and began to suck his fingers. Her eyes widened aggressively as though to say, *This is the only way you're going to keep me silent.*

They moved onto the window seat. She got his pants off while still working his fingers in her mouth. In the dim light, the perfect *O* of her lips looked like a garish red slash through a monochrome landscape, her mouth indecently full of him, stretched.

When she came, his hand wasn't enough to keep her quiet. She grabbed the sleeve of his sweatshirt and screamed into it, the aftershocks shuddering through her like a meteorite disturbing a lake.

Afterward, they lay side by side, exhausted, in no hurry to rejoin the party. Quinn felt his body pulling him toward sleep. In this twilight, his mind drifted, pulling together impressions, camera angles, the alien naturalism of both the house and these people, the way Larisa and her parents were so much themselves, even here where it would've been easier if they'd tried to blend in.

"Did you ever think about staying?"

"Here?" Larisa sounded incredulous, but after a beat she shifted her shoulder to adjust the pillow behind her. It felt like a concession. "I had planned to stay."

"What happened?"

"Several things. My mother and I had a big fight. The doctor I wanted to do research with during residency retired early, and the only other person I could've worked with here thought I was a Valley girl who spent her summers on yachts and European nude beaches."

"That doesn't sound implausible."

"But she didn't know that for *sure*, and she still judged me."

"You could've found a way around that."

"I did. I switched from clinical psychiatry to emergency medicine. Hannah and I moved into a house. I went on a couple dates with a guy who worked at the hospital."

"It didn't get serious?"

"He died in a car accident."

"What?" Quinn laughed, certain she was joking.

"He died in a car accident."

"Larisa. I'm sorry. That must have been . . . " He didn't know how to finish the thought without sounding trite. Why hadn't this come up? Quinn was wide awake now, his brain rumbling with disjointed ideas, connections that felt like they wanted to be made but couldn't.

"Anyway, it wasn't a great situation because technically he'd been dating Hannah first, then he kind of went behind her back and asked me out. I didn't find out until later. And after that, Hannah didn't want to live with me. She'd thought he was going to be her person."

"Oh."

"Yep."

"But you're still friends, right?" He turned to study Larisa's face, bisected with tulip glass.

"Yeah, we're friends. I mean, I've gotten a few messages from her that sound like she's excited to see me. I guess she's bringing a date. So, that'll be something."

"Why?"

"That boyfriend who asked me out is pretty typical of Hannah's taste in men."

"Not great?"

"Nope."

"But you wouldn't try and steal him again?" He was teasing her because it felt the only thing he could do in response to this new story, which seemed so unlike the Larisa he knew.

As minutes ticked by and Larisa remained silent, absorbed in her own thoughts, he wondered what exactly he knew about Larisa's life during medical school and her relationship with her cousin. It should've felt like a serious thing, family drama, a man who'd died. But somehow it all drifted through him as though netted in a dreamscape. The boundaries of his thoughts had become porous with obscure connections, all of them colored by the descending ecstasy of sex, of the miracle of Larisa's body. He thought of a girl he'd known in high school who'd been exceptionally beautiful, as though the horrors of adolescence, including all its uncertainties and insecurities, had passed her by. She'd seemed to walk on clouds down the school hallways. She had admirers more than she ever had friends.

What would it be like to be Larisa's cousin? he wondered. *Always in her shadow.* And while Quinn fully expected, even wanted, to orbit in Larisa's shadow, he thought not everyone would want that. Some people who had higher opinions of themselves might even nourish a dangerous resentment.

Chapter 19

An Invitation

Larisa woke to pristine sun shining through the hotel room window on Christmas morning. They'd stayed late at Bet's party. Quinn had wanted to explore the house. Eventually, they'd found Bet's husband, who'd given them an official tour, telling them bits and pieces of its history. Quinn had asked studious questions about architecture, weather, and the sun during daylight hours. And Larisa had enjoyed watching him.

Now she watched the sun wash color across his pale face as he slept and resisted the temptation to wake him, even though all she wanted to do was watch that slow animation of his body coming to life, the flicker of his eyelashes on his cheeks as they fluttered open, and how he'd look at her for the first time that day.

Last night, he'd told her that he felt liberated being out of LA. To some extent, she felt the same way. But she had more to worry about than he did. Bet had behaved as though she'd been told something terrible about Quinn. *Hannah has gone ahead of me and poisoned them all,* she thought. It might not matter. Her father's family was many things, but they wouldn't turn on her and her new boyfriend unless provoked. And Quinn, for the first time since they'd met, seemed completely at ease, as though the past eight months hadn't been an unending hell of triggers and stress.

He'll be charming. Whatever Hannah said won't matter.

Quinn stirred. Larisa watched breath animate his body,

listened to his contented sigh as he rolled into her side of the bed and drowsily nuzzled his face against her breast.

"Morning."

"Hmm, yes," he murmured. "How long do we have?"

"A couple hours."

"Hmmgoood." He still hadn't opened his eyes, but his hands came for her, digging her out from beneath the tangle of sheets. Worshipping hands that flitted as light as dragonflies across her skin, setting off her own bodily awakening. He dragged his chest over to hers and began to plant soft, morning-breath kisses on her breastbone.

"We could order room service," she said.

"Later. Have to work up an appetite." He moved down to her stomach, took her hips in his hands.

"Quinn?"

He looked up at her, chin on her navel, a devilish glint in his eyes as though his first thought upon waking was how he would pleasure her.

"I love you."

He grinned his rarest, lit-up-his-whole-face, looked-like-a-little-boy smile. "I know."

"No matter what happens."

For a moment he stilled, as though he wasn't sure how serious she was being, and if he needed to also be serious. "What's wrong?"

"Nothing."

"You're not in the mood?" he asked.

She laughed softly. An absurd question given that stress and terrible life events seemed to send her libido into overdrive. But she appreciated his consideration. He was so gentle. So much more than she deserved.

"I just want to be able to stare at you every moment we're allowed to be alone today."

"So, you don't want me to take my"— he stuck out his tongue—"and put it"— he pointed down to her pubis. "Fine."

He crawled up to her head and leaned his weight on one arm. His free hand stroked the line of her mouth until she parted her lips and allowed him to slip inside, two probing fingers along her tongue, filling her.

"You're not looking at me."

She lifted her eyes, tilted her chin up, so her gaze was full of him looking down at her.

"I don't know what you're after," he said. "I'm not that much to look at."

When he removed his fingers she said, "I disagree."

Her gaze caught on the movement of his fingers trolling down her stomach to reach softly between her lower lips, to slide their slow sensuous weight into her.

"You're not looking at me."

Larisa snapped her gaze back up to his face, laughing at the disappointment in his voice. The laughter stopped short as his fingers began to stroke her in earnest. She reached for his briefs and found the bulge there, straining to get involved.

"Take me," she whispered, as she yanked him free, took him in her hand, and guided him to her occupied entrance.

"Slow down," laughed Quinn.

"No. Now." She knew he was more than ready. He was trying to prime her and didn't realize she wanted more than his tender attention. As soon as he was in position, she surged her hips forward, swallowing his length faster than she ever had. Quinn's eyes drifted closed as he moaned.

"Look at me." She slapped his ass as she continued to pulse around him, rough, hard thrusts that drove him deeper and deeper, stretching her more than he'd ever allowed when she left him in control.

He pulled his eyes open. With one hand at his hip, she pressed him into a rhythm until their bodies steadily slapped against each other. She drove her other hand into his hair at the back of his head, drawing him down so their faces were inches apart.

"Harder," she whispered. "Harder," as though chasing an oblivion that would erase everything she feared.

The Kahn family farmhouse sat on the edge of a preserved woodland an hour drive from the city. Or it felt like an hour to Quinn, who'd washed himself top to bottom twice in the shower, but still couldn't shake the feeling Larisa's parents could smell what he'd been doing to their daughter that morning.

After they cleared the city limits there'd been nothing out the window except a long flat white. He'd never seen so much space, so much land just spread out and full of nothing. He pictured Larisa running naked in the snow. Her toes and fingers and nose turning pink. He imagined rubbing it in her hair and the hard line of her voice as she commanded him to stop.

Think about something else, Quinn. Heaven help him, he was getting hard. It hurt; she'd run him ragged.

Gunter and Suzette sat in the first row of captain's chairs, both occupied on their phones.

Larisa sat beside him on the back bench of the hired SUV not doing anything. She'd been quiet since they'd transitioned from bedroom delight to preparing for their day. They'd shared a room service breakfast that hadn't been anything close to the room service at the Palisades resort where Jaden had gotten married, but it still felt like luxury. To sit in a car that smelled gently of pine and have a stranger drive him felt like luxury too. *This could be the rest of our lives,* he thought. Traveling to new places, room service, hired cars, sex.

Rough sex. He blinked away an afterimage of Larisa slamming her mouth against his. The way she'd sucked his lower lip between her teeth, the sounds she'd made when she passed beyond words. He felt stretched and wobbly, the high still echoing through his mind even as he wondered what had prompted her to drive him so hard, to look at him like she was starving only for him. He couldn't help but feel he'd never be enough for the hunger she'd unmasked that morning. If he'd dared to look at it too closely, he might have roused his old worries that he wasn't enough for her, that eventually, she'd want more than he could give.

We'll come back and do it again tonight, thought Quinn. *I'll be ready this time.*

Sometime around the forty-minute mark, beginning to feel they were driving off the end of the continent, Quinn asked, "How far do they drive for food?"

"There's a town with a co-op," said Larisa. His question seemed to pull her out of distracted thoughts because she looked around and caught a glimpse of Suzette's phone screen over her shoulder. "I see what you're doing."

Suzette put her hand up to cover her screen.

"My answer's still no," said Larisa.

"It's better to have a plan in place in case you change your mind. What do you think of this one?" Suzette twisted around to show Larisa an image of a runway model wearing a miniskirt and shell top. "Simple. Elegant. Mature."

"All the things I'm not. Don't go around today telling everyone we're going to Milan."

Suzette shrugged. "You know I'm invisible here, darling. No one cares what I do. I'm just the wife and mother."

"You can leave after we eat," said Gunter.

"Leave by myself and let you all talk about me after I'm gone?"

Finally, a roof on the horizon. It became a house that looked more like a regular house than a farmhouse, brick and siding, and modern windows, with an addition tacked onto the side that looked new, a detached garage bigger than garages as Quinn knew them, but definitely not a barn. He'd been expecting a barn, maybe with a tractor parked in front even though that would've been ridiculous. It was winter. There was a foot of snow on the ground.

"Are we there already?" asked Gunter. "I love roads with no traffic. Magic."

"Promise you won't go back for seconds," said Suzette, as they climbed out.

"It's a holiday, Susie."

Larisa's parents walked ahead of them into the house. Quinn was ready to follow them, but Larisa held him back.

The driveway was covered in a fine dusting of powder that melted under her boots as she turned in a circle, swinging him around with her. The house and its driveway looked down on open space he assumed were fields. He could see all the way to the horizon in one direction. And to his left, farther down the road, a collection of buildings he supposed was the nearest town.

"Are you happy or worried?" he asked.

"Why would I be worried?" Larisa cast him one of her dazzling smiles, a performance smile, but knowing that didn't make it less effective. His heart swelled in his chest.

"I'm happy to be here with you."

"We'll see how you feel in five hours." She gave him a severe look. "No sex here today."

"You sure?"

"Yes."

"Fine." He'd had more than enough that morning.

"It's possible Hannah will be hostile."

"I'll protect you." He grinned. After what they'd been through, he could more than handle one disgruntled cousin.

"Toward you."

"What have I done?"

"She's just unpredictable."

"Are you going to protect me then?" he teased.

"I will try."

"If we end up absconding early, we'll have to take your mother with us."

Larisa rolled her eyes. "She likes it here. Everyone asks her for fashion advice. The last time I came with them, she brought a bunch of her old clothes, and we had a mini fashion show."

"So, we can abscond on our own?"

"We'll see." She pulled at the edge of his sweater, plucked away an invisible cat hair. "Are you good?"

"I am."

She nodded. He had the distinct impression she was stalling, though he didn't quite understand why. A very large bird circled in the sky just like they did in the movies, usually to foreshadow something bad happening, unless it was one of those scenic stories filmed in Montana where giant birds in the sky were just atmospheric. Quinn couldn't think of a movie he'd seen about Minnesota. It wasn't a place where he pictured woods and long stretches of empty pristine white. Just as the quiet began to morph into something a little disconcerting for his urbanized senses, Larisa pulled him toward the house.

The peaceful emptiness of outside vanished as soon as Quinn stepped across the threshold of the front door. A mountain of shoes covered the floor in the atrium. Three people seemed to be shouting at once. There was a child in distress, and a mother yelling at them to be quiet at the top of the half staircase that led up to the front room on the left. Up ahead, down a narrow hallway with snowshoes and poles attached to the wall, there was a wave of heat, more shouting, and very loud music from *Home Alone*.

"Don't stand there all day, come in!"

"Larisa's here!"

"Larisa's here!" someone echoed. And then people were pressing in. An elderly woman peered at Quinn over the rims of her glasses.

"This is Quinn," said Larisa. "Quinn, this is my Great-Aunt Gertrude."

"Skinny," observed Gertrude.

"He's the one who cheated with his ex-girlfriend," said a

middle schooler wearing headphones; he spoke louder than needed.

"Hush," snapped a woman who turned out to be Kristen, Gunter's youngest sister. "That was a misunderstanding."

The middle schooler's twin wedged his way forward and gaped at him. "Do you like weird sex? Does Aunt Larisa like it too?"

"Oh-kay, well here you are." Kristen gave Larisa a hug. "I've been trying to teach them not to believe everything people say about you."

"It's fine," said Larisa.

A teenage girl came up behind them. "I saw the stream in April. It was hot. Will you sign a screen grab after we eat?"

Larisa squeezed Quinn's hand and pulled him with her as she followed Kristen.

At the end of the hallway, the first floor of the house became an open plan with a long central room and archways into smaller, adjacent rooms. It would've felt spacious if not for the tables and chairs crammed in and all the living room sofas braced up against the walls, drowned in winter coats. People were everywhere, and they all looked vaguely similar in the way that some families do, the same bones, the same chins, the same generalized largeness that'd contributed to Gunter's reputation as a hard hitter in Hollywood, but here felt ordinary. Both Hans and the fourth sibling Lena were taller than Gunter and wider. All the Kahns, even the children, moved through the house like they were in charge. It was easy to spot the spouses. One was in the kitchen wearing an exhaustion that looked like they'd been through three holiday dinners already. One was pressed up against the door to the back deck. One was at the far end of the central room, over by the tree, holding his head in one hand, crunched in on himself as though braced for a storm.

And then a storm of children did blow through. Someone had given them lightsabers and capes.

The Christmas tree was impressive enough that it would've

claimed Quinn's full attention if he'd felt he could move without bumping into someone or stepping into the path of someone running to finish an important task. He planted his feet and held on to Larisa's arm, and still the scene swam past his vision, refusing to center itself. So many people, so much movement. He met their hostess, Alison, and her daughter-in-law, both in matching aprons that labeled them as COOK and COOK's ASSISTANT with cartoon, headless chickens on the bibs.

"Oh, yes. You're the one Hannah was talking about," said the daughter-in-law—he hadn't heard her name. She narrowed her eyes with warning like she'd be keeping an eye on him.

Somehow Larisa moved them backward and up to the front room where the din died down. The mother—one of Larisa's second cousins—had corralled her upset child, so they only had to maneuver through clusters of people chatting and a teenager showing off a puppy that didn't want to be held. Finally, they came up to the central rooms from one of the archways. Larisa threw out her hands to present him to the Christmas tree.

"Our one and only old-world tradition," she said. "Except for the family names of course."

The tree had been strung with a strand of white electric lights and hung with glass balls just like any other tree, but the gold-robed angel at the top, with a glare as fierce as a nutcracker, looked handmade. The edges of the tree branches were trapped with garlands of twisted white fabric that Quinn's imagination told him could be nineteenth-century bedsheets. On closer inspection, he saw the glass balls had been hand painted and were chipping from age. The ornaments also included glowing blue star frames that fit around the white lights, white-frosted pine cones, and festively dressed little wooden people. Beneath the tree, a miniature city of boxes poorly disguised all the gift cards.

"Want to help me carry ours in?" she asked.

Quinn followed her back the way they'd come, relieved for any excuse to be away from the chaos.

"It gets better once everyone sits down to eat. But still noisy."

She looked at him like she half expected him to take off running down the road.

"I'm fine."

She continued to give him the look as she walked backward toward the car and knocked on the driver's window.

"What? You think I'm like one of those glass balls? The wind comes along, and I shatter?"

"I think maybe you have less resilience than some people. But that's fine. It just comes with trauma."

He stopped short. It was the first obviously therapist thing she'd said to him since she'd stopped being his therapist. And even when they'd been working together in that capacity, she'd never said anything that sounded so blatantly dismissive. As though he wore a disease label on his sleeve, and it went ahead of him explaining his behavior.

"Sorry, what?"

Larisa had her head in the driver's side window, talking to the driver. She pulled out and walked around to the back of the SUV as the tailgate began to beep and lift. "It seems like they've decided they don't like you."

"No, what you said before. You think I lack resilience?"

An impatient look flickered across her expression. "No, I just think things have been hard. And I want to protect you. It looks like Hannah has been fanning some flames."

She picked up a carboard box wrapped like a giant present and handed it to him. The fact that she'd given him the smaller of two boxes suddenly seemed significant. He watched Larisa expertly pick up the larger box and hold it with one hand as she closed the tailgate.

"I don't have trauma," he said. "And even if I did, it would've given me more resilience rather than less."

"Okay. Yeah, that's probably true."

This response, Larisa obviously backtracking, just made him more irritated.

"Is that what you think?"

"I shouldn't have said that."

"You think I'm traumatized, and that's why I have so many issues with people."

"I don't think that."

"I'm fine. I'm having a good time. I don't see why you're so worried—"

"Let's just drop it. There's a car coming."

Quinn heard the crunch of snow compacting. He peered around his box to see a blue Camry pulling up the driveway. A regular car, much older than anyone in his new life would ever think of driving. There was even rust inside the passenger side wheel well. And in the passenger seat—

"Oh fuck."

"What?" Larisa had turned and was already halfway to the front door, apparently using the car's interruption as a way to extricate herself from the conversation.

Quinn turned and followed her, almost running, hoping it didn't look like he was running. He wanted to take Larisa and run and hide. His mind scrambled for a plan. They would go out the back door and run around to the driveway, ask the driver to take them away. If he moved fast, Larisa wouldn't have to know.

They waded through all the people in the front room and returned to the tree in the central room. Larisa began to unpack her box. "You can set them anywhere. There's no real organization." She glanced over his shoulder, watching.

"Let's go back outside," said Quinn. "Show me the back deck." Quinn pulled at Larisa's arm, but he wasn't fast enough. The chorus of arrival chaos that had greeted them the first time they'd entered the house now erupted to welcome the new arrivals.

"That sounds like Hannah." Larisa straightened her blouse beneath her quilted coat. "Whatever she says, she doesn't mean it. She's actually a very nice person."

A small cluster of people had clogged the opening of the hallway into the big central room. For a moment, it meant the center of their focus couldn't be seen from the tree. But then someone called that something was burning in the kitchen and a few people broke off to go see about it, and there they were, a woman who looked like all the other Kahns—fair hair, blue eyes, and the kind of thick body type that survived in cold climates. And beside her, outclassing Larisa and both her parents with a velvet dinner jacket, crisp cream cravat, cameo pin and gloves, stood Lucas Onslow the Third.

"Food's ready!" called Alison. "Everyone claim a plate and come to the kitchen."

People from the front room began to flow in, pushing Larisa and Quinn forward. Someone put plates in Larisa's hands. She handed one to Quinn. He tried to ask her what they should do, but they were moving too fast. Children were running by. The jostle of people kept pulling them apart.

"Hey! No cutting in line."

"First dibs on the legs!"

A brawny teen, whose elbows were level with Quinn's eyes, pushed between them, then belatedly apologized.

In the kitchen, the line organized itself past the hot dishes on the counter, and Quinn was able to lean in and say, "What the fuck?" in a voice which had seemed quiet enough until the man in front of Larisa—one of the spouses—turned and glared at him.

"Do you mind? There are children." He shook his head. "Coasters."

"We can't leave," Larisa whispered back. "The car's gone. He was leaving right after we got the boxes."

"Can't you borrow one?"

A space opened up ahead of Larisa as she stood, staring at his shoulder like an answer was written there.

"Keep the line moving, we're starving here!"

"How can he be here?" Quinn tried to spoon a small amount of mashed potatoes onto his plate, but ended up flinging the spoon up into a shelf of cookbooks. It stuck for a moment then clattered to the floor, leaving a smear of white fluff on *The Potato Primer* in the process. Three different people rushed to get a new serving spoon.

"I don't know," hissed Larisa.

"What are we going to do?"

Larisa shook her head. "Smile and pretend nothing's wrong."

This was Larisa's first response to any kind of social-situation crisis. In the past he'd been reassured by it, had even felt protected by how good she was at pretending everything was fine. But this was not remotely fine. And he knew, he absolutely knew that pretending wouldn't save them today.

They took the first two empty seats they found at a table already mostly full with people Larisa must have determined were safe: Kristen and her husband Dan, Great-Aunt Gertrude and her sister Great-Aunt Violet, and Lena, Gunter's divorced sister.

Which left only one empty seat at the table. Quinn took a breath and slowly let it out. *We're fine. This is fine.*

Hannah's possibly lesbian sister, who was also a kindergarten teacher, passed by, surveyed the possible places to sit, looked at Lena, and said, "Aunt Lena, come sit with me at the kids' table. Someone needs to protect the tree with me."

And then there were two empty seats. And just like they were following a script, Hannah and Lucas slid into them. Hannah smiled at Larisa from across the table like a cat who'd already trapped the mouse.

"How nice to have new faces around," said Violet, who seemed the younger and more alert of the two great-aunts. "We should do introductions after we pray."

Hans emerged from the kitchen doorway with a megaphone and said, "Everyone! Forks down. Hands folded. Eyes closed. I'm saying grace. Whoever steals someone's food while I'm talking will burn in hell for eternity. I'm looking at you, Ronnie."

A spattering of laughter, then everyone bowed their heads and closed their eyes except, of course, Quinn, who wouldn't have closed his eyes in this moment even if he were on the verge of death, praying for last minute salvation. An unnerving stillness descended over the room. Across the table, Lucas also kept his eyes open. They stared at each other until Lucas began to smile.

Words filled Quinn's mind, as embodied as though Lucas was speaking them in that moment. *I want to bend you over a table and fuck you while she watches.* A spark twinged along the inside of Quinn's leg, another at the base of his spine.

Hans said, "Amen!" and the room came to life again, a burst of activity and chattering dinnerware and conversation.

"Introductions!" called Violet. "Gertie, you first. You're the oldest."

"Am I still?" asked Gertrude. "I thought someone had passed me. I'm Kristen's mother's sister. I live here in the basement. They let me out on holidays."

"And I'm Violet, Kristen, Hans, Gunter, Lena, and Lizabet's mother's older sister. What? They should all be named even if they chose not to sit with us. I live at my apartment in the village and keep the little free library." She picked up her fork and waved it at Larisa to her left.

"I'm Larisa, Gunter's only child."

"And what do you do now, Larisa?" asked Violet.

"I'm in counseling."

Hannah made a noise like she was swallowing back laughter. "Do you have all your patients sign NDAs so they don't go to the police?"

"All that is covered under HIPPA actually." Larisa smiled sweetly at her cousin. "And this is Quinn, a friend of the family. He's just starting out in the film industry. My father's mentoring him."

"Ah, another producer," said Violet. "Maybe you can explain what Gunter never can. What does a producer do exactly?"

"Everything." Quinn felt heat growing on his cheeks. They

were all looking at him and he wanted it to stop. "I mean, it depends on the production, but generally a producer is there to help make the vision of the director happen."

"Did that help answer it?" asked Gertrude.

"Nope, but it sounds like work," said Violet.

"So, you're not dating right now?" asked Hannah.

"We weren't ever really dating," said Larisa. "It was a publicity thing."

Under the table, Quinn reached for Larisa's knee. He'd follow her lead, but did she think Lucas was going to buy the lie?

"You broke up from a fake relationship this spring, then again a few months ago?"

"Seems like you have plenty of time to keep up with the LA gossip," said Larisa. "What are you doing now, Hannah?"

"I'm a traveling phlebotomist for Mayo. I don't actually have time to read any news. But when we were driving up, Lucas was telling me about the baby." Hannah made a sad face like she was watching an ASPCA commercial. "That kind of situation would put stress on any relationship, but yours has always been a little fragile, right?"

"Oh, Larisa." Kristen reached for Larisa's hand and squeezed it. "I'm so sorry."

"It wasn't Larisa," said Hannah. "It was that actress who was Quinn's real girlfriend this spring. She lost his baby."

"It's Dan's turn," said Larisa.

In true Kahn-spouse fashion, Dan shrank into his seat and looked to his wife for direction. Kristen began to talk in short, confident sentences about his job, their children, but Quinn heard none of it. He was looking down at Larisa's hand holding her fork, resting on the table between his plate and hers. It was shaking. He blinked and it looked like the entire table was shaking.

"I need to talk to you," he whispered.

"And next?" said Violet.

"I'm Lucas. I'm an account manager for a lobbying firm in

DC." His voice was like honey that had been heated by sunlight. It radiated across the table like a spell. Quinn almost heard the soft sighs around the table as the others were drawn in.

"Oh, you have an accent!" said Gertrude.

"I'm originally from England. But now my work takes me all over."

"And how do you know Hannah?"

"Through Larisa, actually. We dated when she was in college."

"Larisa, I need to talk to you," said Quinn again.

"Wait, what?" Kristen's gaze swiveled between Lucas and Larisa. "I'm confused."

The table *was* shaking. Quinn was jiggling his knee against the support, and it was making everything shake. He felt Larisa beside him, a boiling volcano about to explode. He reached for her hand without caring who saw. He needed her. He needed to feel that she was as surprised as he was. He wanted her to tell him it was a lie.

But she wasn't. Like some kind of superwoman, she'd already stepped past it, was pretending it hadn't happened.

"And such a nice dresser," said Gertrude. "In my day, a man who dressed well was a keeper." She winked at Hannah.

"We just celebrated our second month anniversary," said Hannah.

"Oh please," said Larisa. "Don't pretend to be that stupid. The only reason he's with you is to get to me."

"Because it's so hard to think he'd want me over you?"

"Because all he does is use people."

Across the table, Lucas kept his eyes on Quinn as though the two cousins weren't half out of their chairs shouting at each other. His eyes answered all of Quinn's questions.

Yes, she knew.

Yes, she hid it from you.

No, she never planned to tell you.

Quinn scraped back his chair and jumped up, began to weave himself between the chairs, not apologizing to people who had to scoot in for him to get by. All he could think was that there were too many people, the air was too hot, the room too crowded. He had to get out. He expected Larisa to follow him. When he made it out to the driveway and found himself alone, he began to walk to the street. He would go to the town and call a cab to go back to the hotel. He would wait for her there. No, he would book a flight back to LA. He would.

He would.

He had almost been a father.

Cold wet seeped into his shoes as he reached the road and began to make his way along the snow-packed shoulder.

Parish had been pregnant. It didn't seem possible. They'd always been careful.

They'd been careful except for that one time. The last time, when she'd drugged him at lunch and—

"Oh God."

He pulled out his phone to call her and realized he'd deleted her number. He thought Sid probably had it. Sid kept everything. But if he called Sid, he'd have to explain he was walking down a country road in northern Minnesota without a winter coat on Christmas Day. *Lucas is here*, would've been his answer, but it was one Sid wouldn't be able to parse.

Lucas had come to Christmas, and he'd convinced Hannah to stage an ambush.

An ambush that was probably meant to result in exactly what Quinn had done.

But he couldn't go back to the house. He couldn't sit next to Larisa while she ignored him, knowing she'd kept this from him. For how long? *Why does he know?*

Quinn's feet were soaked through, toes burning with cold, but the town was within reach. He passed a gas station and the long, trough-shaped barn of the co-op. A main street began to materialize. He looked at his phone. Larisa hadn't called. There was no sound of a car coming up the road behind him. She was probably still at the table fighting with Hannah. Fighting about Lucas. He was so fucking tired of Lucas.

Norseman Bar and Grille was the only place open. Quinn was surprised to find most of the tables inside full. A family of three sat eating dinner at the corner table. A group of men, younger than him, wearing hoodies and flannel were drinking and throwing darts. Two wall-mounted TVs showed the Packers-Bears game. At the base of one, a dozen or more people decked out in green and gold and too many foam cheeseheads booed at the screen.

Quinn slid into a seat at the bar.

"What can I get ya?" The bartender looked like an off-Hollywood version of Pat Garrett with a handlebar mustache and a sweaty bandana tied around his neck.

"Club soda."

The bartender peered at him. "Where you from?"

"Why does that matter?"

"You look like you need something stronger than bubble water."

Quinn closed his eyes and pressed his palms against them. His feet were frozen. His stomach felt like it had been sliced into layers and stitched back together in the wrong order. As soon as he thawed out, he'd be in the bathroom waiting to puke up the four bites of Christmas dinner he'd managed to eat under Lucas's watchful gaze.

"Just get me the fucking water!"

"Whatever," said the bartender.

"With lemon, if you have it fresh."

Fussy, thought Quinn. And then a new thought. Larisa's voice in his mind. *Lacking resilience.*

Fragile.

Lucas arrived in the middle of Quinn's third club soda. The smell of him came in with the bitter wind of the bar's door opening and blowing shut. A smell like flowers, but not any that Quinn could name. Flowers and fresh-cut wood. He didn't look up as Lucas flipped the tails of his coat out behind him and slid onto the adjacent stool.

Don't panic, Quinn told his pounding heart.

"Two bourbons on the rocks. Unless you have an unopened red wine of a French vintage before 2005?"

The bartender laughed like Lucas was the funniest customer he'd ever seen.

Across the room, the football fans cheered.

"I would like to apologize for the scene at dinner. I'd hoped to avoid such a crass method of revelation."

Quinn threw back the last of his drink and motioned to the bartender that he wanted another. His stomach felt sloshy and pressurized from all the carbonation but having a drink would give him something to do to hide his firing nerves and racing pulse. It'd been one thing to sit across the table from Lucas. Sitting at an adjacent bar stool with the man's knees inches from his hip was something else.

"When it became clear that Larisa intended to hide it from you, I felt I should step in."

"When did it happen?" asked Quinn.

"Tuesday, last week. Or I suppose two weeks now since it's Sunday."

That Tuesday Quinn had reluctantly left Larisa to go to his therapist where they'd talked about his childhood dream of becoming a writer, and how that had faded after his mother left. Then there'd been the emergency meeting at the studio. Larisa had been out most of the day, working. He hadn't seen her until Thursday at the premiere.

"Boy or girl?"

"Girl."

Don't trust him. And yet Quinn's throat tightened with an

emotion he couldn't name. Until two weeks ago, he'd been a father.

"I've never thought about having kids," he said.

"Perhaps you were spared the mistake."

The bartender brought him a fresh water. Quinn stared down at the bubbles rising up between the ice cubes. It didn't feel right to call a baby a mistake. But there was some part of him that felt relief.

"Did Larisa tell you?"

"I have connections."

"Connections?" Quinn laughed. "Why would someone like you bother? I mean, really. You're in New York. You're in LA. You're in Minnesota. You're watching my ex-girlfriend, Larisa's cousin, and me. Doesn't someone like you have something better to do with your free time?'

"Someone like me?" Lucas smirked. "Who exactly do you think I am?"

"A businessman with a lot of commitments and important people who expect him to get results."

"Bravo. You understand me exactly."

"You didn't answer my question."

The bartender came by with Lucas's drinks. Lucas ran his finger over the rim of one as though evaluating the quality of the glass. "What do you think is the answer?"

"Don't play games. You've ruined my Christmas. I get a straight answer."

"Larisa ruined your Christmas." Lucas moved one of the glasses toward Quinn. "Drink with me. A toast." He raised his glass. "To broken hearts."

One sniff of the amber liquid told Quinn what he'd already suspected. His heart was pounding a 200-meter sprint through his chest, but he couldn't help but smile. When Lucas had rimmed the glass, he'd left a chemical residue.

"Do I have one of those faces that says, please do whatever you like to me?" Quinn twirled the liquid in the glass, set it down, and reached for his water. "I've already been drugged and kidnapped once this year. She was better at it than you. She knew I don't drink."

Lucas gazed at him, a steady, unflinching intensity that existed outside of everything else, as though he didn't hear what Quinn was saying, didn't see his hands, or the drink left untouched. Finally, he said, "That girl was selfish. She would have ruined you with her baby. I'm not."

"Not selfish?" Quinn sipped his water, tried to breathe. He was sweating in his already wet clothes. Would Larisa come and find him? Is that why he was still sitting here? Was he waiting to be found in a compromising scene with Lucas?

Maybe it was more than that. He was still sitting here because he needed a resolution. He didn't want to walk away and continue living with this man looking over his shoulder.

"I have a gift," said Lucas. "I can see past who people think they are. I see what they could be. Sometimes, the process begins with force." He leaned forward and rapped Quinn on the shoulder with his knuckle. "I have to break open the hard shell to reveal the soft, tender parts."

Quinn resisted the impulse to recoil. His heart leapt in his chest, so forceful now against his ribs he felt like an animated character with a heart shape trying to escape from his body.

"Are you going to leave her?" asked Lucas.

"Why would I do that?"

"She lied to you." Lucas looked impatient, as though in his mind the ending of this scene had already been written. They were supposed to be going through the requisite beats, but Quinn had gone off script.

Quinn toyed with his drink. There was a sour taste in his mouth. He felt dizzy in a way that felt familiar, like he had fallen into an old dream. Nothing about this scene felt determined. If anything, he felt the possibilities were too open, the writing sloppy and confused. He was scared out of his mind, but also strangely calm. The way Lucas was looking at him made him feel powerful, as though he was in control of the next steps.

An illusion? Possibly. Lucas had orchestrated everything to this point, to what extent, Quinn didn't want to imagine, but it seemed clear he'd been envisioning this for a while, maybe since New York. Which meant everything Larisa had done since then to try to protect them had been useless. Their paths were always going to draw them here, to this moment.

He wants me to leave her and go with him.

At first blush, it sounded ludicrous. Quinn would absolutely never consider it.

But then his mind skipped ahead, to that night, the next day, going home with Larisa, trying to find things to say, realizing she wasn't likely to stop keeping secrets from him because she was always going to need to protect him.

Lacking resilience.

Fragile.

She has no idea who I am, thought Quinn.

It wasn't her fault. But how was she ever going to find out if they kept moving forward, trapped under the glass dome of Lucas's panopticon. Something needed to happen to break them free.

Lucas had given him an invitation. It came without the suspicion that would have limited Larisa if the CIA had pushed her to return to him. But Quinn could do it. He could follow the script Lucas had written and play the spy. And maybe, maybe if he was lucky, he could remove Lucas from their lives.

Quinn shivered.

"Can we get some hot water?" Lucas called to the bartender. "You shouldn't stay in those wet clothes." He leaned forward and began to pull the zipper on the front of Quinn's sweater. When Quinn lurched back out of reach, the room spun. The bitter taste rushed along his tongue even stronger than before.

"You dosed my water along with the bourbon," said Quinn.

"The bourbon was just a game." Lucas's eyes glinted with

dark delight. "I was curious what you would do with something obvious."

"What did I do?"

Lucas tilted his head to one side as though studying a specimen. "Nothing I can see. You're a cipher Quinn VanderVeer."

"So, you took the choice away."

"There's still a choice. I'll honor whatever you decide."

"What choice?" Quinn's tongue felt thick in his mouth. His eyes skittered over to the bartender, then to the football fans, everyone absorbed in their own little worlds. If eyes looked in his direction, they were focused on Lucas. Quinn's need to be rescued was virtually invisible.

I'm tired of being rescued.

"Come with me to Florence," said Lucas.

"I have to work."

"That can be managed."

Quinn tried to stand and found his legs unstable beneath him.

"Surrender." Lucas's face swam before Quinn's vision, both near and far at the same time. "Let me do what Larisa won't."

"What choice?" repeated Quinn.

"I have a car outside. I'll drive you back to the Cities, leave you at the hotel, and you can carry on with Larisa, knowing she's spent your entire relationship lying to you. Is that what you want?"

Another right answer, as though Lucas was laying out breadcrumbs for Quinn to pick up. *He's an arrogant little prick,* thought Quinn. Even in the haze of his addled mind, he felt the power in this observation. It was something he could use.

"You're going to be asleep in a few minutes." Lucas was holding a steaming mug to Quinn's mouth, guiding him to drink the hot water the bartender must have brought. Quinn had lost all awareness of other people. He felt only the looming presence of Lucas before him. And between them, the yawning chasm of his choice. All he had to do was step forward into Lucas's waiting arms.

"Florence," said Quinn.

"You're certain?"

"Take me." Quinn closed his eyes and felt the fog of chemical sleep crowd into his mind. He thought of Larisa that morning, splayed across the bed in their hotel room, slick with sweat from their exertions, eating raspberries. How they'd stood in the bathroom and brushed their teeth side by side, making faces at each other to see who would spew toothpaste at the mirror first.

Forgive me, he thought. *I'm doing this for us.*

Chapter 20

Christmas in Flames

"Because it's so hard to think he'd want me over you?" Hannah had said.

And Larisa had almost-yelled back, "Because all he does is use people."

"You'd be the one to know about using people," Hannah had said at full-fighting volume, which probably wouldn't have been enough to silence the room, except Quinn had stood up and ran out. Rather, he attempted to run out and was stalled by having to maneuver through all the chairs.

Larisa should have stopped there, used the natural interruption of Quinn's departure as a pause to wind herself back into some semblance of composure. Instead, she said, "You're right, I know how to keep men from walking all over me and leaving me with nothing."

"What's happening here?" asked Alison from the adjacent table.

"Nothing," said Kristen. "We're going upstairs." She gave Larisa a look, then stood and pulled Hannah's chair back from the table.

"I have nothing to hide," said Hannah. "Everyone should know. There's nothing wrong with it. I'm dating Larisa's ex. There! Now everyone knows."

Kristen led Hannah toward the stairs. Larisa followed. The last she saw of Lucas, he'd forked a bite of stuffing into his mouth and was chewing thoughtfully as Violet patted his hand in sympathy. It was a little like watching a movie of her worst nightmare, except Larisa hadn't ever articulated her unending, nameless dread in such detail. The little things shocked her more than his presence alone. That her great-aunt was touching him. That everyone was acting like he was a nice, reasonable person. That he ate stuffing.

Upstairs, Kristen sequestered them in the main bedroom. "Alrighty, let's just take a breath and remember that you love each other. And that family is stronger than anything else."

Larisa stalked to the window. The main bedroom looked out on the backyard, a blank stretch of half-melted snow and the tree line of the preserved woodlands. *Quinn doesn't have a coat,* she thought. *He'll have to come back inside soon.*

"I love you," said Hannah from the opposite side of the room.

"Alright," said Larisa. "I believe you. But what the fuck were you thinking?"

"Larisa, language!"

"I wanted to be happy for once." Hannah crossed her arms over her chest, planted her feet, as though she had the moral high ground.

"It's obvious what he's doing. I bet he contacted you."

"So?"

"And he told you this story about how I've fallen for a terrible person."

"I knew that already," said Hannah. "We get the news here, you know."

If you were that worried, why didn't you reach out in April? wondered Larisa. But she kept the thought to herself. Hannah had never been one to take the initiative in their relationship.

"When did Lucas tell you about the baby?"

"Last week."

"And you felt you had to save me."

"He asked for my help." Hannah glared at her. "He still loves you. We both want you to have good things in your life."

The last time they'd spoken, Hannah had said Larisa had

received more than her fair share of good and squandered it. It hadn't quite been a fight that time, but Larisa had been surprised by the potency of Hannah's resentment. That had been the Christmas right after she'd finally managed to detach herself from Lucas. She hadn't been her best self.

"You brought a date to Christmas dinner to undermine Larisa's relationship?" asked Kristen, whose bewildered expression mirrored the aunts', as though this revelation of the machinations of young people was simply beyond her. Any minute, Larisa expected her to say, 'kids these days.'

"He's already ruined her," said Hannah. "And she couldn't stay away from him. It's for her own good." She paused to let the words sink in, the exact words Larisa had used when Hannah had caught her with her then-boyfriend, though the context was different. Not at all comparable, in Larisa's opinion. Her actions hadn't been premeditated. And they hadn't been coordinated with an arms dealer.

"Quinn's not going anywhere," said Larisa.

"Then what I've done shouldn't matter, eh?" Hannah smiled bitterly. "I'm sure whatever the two of you have is stronger than a surprise baby. Maybe he'll even come back from the dead after a mysterious car crash."

Kristen sat down on the bed and blew out an audible breath. "You two." She shook her head. "It's Christmas."

Something false flickered across Hannah's expression. Larisa could only imagine what she was hiding. In this moment, a different version of Larisa might have softened, might have pleaded, might even have shed tears and said, 'if only you knew what I knew,' and 'let me spare you this.' But Larisa wasn't that kind of person. And she and Hannah had walked too long down the road of Larisa's patronizing protection when it came to men. Hannah no longer listened to Larisa's advice. She wasn't likely to start again now, the one time it mattered the most.

Larisa's heart ached. "I'm sorry," she said. *Sorry I introduced him to you. Sorry I ever met him.* Sorry would never be enough.

"Hannah?" asked Kristen.

"I'm sorry for disrupting dinner."

Kristen hesitated, possibly deciding if she was going to accept their lackluster steps toward peace. "You should go down and apologize to Alison," she said. "Maybe the four of you could have a sit-down after dessert. I think that would be nice, get to know each other as couples."

Out the bedroom window, a pair of deer ventured out from the tree line. Larisa supposed if she lived in a place where deer wandered in backyards, maybe she'd have a simpler idea of how people related to each other. *Maybe it's just me,* she thought. *I'm ruined.*

"Were the pies left in the oven?" asked Hannah.

The air smelled of woodsmoke. Larisa thought she could break the tension by laughing that her cousin would conflate burning pies with woodsmoke, but then Kristen stood up and went to the door.

"I brought them with me from the house—" When Kristen opened the door the smell of burning intensified. Larisa caught a distinct undercurrent of pine.

The smoke detectors began to wail, and Larisa understood the smell of pine meant the Christmas tree was burning. She thought *Ah, Lucas has set it on fire.* For a moment, the thought existed in suspended time, an interesting idea that she circled without making any of the obvious connections. Even as Kristen and Hannah ran out of the room, Larisa's mind resisted reason. She wondered if all her carefully wrapped gift cards would be ruined, and if the metal folding chairs at the tables nearest the tree would burn.

Obviously not.

Then it came to her. Because Lucas did nothing without purpose.

He's leaving and he doesn't want us to notice.

She rushed downstairs to find a bedlam of shouting and coughing and smoke thick along the ceiling, but also drifting down to smog the air people were breathing. People pushed her from every direction, some of them moving the tables and chairs, others trying to pass Tupperware full of water from the kitchen. Larisa fought to reach the front hallway. The air was clearer there; the front door and all the windows in the den had been opened to help feed a fresh breeze of oxygen to the fire.

At the end of the driveway, she caught a glimpse of taillights as Hannah's Camry descended to the road.

Hours later, after firefighters and police interviews, the family sat on the back deck under heat lamps and electric blankets and ate slightly smoked pumpkin and pecan pie. No one had much to say. The exhaustion had set in and now there was a feeling of going through the motions so they could all scatter back to their individual families and freely discuss what had happened.

No one had seen Lucas start the fire. Cousin Erik had heard a pop and seen a spark like an electrical short. But being the most oblivious version of a nineteen-year-old male, who had also been starving, he'd ignored it. Electricity was so advanced these days, everything came with fail-safes, he'd thought. Cousin Tonia had felt the breeze of the windows opening and complained to her mother, who'd shushed her and said she should've worn her sweater over her nice Christmas dress; Hans always kept the thermostat down to save money.

Even the smoke had gone unnoticed for much longer than seemed reasonable. But Larisa hadn't been there. And her family, as a species, wasn't the suspicious kind. They hadn't lived her life. They hadn't thought to worry over what kind of man Hannah had brought into their house.

But now, as their tongues squished pumpkin-flavored sugar along the tops of their mouths or chomped pecans that tasted like a campfire, the culprit was clear.

"He seemed so nice," said Violet.

Larisa sent another text to Quinn, some small part of her holding on to hope that he wasn't responding because he was angry with her.

Please just be angry.

"Sorry if I missed this," said Hans. "But how do you know this man?"

"We dated when I was in college," said Larisa. *And technically, we were together and not together while I was living here.*

"And why did he start a fire in my living room?"

"I don't know."

"It seems obvious that he and Hannah have absconded," said Kristen.

"But she left after he did," said Cousin Becca. "I saw her with a suitcase in the smoke."

"They'll be stopped at the airport," said Gunter with the authority of a man who got things done.

Larisa's parents, not surprisingly, seemed more embarrassed than shocked. They'd sequestered themselves at the edge of the deck where it was coldest, as though this was their penance for having a daughter who ruined holidays. Larisa wondered how long they'd been like this, resigned to the possibility of chaos she brought into their lives. She liked to think the nature of celebrity had given them these shock absorbers before she'd added her particular messiness to theirs. Scandal was part of being public people.

But none of their scandals had ever involved arson, or a live-streamed bondage video, or even secret babies. *And they don't even know about the kidnapping,* she thought as she looked at her dark phone. No one seemed to remember that she'd come with a date, and that he was also missing.

"But do you think he's honorable?" asked Alison, as though she'd read the line from an Austen novel.

"What does honor mean now?" asked Kristen. "She said he'd planned this with her, to help save Larisa—"

"Always Larisa," huffed Hannah's married brother. "It's like she's in love with you. And you never did a thing about it."

Larisa arched a placid eyebrow and waited for her cousin to realize how he sounded, then she said, "I don't think I'm responsible for Hannah acting like this, but I'm willing to pay for the damage to the house." She looked to her uncle, who waved her off. Money was not going to solve this.

"Do we know where he lives?" asked Alison. "If the police don't stop them at the airport, what will happen?"

"They will be tracked," said Gunter. "People can't just disappear. Worst case, she's back by New Year's."

Larisa's phone vibrated. One new message, followed shortly by a second.

The first message was a picture of Quinn asleep in the overstuffed chair of a private jet, a blanket tucked up around his chin, slipper socks on his feet.

> Lucas: He chose to come. Don't bother us.

Without thinking, Larisa dialed back the number. "I'm going to kill you, you motherfucking bastard!"

Silence.

When she looked at her phone, she saw the line had clicked open, then disconnected two seconds later. Just long enough for Lucas to hear her rage and know for certain what she'd tried so hard to keep a secret. She loved Quinn more than anything else. And when the time came, she'd do whatever Lucas asked to keep him safe.

Please Leave a Review

So glad this book found you! If you enjoyed reading it, please leave a review on Goodreads and Amazon if you use them. Please also tell people about this book. Books are sold by people talking about them.

Cheers, Jaye

You're welcome to post about Terrible Love all you want on your own socials, but if you want a dedicated place to discuss this, and my other books, with your fellow readers, join my private, member-only reader group on Facebook.

Coming Winter 2023!!!

Casta Diva

Quinn is in Italy with Lucas determined to find a way to detach him from Larisa and from their future together. But he has no idea what he's in for, or how far Lucas will go to test his resolve. He certainly doesn't know that Lucas has contacted Larisa and pulled her into his business dealings and that she is making plans of her own to get Quinn back before he falls too far into Lucas's world.

Sign up for my mailing list to receive early offers and announcements.

Acknowledgements

Land Acknowledgement - Terrible Love was written on the ancestral land and traditional territories of the Omaha, Oto, and Pawnee Nations. They are the original custodians of the land on which I have lived and worked while writing this novel.

Special thanks to my intrepid beta reader Hannah Gage whose close reading and thoughtful questions made this book better.

Thanks to Sarah McGuire my editor, and to Damonza Designs for the great cover and banner, and to Clara at Author Tree for taking my Word doc and making it look like a book.

Thanks to Kelsea Reeves for her excellent sensitivity read and insights.

Lastly, thank you to the wonderful bookstagram community who posted such beautiful images of Elaborate Lives and launched this series off to a great start.

About the Author

Jaye Viner lives on what used to be the plains of eastern Nebraska with a tall human and three fur bombs. She knows just enough about a wide variety of things to embarrass herself at parties she never attends. Her short fiction has been published in Drabblecast, Everyday Fiction, The Rumpus, and Others. She is the author of *Jane of Battery Park* and the *Elaborate Lives* Series. Find her on Instagram @Jaye_Viner or her website JayeViner.com

Milton Keynes UK
Ingram Content Group UK Ltd.
UKHW042140020823
426203UK00005B/287